T0274369

THE SMOKE THAT THUNDERS

Erhu Kome

THE SMOKE THAT THUNDERS

ACCORD BOOKS

NORTON YOUNG READERS
AN IMPRINT OF W. W. NORTON & COMPANY
INDEPENDENT PUBLISHERS SINCE 1923

For my angel baby

Printed in the United States of America
First Edition

For information about special discounts for bulk purchases, please contact W. W. Norton Special Sales at specialsales@wwnorton.com or 800-233-4830

Manufacturing by Lakeside Book Company
Book design by Hana Anouk Nakamura
Production manager: Delaney Adams

ISBN 978-1-324-05265-4

W. W. Norton & Company, Inc., 500 Fifth Avenue, New York, N.Y. 10110
www.wwnorton.com

W. W. Norton & Company Ltd., 15 Carlisle Street, London W1D 3BS

1 2 3 4 5 6 7 8 9 0

THE SMOKE THAT THUNDERS

1. QUBI
2. UVWIE
3. EMEVOR
4. BURUTU
5. OKPARA
6. IKOT
7. EFFIOM
8. MBIABONG
9. IGA
10. EYO
11. QUA'I
12. EWUARE
13. IDUMOWINA
14. OREROKPE
15. KOKORI
16. INNUERE

A. RAINBOW ROCKS
B. EWUARE MOUNTAINS
C. CROOKED FOREST
D. TEMPLE OF ISO
E. WOLFDEN HILLS
F. OREROKPE SANDS
G. DJONE FOREST
H. ORON FOREST
I. INNUERE FOREST
J. TEMPLE OF EGBESU
K. ETHIOPE RIVER
L. DJONE RIVER

OTỌRAKPỌ

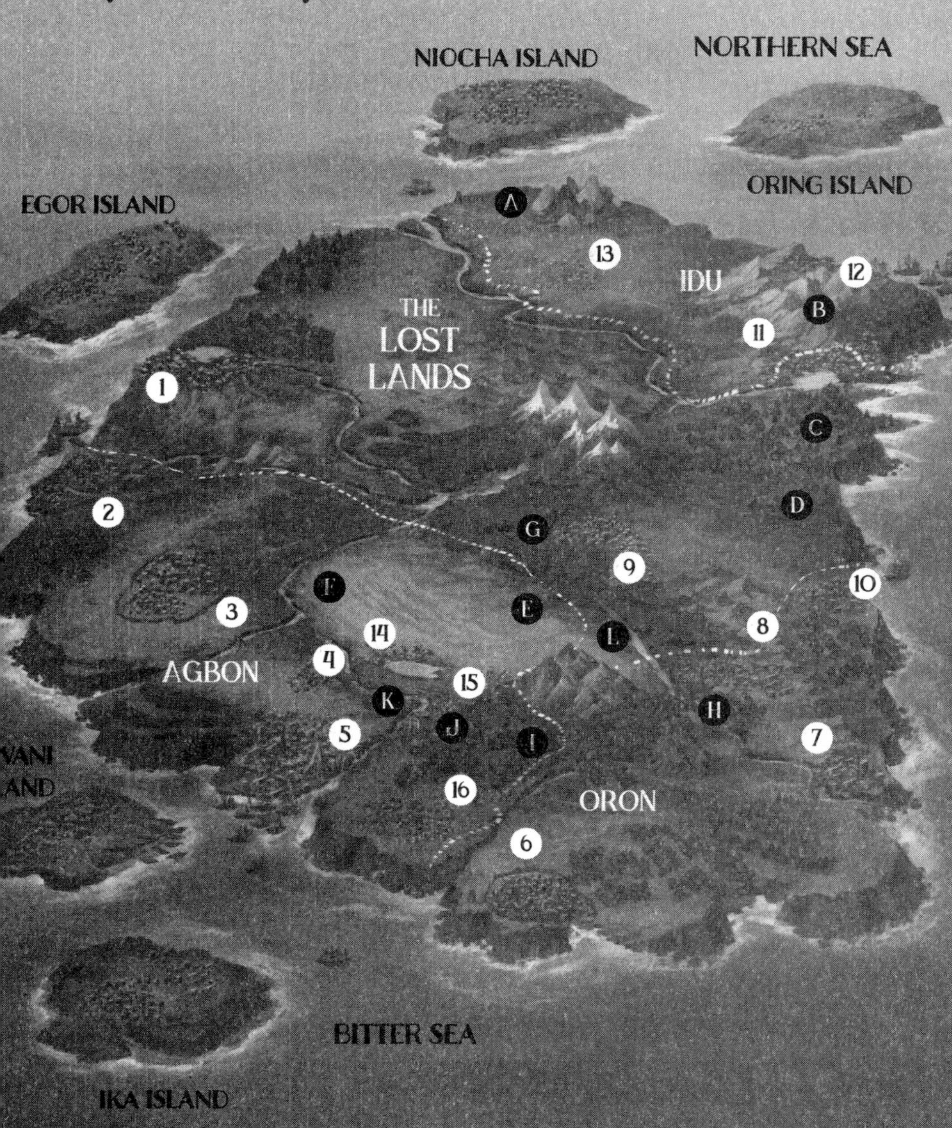
NIOCHA ISLAND
NORTHERN SEA
ORING ISLAND
EGOR ISLAND
THE LOST LANDS
IDU
AGBON
ORON
BITTER SEA
IKA ISLAND
N

1

I WAS THINKING ABOUT RUNNING AGAIN.

Grabbing my sister, Tega, and just bolting out the door and out of Kokori. Then I wouldn't have to be married to whomever my uncle and aunt brought with the best price.

I was distracted from my thoughts by the gust of wind that, along with a light drizzle, was trying to put out the fire in front of me. But the flames remained strong and my pot of vegetable soup kept on bubbling.

I looked out the kitchen window and into the courtyard where we had our meals, drank red spice tea, and received guests. At the entrance, next to some potted plants, were the statue of Egbesu, our protector god with his gilded sword, and a wooden carving of the Ọkan, the Sun Bird spirit that brought wealth, its spiked wings spread wide.

Tega was busy cracking ori seeds out of their shells on a stone slab under the awning of the kitchen. We would later sun-dry them before grinding to get the rich-smelling oil. The combination of the ori oil and a special powder from Burutu got our hair from chin to chest length.

She adjusted her robe around her hands and stretched her aching back before resuming cracking.

Imoni came out of the room she stayed in when she visited. She was my mother's older sister and looked every bit like her. She was tall and plump, and her delicate facial features, enviably long hair, and charcoal-dark skin made her one of the most beautiful women in Kokori.

She had been married for years but had had no children. Her husband, who should have followed the custom of letting her go and marrying another, chose to do the opposite. And even after his death, his family never let go of her.

She had been in charge of Tega and me ever since our parents passed away. Because my father had no sons, we had to remain in the house until we were married.

"The house of Okota Tanomare will stand until you are both married," my father's younger brother, Unika, had declared. He had assumed the role of our father, and Imoni our mother.

Imoni took a look around the courtyard, then headed my way. She adjusted the wrapper she had around her shoulders and breathed out misty cold air. "Naborhi, when you are done cooking, go to the small market and buy some smoked fish."

She handed me a few silver shells through the window. She inhaled and gave me a toothy smile. "That soup smells delicious.

Your cooking and your beauty will fetch an excellent bride price. Your husband will be a lucky man."

I hid my cringe.

Usually, I was glad I looked more like my mother and Imoni than my father. But when my beauty was used to gauge my worth as a woman, I wished I had inherited his icy stare and harsh features.

My father, Okota, had been tall like the uloho tree and menacing like a crocodile. He would curse at the empty courtyard whenever he drank agbagba wine directly from its wooden jar. His breath always smelled bad, soiling the air around him. He would threaten to beat Tega and me but would never go through with it.

"I am not going to hit you foolish girls. And leave a scar that will reduce your bride price? That will never happen."

My mother, however, was not offered the same courtesy.

Sometimes I wished he would hit me so I could have a reason to hit back. Hard. But I remained a good, dutiful daughter, and my mother remained a good, dutiful wife until she died three years ago during childbirth. It was her third attempt to give him a son.

It did not take long for my father to start searching for a new wife, one who could give him an heir. He died from a sudden, painful stomach illness before he could succeed.

By the time the soup was done, the rain had stopped falling. I took a wrapper and draped it over my shoulders before taking a basket and heading out of the courtyard. The stone streets had been washed clean by the rain, and golden droplets of sun warmed the green brick walls that defined Kokori houses.

The small market was a cluster of stalls on the banks of the Ethiope River that sold different kinds of fish and shellfish.

I met Chipo on my way down. My friend carried a basket but wore nothing for the cold. Her smooth, fair skin was illuminated by the ori oil she rubbed in. I was sure that would keep her warm.

"Going to buy fish?" she asked.

"Yes," I replied. "Imoni is with us."

"She always prefers fish." Chipo laughed fondly.

I noticed her half-plaited hair had turned light brown. "What did you do to your hair?"

"I have been soaking it in fora tea. You should see Dabi's hair now. She's been soaking it for weeks, and it is as brown as garden soil."

In Kokori, young girls were free to color their hair and style it whatever way they liked, but not to completion. So whenever I threaded or plaited my hair, it could only be done halfway. Only married women carried complete made-up hairstyles.

At the side of the road, some girls were playing Ten-Ten. Two were faced off, throwing their legs and trying to outsmart the other on the pattern their feet would make.

"When was the last time we played like that?" I asked with a chuckle.

"I cannot remember. But you know I always beat you."

"Who could beat you, Chipo? I never stood a chance."

She smiled imperiously.

"Imoni will not let me play like that anymore." I sighed. "'Your time has to be spent on perfecting your soups and weaving,'" I scold, trying to sound like Imoni.

Chipo laughed. "That sounds like my mother too. 'You have to cook properly.'" She mimicked her mother's nasal voice. "'You have to protect your honor and be ready to serve your husband and his family.'" She laughed again. "Like we do not know that already."

When we got to the small market, we headed to the smoked-fish stall first. The fish were tied in bundles of five and hung from the bamboo roof. The seller, a stout, stern-looking woman, named a price.

"No, I will only pay ten shells," I replied, keeping a straight face like my mother used to.

"Ten is too little for this fish."

"That is what I am willing to pay," I maintained. "My aunt paid eight shells last time she was here."

The woman rolled her eyes. "Twelve," she said.

"Ten."

"I cannot accept ten shells. I paid the fishermen more to get these fish down here."

"Chipo, let us go," I said, taking my friend's free hand.

The woman called us back.

Chipo laughed softly as the woman handed me my fish with a grumble.

"Next time, you have to buy from me and no one else," she barked.

"I will," I said, and Chipo laughed again as we walked away.

We bought Chipo's fresh fish with as little haggling as possible and headed back home. Just as Chipo and I were about to part ways, we spotted our childhood friend Tjolomi. Tjolomi was a year older than us, but she was small and thin so we nicknamed her Atete—grasshopper. Her rite of passage had been the previous year. She would be married soon.

"Chipo, Naborhi," she greeted us cheerfully.

"How is the wedding planning?" Chipo asked excitedly. She always hungered for every detail about these things.

Tjolomi smiled good-naturedly. "My mother and I are going shopping in Uvwie for wrappers and beads."

Jealousy twinged in my stomach. Uvwie was a bustling merchant clan to the west. I had always wanted to visit.

"How lucky," Chipo cried. "I have never left Kokori."

"I cannot believe I'm to be married," Tjolomi said, but her smile looked forced. "It seems like just yesterday the three of us were collecting periwinkle shells and playing in the river."

"Time goes by faster than we realize," Chipo agreed.

"The feeling is overwhelming," Tjolomi continued softly, as if Chipo hadn't spoken. She suddenly seemed to remember herself. "But I have so much to look forward to. I should get going; my mother is waiting for me at the market." Tjolomi hugged us each before walking down the hill.

I watched Tjolomi's retreating figure and shivered.

"Are you cold?" Chipo asked, running a hand up my arm.

"Yes," I lied. "Can you believe she is already betrothed?"

Chipo sighed. "I wish it would happen to me already."

I eyed Chipo carefully, my stomach in knots. This was going to be my future. Asking my friends to be part of my procession, buying fabric and beads for my wedding.

Becoming a wife.

"It will happen for you sooner than you think," I murmured. I wasn't sure who I was speaking to.

We parted ways and I hurried along the path home.

Raised voices greeted me the moment I stepped into the courtyard.

"Can you believe Tamunor has stopped going to the sankore? His father is livid," Imoni cried.

Tamunor stood beside my aunt, looking exhausted. Tega was still outside the kitchen, cracking ori seeds.

We were related—something about our ancestors marrying sometime—but he did not look much like us except for his small lips. He had a thin, pointy nose and big, bright eyes that made him look handsome for such a skinny boy. We just called him our cousin. He was fifteen, the same age as Tega, but he liked to pretend he was older than the both of us.

"I got bored. I know how to write in Iagbon. I can speak and write a little bit of the Traveler's Tongue. That is all I need to be a builder, just like Okota."

Imoni gave him a nasty look.

"A builder? You no longer want to be part of the Osusu?"

The Osusu was Agbon's guild of merchants.

Tamunor grunted, avoiding Imoni's accusatory gaze.

"As a merchant, you could have easily become a minister,

working in the king's court. You could have held more power than the orosuen," Imoni scolded him, shaking her head. "Your father will be disappointed."

Tamunor muttered quietly, "My father is already disappointed. He is always disappointed."

"Whatever it is you want to become," Imoni said, "you need to learn. You have to go back to the sankore."

Tamunor rolled his eyes. "I don't like it there. Maybe Naborhi can replace me."

Tega's gaze snapped to mine.

"Tah!" Imoni scoffed. "Girls have no need for a sankore. Their only duty is to their homes and their future family. A girl who is eager to eat fufu will have it stuck in her throat. If Naborhi goes to a sankore, who will take care of her husband, her children? A woman's place is in her home. Nowhere else."

Tamunor shrugged and joined Tega, helping her with the last of the ori seeds.

I dropped the fish in the kitchen and stared at Tamunor in shock. What was he thinking? He had an opportunity to learn, an avenue for escape out of this village, and he was taking it for granted. I never took my lessons with Moyo for granted. Every day I was grateful the old man had decided to secretly teach me how to read and write.

Only Tega knew about Moyo, but we never really talked about it. She knew how much I'd wanted to attend the sankore. The first time she had seen me practicing my writing, she had been surprised, but she'd accepted it immediately and had kept it secret since.

When I'd tried to teach her how to write, she had flat-out refused. No matter, I'd decided. I was going to learn enough for the both of us.

"How much was the fish?" Imoni asked me, coming into the kitchen.

"Twelve shells," I lied.

The two shells would be added to the pouch hidden away in my room, to be saved for when Tega and I left Kokori. A shell here, two shells there, and I had grown quite a sum.

When the time came, Moyo would pretend to be our father and help us get a boat that would take us out of Kokori to Iga, a settlement in the Lost Lands where Moyo had once lived. He was sure we could find work on the farms and get a place to lay our heads easily, so we could stay there until we decided what to do next. He mentioned the kindness he received from the Igan people and how well they treated girls and women.

Such a simple plan. If only it were that easy to carry out.

For one, I did not have enough money for both me and Tega.

And, most critically, Tega was not willing to leave Kokori. I just had to convince her.

"Tamunor," I called out into the courtyard. "Will you eat taro or yam with the soup?"

"Taro," he replied. "Please make sure you fill the plate. I'm so hungry."

"You're always hungry," Tega teased, and Tamunor elbowed her.

"Naborhi," Imoni said, coming into the kitchen with a tray of melon seeds.

"Yes?"

"You have to remove the shells for tomorrow's meal."

I wished I could break melon shells with a smile on my face like Tega always did. She was always willing to please Imoni and Unika.

I swallowed my grumble and said, "Yes, Imoni."

After Tamunor had gone home, I settled near the courtyard fire to fight off the evening cold.

"Your uncle is thinking of putting new tiles here on the courtyard floor," Imoni said to me as she placed a pot of milk over the flames. "When your suitors and their families come, they will know we have taste."

"Are we that rich now?" Tega asked, laughing.

"Your father's boats are bringing in more money than before."

"Because people hardly knew him," I retort.

"Naborhi, you cannot speak so bluntly."

"It's the truth. He was a well-respected man but he didn't deserve it. It's only fair his death brings in money."

My father was dirt who feigned nobility in public but became something else inside the walls of his home. His death had done more good than his life.

"Your father tried to be the best man he could."

"Well, he did not try enough."

"Do not call the forest that sheltered you a jungle."

"But he was. He was a jungle."

Imoni refused to discuss my father any more, and instead prattled on about how maybe we should let go of the idea of new tiles that was sure to use up a lot of money. She suggested Unika save the money instead for my wedding and for days when the business did not do so well.

"When can I go to Okpara to see the boatyard?" I asked.

Okpara was the capital of our kingdom, Agbon. It was a sprawling coastal city that had the best ship-makers. I remembered the last time I was there with my parents. I had thought the castle of the king was the second most beautiful thing to see in the city, second only to the giant statue of Egbesu overlooking the city from a nearby mountain.

But what I loved most about Okpara was its boatyard. I was fascinated by the coordination of the men as they moved, assembling huge logs and wooden planks to create something wonderful. Their ships were used to explore the little-known islands far beyond the Bitter Sea.

"Your uncle may come tonight, so ask him then."

"Why is Unika coming?" Tega asked, pouring me a glass of the now-warmed milk before helping herself.

Imoni shot an unreadable look my way as I took a sip. "He has business to tend to."

Something about that look curdled the milk in my stomach.

2

UNIKA ARRIVED BEFORE THE EVENING MEAL AND JOINED US. He'd brought Imoni part of the profits made from the boats.

"I have found a man for you, Naborhi," Unika said, dipping his cut of usi into the amiedi, grabbing some fish and periwinkle along the way.

I continued to eat as if I had not heard him. I wanted to tell him he should be looking for a wife for himself instead of looking for a husband for me.

Tega looked at me, waiting for a reply. I continued to eat, ignoring them.

Imoni broke the silence. "Who is he?"

"His name is Fynn, the youngest son of Sayo Goredenna, the salt merchant. He is very interested in Naborhi and would like a meeting. The Goredennas are a good family. Wealthy too. The father of your suitor is a good man."

"And my suitor? What is he like?" I asked.

"Fynn?" He lifted his chin, scoffing. "Young men nowadays are vain and impatient. They lack discipline, but Fynn will do just fine."

A clever way to avoid answering my question. If he had any reservations about this Fynn, he was not willing to share them.

"Tell them we will set a date for the meeting," Imoni said.

"Good. I will be going back to Okpara tomorrow to drop off some uloho with the workmen."

Ships made from uloho were without match, but the wood was extremely pricy.

"I will go with you," I said. "I have not seen the boatyard in a long time. I—"

"You should be honing your skills as a homemaker," Imoni cut in.

"Imoni, please," I begged. "Let me go."

She shook her head firmly.

I turned to Unika, but he shook his head as well.

"Maybe some other time," he said, putting a piece of meat into his mouth. His tone didn't give me much hope.

Two days later, Sayo Goredenna and his wife, their two eldest sons, and their last son, Fynn, visited our house.

I greeted them separately, as was customary, making sure to bend my knees properly. I observed Fynn closely. He must have gotten all his looks from his father, because he shared few similarities with his mother.

He was maybe eighteen or nineteen. He was tall and thin. He was good-looking, but not as good-looking as he thought. He carried himself with a pompous air, looking around the courtyard like he owned it and everything in it.

I didn't need to be present during the preliminary talks, so I made my way up to the roof. I sat down in one of the chairs we kept up there, taking in the view of the Ethiope.

To the south sat the grand temple of Egbesu in all its glory. It had been built by Orosuen Khefre the Unmoved after the invasion of the Lost Lands as a gesture of peace to honor the god after such a tumultuous time. The temple was carved out of a single rock to form columns, bridges, secret doors, and statues. The priests of Egbesu lived within it and took care of it. They wore nothing but long orange tunics, and their heads were completely shaved to display their tattoos of the Ọkan on their scalps.

My peace was disturbed by the sound of Fynn coming up the stairs. I slowly stood up and clasped my hands in front of me.

"So you are an orphan," was the first thing he said.

What a marvelous conversationalist.

"Yes," I replied stiffly.

"And your father had no heir? What a pity."

I wanted to bite back that he was speaking to Okota's heir, but I said nothing, observing Fynn's every movement.

"Father really wants you to be my wife," he said, strolling toward the edge of the roof. He turned round. "I guess your uncle made an impression on him." He stroked his chin and flashed a smile my way. "Or perhaps it was you who made the impression."

He expected a reply, but I continued to stare at him, chin up.

"Why are you looking at me like that?" he asked, his eyes narrowed.

"Just observing," I replied calmly.

"Your bride price is going to cost us a lot, but Father says it will be worth it."

"Do you think it will be worth it?"

His eyes narrowed again. "I say a bride is a bride, no matter how many bucks you have to kill," he quipped, smiling again.

"It's goats," I corrected sharply. "No matter how many *goats* you have to kill." How could he mix up such simple words?

His brows went up and his nostrils flared in surprise.

For Imoni and Unika I lowered my gaze, feigning shyness. "Well, as your bride, I'd hope to bear you many sons someday."

From the corner of my eye, I saw him straighten and nod approvingly.

"That is all I want."

"That is all I want too." I plastered a smile on my face, still looking down at my hands.

"What are your skills?" he asked briskly, putting his hands behind him and pushing out his chest like a turkey puffing its feathers while strutting about. "You can weave, I assume, and perfectly tend a garden. Can you cook well? I like my yams pounded smoothly, no lumps. You can do that, right?"

I nodded, my hackles rising at his inquisition.

"Melon soup is my favorite. You can prepare it, right? I like the hand-broken melon seeds, not the ones broken by a mill. You can do that too, I assume? Your aunt should have taught you."

"Yes," I answered through gritted teeth.

He grinned. "Good. Oh, and I think my father is going to have you stay with us for a while."

I startled. Not every family required this, but some more traditional families required the bride to live with them to find out how good a daughter-in-law they were going to get. It was a test, and one I resented immensely.

"You can prepare my breakfast before my father and I leave for his shops and have my lunch ready for when I get back," he declared, droning on.

My hands balled into fists.

He placed a hand under his chin and looked up, thinking.

"I like red spice tea," he said cheerfully, "Can you make red spice tea?"

I could not take it anymore.

"Yes," I snapped. "Yes, I can do all those things. What about you, *Fynn*?" I stormed closer to him. He stepped back, eyes bulging in shock. "Can you even feed yourself? Can you differentiate your legs from your arms? *I like this. I like that,*" I mocked. "But can you even speak your own language? *Bucks?* Everyone knows it's goats!"

I swung my arms out with that final word, and Fynn stumbled back from me. I was practically trembling with anger, and he took me in with a stony expression.

"My father will hear of this. And your uncle too."

He shook his head and hurriedly descended the stairs, mumbling to himself. I sat back down in my chair, the sun low in my eyes, and enjoyed my solitude.

My presence was not requested during the talks, and that was one of my prayers answered. After the Goredennas left, Imoni, Tega, and I sat down to eat.

Imoni did not wait long to pounce.

"What did you say to Fynn?" she demanded.

"Nothing." I kept my voice even.

She grumbled, shaking her head. "Don't think I don't know you're trying to scare that boy off. Fynn seems unsure about you, but his father does not."

I looked up at her sharply. "And?"

"It is good his father is so interested in you. It means we have no problem no matter how you try to send Fynn running with your attitude."

I swallowed a smile but Tega laughed loudly, head thrown all the way back. When she caught Imoni's glare, she covered it with a cough and quickly drank some water.

"It is not funny," Imoni chided. "I have been waiting a long time for you to be married so you can start your family. Look at you—there is nothing wrong with you. You are beautiful, your cooking is excellent, no man has seen what is between your legs, and no man will unless he is your husband. You will respect Fynn and his family." She took another bite, seeming to settle on something as she chewed. "Soon you will be betrothed to him, and once you complete your rite of passage, you will be married."

The thought of being married to Fynn sent my stomach churning so violently I thought I would vomit.

All of this with Fynn and his family was not what I dreamed of.

I wanted to travel the world. I wanted to see the smaller islands to the north and find out if it was true that some of their people really had gills. I wanted to see the Lost Lands and wander through the Igan streets and eat new foods along the Djone River. I wanted to do a lot of things that would not be possible if I remained in Kokori and got married.

The next day I went to Moyo's, even though Imoni was still around.

The sweet smell of bento beans greeted me as I stepped into the field circling Moyo's farmhouse. It was a squat building surrounded by pear trees. I walked down the overgrown pathway until I reached the farmhouse.

The front door was locked. I would have no lessons today.

Two years ago, Moyo had saved me from being thrashed by the Abavo. Back then, I used to sneak into the sankore near the market any chance I got.

I got away with it for months, until one day the macali who taught the boys caught me and handed me over to the Abavo for punishment. But the timely interference of Moyo saved me.

He was not from here, but he had married a Kokori woman

named Ufi, who had run away to Idu soon after she'd been betrothed. She'd wanted more out of life just like I did. She met Moyo and they'd fallen in love, traveling the world together. But she got sick and had wanted her ashes to be brought back home when she died. Afterward, Moyo could not bring himself to leave Kokori. To leave her.

I wondered how someone could love another so. To not even want to be parted even after death.

Moyo was once the head guard for the chief who ruled the Egor, an island clan. When he saved me from the Abavo and learned of my plans to leave Kokori, he chose to teach me to read and write. He also began training me brutally and meticulously.

The world is harsh, especially to women, he had said. Having the upper hand physically and mentally would equip me to take it on.

His expression had turned sad as he told me he wished his wife had been trained to defend herself before she'd met him. It would have saved her from a lot of trauma she'd had to overcome.

When Moyo agreed to be my teacher, it felt like a step toward having some control over my life.

He was a good teacher. He was patient, and he never talked down to me.

He gave me books on the Lost Lands, home of the famed cities of Qua'i and Qubi that were ruled by an okao and an onodjie. These rulers were *elected* by their citizens by means of votes, the equivalent of giving power to ordinary people.

And he told me stories about his many journeys throughout

Idu, and about the Azen, a band of women with magical powers who were commanded solely by the king of Idu.

"I will never forget the first time I saw the Rainbow Rocks," he told me once. "They're just past the city of Idumowina. I could hardly breathe. The boulders are as colorful as the rainbow, stacked atop each other in twos and threes, stretching out for miles. You have to see it."

Whenever I ate my meal or plaited Tega's hair, I imagined we were in these faraway lands, deciding whom we wanted as a leader, deciding where we would travel next, holding books out in public so everyone could see that we could read. I knew those thoughts were just fantasy, but I wished to make them a reality.

Tega, however, did not.

Tega, who had voiced her dislike about leaving Kokori. Tega, who seemed content, even eager, to be married off.

I did not understand her.

Eventually she would realize how little awaited her in Kokori and would want to come with me. I had to believe this.

Because I knew I could not leave without Tega.

I came back home to find Imoni in my room, money in her hands.

I could hardly breathe, feeling the weight of my tongue double in my dry mouth.

I thought I had hidden the money better. How had she found it? Why had she been searching through my things?

"I said let me take a look around your rooms today," she said. "To see what clothes you needed."

Snooping. She had been snooping around.

"Only to find this hidden in a loose part of the wall." She gestured to the open space, the stone meant to cover up the hole lying on the ground next to my bed.

"Where did you get this money?" she demanded.

"It's my money," I replied without thinking.

The vision of Tega and me in Iga started slipping away, ready to vanish. My heart was pounding so hard in my chest I was sure Imoni could see it.

"I know it's your money. I found it in your room. I asked where did you get it? What is it for?"

Her raised voice drew Tega to my room. She stood at the door, watching with wide, panicked eyes.

"Where did she get such a huge amount of money, Tega? And what is she hiding it for?"

My sister kept quiet, just like I did.

"Have you been stealing from me?" Imoni shouted, hands in fists on her waist.

"No!"

"From Unika?"

"No, Imoni. Of course not!"

"Since neither of you will tell me what the money is for, I will keep it for myself. It is mine now. I will use it how I see fit." She moved to put the money in her skirt pocket.

"It's *my* money," I said, my voice cracking. I tried grabbing at her hand, but she quickly evaded my reach, her expression furious.

"Imoni, please—" Tega stepped forward to help, but Imoni shot her a glare.

"How did she get it then?" she snapped before turning to me. "What is it for? Surely since it is *your* money, you would know."

I stared back at her, my tears blurring her image. I could not answer her. I felt cornered, trapped. I had not thought to come up with a cover, and now I was too thrown to even formulate an idea. The only thing I could do was walk away.

I stormed out. Imoni shouted after me and I ignored her. Tega rushed to follow behind. She caught up with me on the street as I hurried toward nowhere.

"I'm sorry," she said, squeezing my arm. "I know how much that money means to you."

I stopped to face her.

"To *me*?" I asked, and the words broke me. My tears spilled down my cheeks, my frustration and pain and *want* overflowing.

Tega's face fell, but she said nothing.

"Is this the life you want to live?" I asked. "One where you can't even have your own money? Tega, I can write and read. Iagbon *and* the Traveler's Tongue."

"I know that." Her voice was small.

"Remember how Mother used to say a girl's mind can't comprehend much? She was *wrong*. I'm proof that we can do much more than we are told."

"This is not about me," she replied, her eyes flashing.

"It is about you, Tega. And me. And every girl in Kokori. I want more than this life. I want more for them than this life," I cried. "Don't you want more too?"

Tega's expression softened as she took my hands.

"This life may not be for you, but I want to be a wife and a mother," she murmured. "That is all I've ever wanted. Just because it is not the life you want for me does not mean that it is wrong."

My shoulders began to shake and she hugged me tightly.

"I cannot live my own life if I am living your vision of it."

My heart felt like it was breaking in two. This was an impossible choice. I was torn between my sister and my dreams.

"I don't know what to do," I whispered into her shoulder. Since when had she gotten so tall?

"You just have to start saving again."

She was right. But I knew how long it had taken me to gather the money that Imoni had confiscated.

"I'll help you. Give anything I can."

Hope soared in my heart before I understood the meaning in her words.

I pulled back to look in her eyes. The sun was setting now, the wind off the Ethiope cool and bracing. "You will not consider coming with me?"

She smiled sadly. "You cannot live your life if you are too focused on mine, Naborhi."

She stopped me from saying anything else by asking, "Did you see Imoni's face when you tried to take your money?"

I laughed bitterly, begrudging her the conversation change. "I thought she was going to faint."

"More like start screaming." She sighed. "I'm sorry this happened."

"Me too."

More than she could know.

3

THE NEXT DAY, IMONI RETURNED GLEEFULLY FROM THE MARKET with news that spelled doom for me.

"The Goredennas will bring wine tomorrow. Once you accept the drink, you will be betrothed to Fynn. I have already spread the word around to a few women."

My fingers froze around the melon shells I had been removing. Without thinking, I blurted out, "I do not want to get married."

Imoni smiled. It was a reaction far from what I'd expected.

She put an arm round me, her lavender perfume oil trying its best to calm me. "It is normal for a bride to feel this way. But you will get excited once the gifts start pouring in. You have until the end of the year to get used to the idea. Do not worry."

But of course I was worried. Worried for myself and my future and where my decisions might lead me to.

I could not sleep that night, and by morning I had a headache. There was nothing else to do but go along with what I was told.

That evening, Imoni hosted a small gathering to witness the betrothal. Chipo came, smiling from ear to ear as Imoni helped me get ready. I wore a beautiful ivory dress, and Chipo had done my hair in gorgeous half braids.

She held my hand in hers as Imoni applied makeup to my face.

"You look so lovely. Fynn is a lucky man," she gushed, her eyes bright and playful. "I hope soon it will be my turn."

The ceremony was brief and rather anticlimactic for how much I'd been dreading it. Sayo Goredenna poured me a glass of wine from the cask that his family had brought. I held it in shaking hands as I looked first at him, then at Imoni's encouraging gaze, and finally to Fynn, his expression flat and unreadable.

I swallowed down my fear and panic along with the wine. I was betrothed to Fynn.

The next day, Imoni left for home and I went to Moyo's. I filled my mouth with bento beans from his field until my fingers and teeth turned purple.

All I could think about as I chewed was Fynn's gleaming eyes after I'd finished the wine. I would have to see his smug face every day and treat him like a good Kokori wife should. Maybe even spoon-feed him if his hands got too tired.

Moyo opened the front door. He was tall and built like a tree, with light brown eyes and a strong nose, his face slightly wrinkled from the sun. I had no idea how old he was. "Good, you are here. We will continue with your writing."

"I have been betrothed to Fynn," I blurted, gagging. "Fynn!" I wanted to throw up.

I picked up a stick and beat the dead bento-bean stalks he had propped up against the wall of his house. Anger filled me up and made my skin hot. Moyo watched me as I pummeled the stalks into the ground, not once trying to stop me.

When I finished, Moyo took the stick from me, leaving me breathless and ashamed.

I clenched my fists so tightly it hurt. "I hate this! I hate it so much! I do not want to get married to Fynn or anyone else."

My hands shook so much I had to clasp them together, fearing they would fall off.

"Naborhi, come inside," Moyo said in a soft voice. "Sit down."

He offered me a chair and some water. I worked to quiet my racing heart.

"Imoni took my money. And Tega won't come with me. How am I ever supposed to get to Iga now?"

Moyo sighed, sitting down in a chair opposite me.

"Have you considered leaving without your sister?"

My response was immediate, a gut reaction. "I won't leave my sister alone."

"But she won't be alone."

I swallowed thickly. "It's my job to take care of my sister. I won't leave her."

Moyo folded his arms and sat back in the chair, a serious look on his face.

"You may have to. And it would be best if you considered that."

I couldn't think about it anymore, or I would fall to pieces. So I moved to the table, where Moyo had already placed out sheets of paper and a pencil.

I got to work.

"Will you leave with me?" I asked Tega when I returned home. I was lying in bed; Moyo had run me through hand-to-hand fighting drills after my writing lessons. My arms were aching, but my temper had quelled.

"But you are betrothed to Fynn," was the first thing she said. She was standing at the doorway to my room, partially blocking off the rays of the evening sun. She looked surprised for a moment. "I had thought . . ." She shook her head and furrowed her brow at me. "You've heard the stories about Iga. It's lawless and chaotic."

"Words spoken by people who want to keep us trapped. To keep us from ever looking outward."

She folded her hands across her chest. "What would we do in Iga?"

"Whatever it is, it will be our choice to make."

She cocked her head and sighed. "It doesn't seem like you've thought things through."

"I have thought things through. With the money Imoni took

and a little bit more on top we could have made it to Iga and planned further from there." I reached out my hand to her. "We would have choices there, Tega."

She joined me on my bed. I could see the pitying look in her eyes. I was sure it was not unlike the look I was giving her.

"Do you want to end up like our mother?" I asked.

"I will not end up like her."

"How do you know?"

She didn't answer. Still, I was not going to give up on her.

The next day I went to Moyo's again.

He had brought out his chestnut mare already saddled into the field to perfect my riding skills. The first few times learning how to ride had been tough—and once I had even sprained my wrist. After a few days, I'd succeeded in mounting the horse and learned to steer while trotting. Now I was sometimes more comfortable on horseback than I was on my feet.

I stood beside the horse, brushing her left side. "Nour, I am happy to see you."

The horse snorted and bobbed her head.

"You will go riding today," Moyo said by way of greeting.

"I thought we were training today."

"This is training," Moyo retorted, and I hid a smile.

Without any warning, he threw two oranges from his pocket at me, and on instinct I easily caught them.

"It is because you can do that, that is why you are riding. Your reaction gets sharper each day. I want you to go to Innuere to get me some ori fruit."

I tossed the oranges back to him and placed my left leg on the strap and mounted, keeping my back straight and adjusting into a balanced position. Moyo followed on the ground as I got Nour walking.

"Do not slouch and make yourself smaller. You tend to do that sometimes. Remain upright, keep your back straight and head up. Do you have your daggers?"

I nodded, shifting my shoulders. He had gifted me twin Assegai daggers last year. I kept one strapped to my hip and one on the other thigh.

I started with a nice trot, moving around the clearing, a soft wind caressing my cheeks. Then, I pressed my heels and calves against Nour's belly to urge her faster. The feeling was exhilarating.

I wanted to go even faster, so I made a clicking sound and applied more pressure with my legs. Nour went into full speed and I waved goodbye to Moyo as we raced out of the clearing and into the woods.

We rode along the path toward Innuere at breakneck speed. It felt like I was flying, like if Nour and I could move just a little bit faster, we would take to the skies and I could escape all my fears and my pain. Like I could leave Kokori behind and escape my stifling, dreadful future.

I did not realize we were lost until Nour came to a jolting stop, and it took all of Moyo's training for me to keep my seat.

"What is it, Nour?" I murmured, running a hand along the mare's neck.

She huffed uneasily, and I glanced around the lush forest, the air sticky with heat and humidity.

Something tugged at my belly, my attention drawn to a small patch of sunlight deep within the trees. I dismounted and led Nour toward it, entering a small clearing in a grove of ancestor trees.

Rays of soft sunlight caressed the moss-covered trees, casting shadows of their leaves on the damp soil. Birds called to each other as they flew from one twisted branch to another. I walked a little bit farther, avoiding the thick roots that wove in and out of the ground.

From here, I could see past the forest to golden-brown grassy plains and, beyond them, the imposing border of the Oron Forest.

No one from Kokori dared go near the Oron Queendom. Thirty years ago, the King of Agbon broke off his engagement to one of the Oron princesses, shattering political relations and starting a feud that was still causing discord. Anyone from Kokori found in Oron would be killed on sight.

Staring at the enormous trees that had been there for ages, I wanted to go there. To cross the threshold and plant my feet in the soil and breathe in the woodsy air. I wanted to go where no Kokori woman in the past thirty years had been and lived to tell the tale.

Then I saw something move within the grassy plain. The creature was fast at first, then it slowed down. It stopped when a gust of wind moved the blades of grass. It began to move again, then suddenly collapsed, disappearing from sight. The hair on my arms rose.

The tugging in my belly beckoned me forward, and I approached the creature, careful not to make any sudden movements. I scanned the Oron Forest for signs of archers, for any guards ready to shoot me dead.

Then I got close enough to see the blood. On the ground, nearly hidden in the tall grass, was the most beautiful creature I had ever seen.

It looked somewhat like a fox. Most of its fur was a brilliant sunset red that gave way to white fur on its stomach. It had long whiskers and dark rings around its eyes, with a long bushy tail. It was small, no bigger than my two fists, and it was curled tightly around itself, purring and wrinkling its nose. I edged closer, my hand just touching the dagger sheathed at my hip. The animal purred again, then made a sound more like a whimper. It turned to its side slightly and I could see a bloody smear across its shoulder. Gently, I picked the creature up and ran as fast as I could back to Nour, who was shifting anxiously on her feet. We had to get back to Moyo's house. He would know what to do with this . . . thing.

Moyo was outside smoking a pipe when I arrived with the creature.

"Good, you're back," he said. I stumbled as I dismounted but quickly regained my footing and raced toward him. He put out his hands to slow me. "What is the hurry?"

"I found this in the woods. Do you know what it is?" I shoved the animal into his face. "Can you help with the bleeding?"

Moyo looked at me strangely. "What are you showing me, Naborhi?"

"This," I said, looking at the animal and raising it even closer to his eyes.

Moyo was looking worriedly between my hands and my face. "There's nothing in your hand."

I looked at the animal again and back up at Moyo.

"Naborhi, are you all right?" he asked. He leaned over to look into my eyes.

"Moyo, you are spinning."

I staggered, and Moyo lunged to catch me.

I fought hard to stay conscious, but it was futile. Everything faded to black.

I dreamed of the creature.

I was back in the clearing, running through the trees. Ahead was the creature, only it was bigger and taller than the surrounding trees in the encroaching fog. It stared at me for a long time. I felt like it wanted to speak to me.

Then it turned around and disappeared.

I opened my eyes after what seemed like a lifetime to see the creature sleeping on my stomach. I could not tell if it was my imagination, but it seemed to have grown and its injury was no longer there. I was still in Moyo's house, lying on the bed, but his books had been moved away and the room looked cleaner. There was still some meat cooking over the fireplace; the appetizing smell made my stomach rumble. I turned to see some thick, seedy honey bread in a bowl on the table.

Tega had been around. Only she could make bread like that.

The door opened and Moyo stepped in. He looked relieved to see me awake.

I sat up and the creature stirred, purring. It leapt to the ground and started walking around as if inspecting the place.

"Your aunt and sister came by. I had to let them know you were here. They had not left your side until today. They went home to have a proper meal, a bath, and a change of clothes."

"What did Imoni say?"

"She asked what you were doing here. I told her I found you near my field and treated you. She fetched a priest of Egbesu, who said it was best you remained here until you found your legs again." Moyo paused, taking a deep breath. "Your aunt was furious you were here."

"Of course." I glanced at the bread. "How long have I been here?"

"It has been two days since you decided to fall asleep in my house."

"What?" I yelped. "Surely it cannot be two days."

"But it is." Moyo perched on the edge of the bed, clasping his hands. "There is nothing physically wrong with you. You have no fever or bruises. Nothing anyone can see."

Moyo watched me cautiously before turning to examine the room.

"Are you still seeing it?" he asked quietly. "The creature?"

I looked down at the creature. It had gone near the fireplace and was now stretched across the warm stones.

I nodded.

Moyo rose and went to his dresser to get me a mirror. The front part of my hair had a red streak. Like the color of an unforgettable sunset.

Like the color of the creature's fur.

"I must be aging," I tried to joke, my laugh strained.

"Do you feel ill?" he asked.

I shook my head, putting down the mirror.

Whatever this creature was, only I could see it. And it seemed to have made its mark on me. Either I was going mad or there were some powerful forces involved. I wasn't sure which option scared me more.

"What is happening, Moyo?" I whispered, eyeing the creature.

"I have never seen anything like this before."

For Moyo, who had seen so much of the world, this was a frightening thing to say.

The creature leapt back on the bed, turned several times, and settled on my legs. And with that, I didn't feel so scared anymore.

I could feel its heartbeat and could feel my own too. They resonated as one, one heart shared between two bodies.

Moyo handed me Tega's bread and I ate slowly so as not to upset my stomach. The food was comforting and did well to quell my anxiety.

"You said you found it in the woods? By Innuere?" Moyo

asked, bringing me a cup of water. He looked around the room, not knowing where to focus on to spot the creature.

"Yes, I did," I answered. "But it came from Oron."

Moyo stilled, just long enough that a bit of my unease creeped back in.

"The priest will know what to do," he murmured vaguely. "Now I will go and inform your family you are awake."

Imoni and Tega returned with Moyo. Tega wore a new hair scarf holding up the part of her hair not braided. They brought more honey bread, some beef stew, and a change of clothes. Imoni did not hide her fear when she saw my hair.

"What is this, Moyo?" Imoni asked, surprised. "What is happening to Naborhi?"

"By the gods, I have no idea."

"What is this creature she is seeing that no one else can?" Oddly, she locked eyes with the creature and frowned. I had named it Zuberi, like the loyal dog in the Kokori legend who never left its owner's side. Even after its owner had died, the dog stayed by his grave.

Moyo led her outside, speaking to her in a low voice.

"The color suits you," Tega said, sitting beside me in bed, eyes on my hair.

She then looked around me with both fascination and caution. Looking for Zuberi.

I touched the colored part of my hair and felt the knots. I had a head of hair that always wrestled with combs. My mother had always said my hair took after me: a wild child incapable of staying still.

"I made this scarf yesterday," Tega murmured, touching the patterned fabric. "I didn't know what else to do with you just lying there. You know how I get. I needed to do something with my hands."

"It's very beautiful." I stood with difficulty and wobbled to the door to listen in on Imoni's conversation with Moyo. But they had gone farther from the house and I couldn't hear them.

"We were so worried," Tega said softly.

I turned around and gave her a reassuring smile. "I'm sorry for making you worry. I feel all right. Really."

She looked at me, her eyes darting around. Zuberi was still on the bed. "I can't believe this is happening to you just before your rite of passage."

I snorted, shaking my head.

"Why does our rite of passage have to be a hunt anyway?" she continued. "It sounds so tedious."

"You will get training," I replied offhandedly.

She frowned. "Hunting." She said the word like she was asking herself a question. "Why? Why can it not be dressmaking?" she asked with a pout. "In Uvwie there is a lot of dancing during theirs. I want to dance instead."

I stepped away from the door and crawled back into bed once I realized Moyo and Imoni had walked completely out of earshot.

"Because as Imoni would like to always remind us, it is tradition. And tradition should be obeyed."

"A tedious tradition. I'd rather just get married as soon as I turn sixteen."

I agreed with Tega, but didn't say anything further. Our rite of passage was a method to prove ourselves as strong women able to provide for their homes and families. At sixteen, girls go on a hunt to bring a prize animal back to the orosuen's estate. The orosuen, Kokori's tribal lord, would host a celebration honoring each girl and boy in the village who had successfully completed their rites. There would be wine, music, and dancing, and everyone would eat the meat the girls had provided.

Our displays of strength and cunning were rewarded with a lifetime of being shackled to a husband. I wanted to scream at the unfairness of it.

"During my time I will just bring back a rabbit or snails." Tega was still chattering. "That is all every girl brings back anyway."

"That is not all Imoni teaches us to hunt, Tega," I remind her gently. "Do not underestimate rabbits. They are fast creatures. You have to know how to smoke them out right."

"A wild beast then."

"Whatever you can."

"A red deer like Imoni." She laughed and snorted.

I smiled weakly in return. "If you can."

I felt my anxiety spike at the reminder of Imoni's famed hunt. She was a popular woman for many reasons, but especially for her rite, in which she brought down with only a single arrow the largest red deer anyone in Kokori had seen. The orosuen himself requested she go on to train girls for future rites after her impressive display.

"I know you will bring something surprising. You are Naborhi, after all."

I shrugged. I was not the least bit interested in bringing back anything other than a rabbit.

"I am looking forward to my rite of passage next year." Tega's voice was calm, steady, but I heard what she was hinting at. "In spite of all that."

I looked at her. *She would still be here for her rite.* "I know."

"I know you look further than the rite."

I knew where she was heading.

"To Iga."

"Yes, to Iga. Then I can go anywhere. Everywhere."

"And you will do whatever you want."

"Yes, whatever I want."

She let out a raspy breath, and I watched tears fill her eyes.

"I'm surprised you haven't left already," she mumbled, her tone peppered. She looked away from me.

I frowned. "You know I can't leave you. Mother asked me to take care of you. You're my sister."

She crossed her arms. "Well, you can't leave and you can't stay."

"I know," I whispered. All I could do was face each day as it came.

"Well, good luck," she said bitterly.

I tensed. "Well, you could at least mean it."

She stood up so abruptly I nearly toppled off the bed. Zuberi let out a mewl of surprise, glancing between us.

"I don't want to mean it," Tega snarled.

"Why not?" I had never seen her so upset.

Her lower lip trembled. "Have you ever stopped to think maybe I don't like hearing you say you want to leave? That it makes me sad knowing that you are so unhappy with our lives? That it really and truly hurts to know that I am not enough to keep you here?"

Tears spilled down her cheeks, and my heart, battered and bruised from our previous conversations, finally broke apart.

I drew her back to the bed, her body shaking in my arms as I held her so tightly I thought I would fuse us together.

"I'm sorry," I said. She held me back even tighter. "I'm sorry, Tega."

They were the only words I could say.

4

BY THE TIME THE PRIEST ARRIVED, I COULD NO LONGER SEE Zuberi and I told them all so.

The priest said Zuberi was a nature spirit, most likely from the forests of Oron, and it had lost its way.

"What will happen to Naborhi now?" Imoni asked.

"Nothing. Since the spirit is gone, it most likely will remain gone."

"What of her hair?" Imoni's anxiety leached into her words. I wanted to roll my eyes. She was probably concerned that it would affect my value as Fynn's bride.

"You don't have to worry," he told her. "She is healthy. We should thank Egbesu for that."

Imoni's sigh of relief could have been heard for miles.

Once the priest left, Imoni thanked Moyo and hurried me out of there like his house was on fire.

As we passed the fish sellers and neared my house, I felt a

tug on my dress. I turned quickly, my hand instinctively moving toward the dagger at my waist and finding it gone. Moyo must have taken it so Imoni would not see.

A woman knelt on the ground, her sunken, milky eyes searching mine.

"A few shells will help put food in my stomach." She held out a hand.

"I have nothing," I murmured. "Apologies."

"Kenyatta, how are you?" Imoni asked, as if the girl were not begging on her knees.

The woman nodded with a weak smile. "I am surviving."

"Naborhi, let us go," Imoni urged, dragging me onward, Tega trailing us.

Kenyatta was unmarried, and at a certain age, that comes with its own kind of shame. A woman's family would have no choice but to disown her; no one would be willing to give her any work.

Some of these unwed women were lucky enough to become second or third wives. Most, like Kenyatta, became beggars. I wondered if she had thought about leaving. She could not go anywhere in Agbon. The women were treated no better in any of the kingdom's five other clans. She would have to go far away, as far as the Lost Lands. But where would she start from? Who would help her? She did not even have enough money to feed herself. My heart felt weighed down, and I worried for Kenyatta. I wished I had some money to give to her. She was only eight years older than me.

I resented this world that punished her for being alone.

When we got home, Tega brought out rugs with back supports for us and began making a fire.

Imoni and I sat in silence as Tega put a pot for tea over the fire. I watched my sister, startled by how much her movements reminded me of our mother.

"I am glad you are fine," Imoni finally said as she poured herself some tea. "I will let your uncle know. But no more going to places you should not. No spirit is going to hinder your rite of passage or your marriage." Her voice was almost threatening, like she was daring the gods to try to stop my elevation to womanhood.

I went up to the roof to clear my head.

I settled in one of the chairs and surveyed Kokori through big gulps of cold air. A few houses down, a woman beat dust out of a rug on her roof.

My mind was churning, trying to sort through the events of the past few days, the knowledge that I had encountered a spirit and that it had left its mark on me.

Things felt like they were spinning out of my control, like something was rearranging the threads of my life into a knot, my rite of passage at its center. The closer we got to the rite, the more unfamiliar my life became.

I heard a sound coming from the side of the house, and I jumped up just as Tamunor climbed up over the ledge using the window eaves.

He looked dirty, like he had been playing in mud.

"I came to see how you're doing," he said breathlessly, curling his words in the manner of someone who spent most of his life in Okpara. Kokori people spoke more sharply and slightly more rushed.

He straightened and lifted his hands to the sky, cracking his neck and hands.

I sat back on the chair and stretched my legs. "I'm fine."

"So what happened?" he asked, settling in the chair next to me. "And not the exaggerated version Imoni told my father."

I told him all that happened, and he whistled. "Naborhi, being marked by a spirit is no small thing. What do you think it means?"

I shrugged, trying not to show him how much his words affected me.

"Why are you dirty?" I inquired, changing the subject.

He crossed his legs, one atop another. "I was at Aye's compound. He is building a new quarter for his new wife. She is from Emevor, and is so beautiful that you cannot take your eyes off her."

I gave him a knowing look, and he smiled mischievously.

"You are really serious about becoming a builder then?" I asked him.

He nodded. "I guess."

"Making bricks is hard work."

"But not harder than going to the sankore every day. I could not keep up. I would never do well in the king's court anyway. That is not a place for somebody like me. It takes a certain kind of ruthlessness to be there. I do not have that."

"And Iyo?" Iyo was his closest friend.

"He wants to be head merchant. So he needs to pass the court's test." The side of his mouth curved. "And you, what will you do? Will you keep sneaking off to Moyo's?"

"Maybe."

That provoked a mocking smile out of him.

"Will you tell me the truth? Please. You know I will tell no one," he begged. "What do you do there?"

I trusted Tamunor would not tell anyone. Still, I could not take any chances. I decided to be vague.

"He teaches me things that will come in handy someday. Things that I will need to leave Agbon. Things that would not sit so well with people around here."

He looked pained. "I guess you have a different future planned out than what everyone believes."

"For now, I am content with everything Moyo has taught me and will continue to teach me." It was not quite an answer.

"What if you end up unmarried, a beggar?"

Kenyatta's weathered face flashed in my mind, and my chest constricted.

"I will not."

"Imoni will not let you make your own way. She is so headstrong."

"I know. But I want to follow my heart and see what is out there," I said. "Do the things that will make me happy. I cannot get married and give up my freedom when there is this voice in my head telling me I could do more. That I could *be* more."

"If you leave, how are you going to survive without the help of your family? The world is a scary place."

I pulled Tamunor to me by the hand. He begrudgingly shuffled his chair closer, and I felt my heart swell at the love and worry in his eyes.

"I will be okay, Tamunor," I said to him, smiling. "I just have to believe that."

The next day, Tamunor came around wearing clean clothes. He brought with him three sticks of dried fish.

"Tamunor," Tega cried, surprised, as he entered the compound. "I thought you had gone to Okpara with Iyo like you said you would."

"Iyo had to run an errand for his father. So I brought these for us while I wait for him."

"Take them to the kitchen," I told him, combing Tega's last strands of hair that I was going to braid. "I made ukodo with goat meat in case you want to eat," I added.

He made an excited sound and headed to the kitchen.

"Naborhi," Tamunor said, coming back out to the courtyard and pointing at his plate. "This ukodo is so sweet. I could have three pots of it."

My mother had taught me the secret to making good ukodo was fresh lemongrass and fresh lime leaves.

"I haven't eaten, Tamunor. Please don't finish the food," Tega protested.

"Too late," he said, scooping yams into his mouth and settling on a stool next to us.

Tega squawked in dismay and tried to swat at him, but I kept her in place as my fingers twisted her hair down to the middle of her head.

I stood up when I was done.

"Thank you, Naborhi," Tega said, patting her hair. I touched my hand to hers briefly before gathering my bag and my weapons for training.

"You are going out?" Tamunor asked, drinking some water to wash down his food.

"I am going to meet Imoni and the girls at Innuere."

"Right, training," he stated, cocking his head. "Next year it will be my and Tega's turn. Father told me he has a girl for me."

"Oh, does he now?" I giggled at the thought of Tamunor married.

"Yes. I don't know her name." He sighed. "I don't think I want someone my father chooses for me. I want to marry someone I love."

Tega sighed. "I wish it were that easy."

"That's my dream," he said.

Their longing for marriage made me uncomfortable, and I swallowed thickly.

"I am going. Tamunor, see me off?"

Tamunor followed me as far as he could before he branched off toward the river.

"Good luck!" he called, waving goodbye.

I hoped I wouldn't need it.

"Very gracious of you to join us," Imoni said sarcastically when I finally arrived at our usual spot in the woods between Kokori and Innuere. I hurried toward her and the girls. Imoni held a bow in her left hand and had a quiver of arrows on her shoulder.

"Apologies. I had my hands full of hair."

She looked puzzled but quickly ordered me to help with the setting of the traps. This part of the forest was where rabbits liked to build their homes. The kernel trees were abundant here.

I joined Chipo, who was hanging a net outside a rabbit hole the way Imoni had taught us to. She wiped beads of sweat from her forehead and twisted the edge of the net around a stick. The sun was out in a cloudless blue sky, and the forest was hot.

"The other girls are saying you are marking yourself for failure if you keep coming late," Chipo murmured.

"I say let them talk."

She raised a glistening brow, shaking the sticks to test their depth.

I tried to change the subject. "I believe I can catch a rabbit if I try hard enough. We have caught several before. Imoni is an excellent teacher."

But Chipo wasn't having it. "The girls also think you are full of yourself because you are not taking all this seriously. As if the luck of your aunt will rub off on you without you trying. They think you're haughty because you already have someone waiting to marry you."

"*Fynn?*" I asked disgustedly.

"Who else?"

I looked up at the other girls. They were building rabbit traps, setting baits, and gathering dead leaves for a fire. I wanted to explain that I was not trying to be full of myself, that having to marry Fynn was not something I looked forward to.

"And what do you think?" I asked as I began to hammer the sticks into the ground. "Am I full of myself?"

She shrugged. "You are not. But you have Imoni for an aunt. I expect people have high expectations of you."

I was done hammering. "I am proud of my aunt. I should do well to make her proud of me too."

Chipo shook her head, laughing softly. "I would be twice as nervous if I were you."

"Good thing you are not me," I teased.

"Gather around!" Imoni shouted, walking toward a rabbit hole where a girl named Muto was blowing air into it through a pipe. Smoke billowed from the pipe, filling the hole.

The trick was to smoke the rabbit out through one entrance, forcing them to flee out the other, where a trap like the one Chipo and I had set up awaited it. Or, the rabbit would jump toward Muto and knock her down and she would end up burning her mouth.

The large brown rabbit did the latter.

Muto lay dazed on the ground. The rest of the girls shouted as the rabbit sprinted around, confused by all the people. It was stopped by an arrow straight to its side.

Imoni put down her bow.

"You either do that or you go after it hoping that your knife finds its throat," she barked.

Some of the girls behind me grumbled. One of them was on the verge of sobbing. Muto had her fingers to her lips, testing the raw skin. She nodded at me, and I knew she'd be fine.

"Why is this our rite of passage?" Muto complained, which reminded me of Tega. "The girls in Burutu dance and sing songs. Then they weave blankets that would be used in their homes. It's all a mellow affair. And this is ours," she hissed. "I cannot wait for it to be all over."

Imoni ignored her and stood on the stump of a fallen tree. "We will leave the traps with baits here and move ahead to practice archery."

More grumbling ensued as we gathered our bows and belongings and followed Imoni through the woods.

"You can make all the noise you want," Imoni chided, "but you will do as I say."

Chipo came to walk by my side, rubbing her palms together as we went deeper into the forest. The forest smelled clean, fresh. It had rained the night before, and steam billowed from the forest floor in the heat like the smoke from our rabbit traps. I wiped the sweat from my brow.

"Father has found a suitor for me," Chipo murmured with a shy smile.

I gasped quietly. "Chipo! How could you keep this secret from me? Who is he?"

She laughed before letting out a sigh. "He will not tell me his name or the name of his family."

"Do you have anyone in mind?" I whispered, nudging her with a grin.

She blushed. "I'm not sure," she replied coyly. "But I suppose I hope for Birungi."

My eyes widened in delighted surprise. "Birungi? Chipo!"

Birungi was the heir to the Taokiri fortune. He was the eldest grandson of one of the richest men in Agbon. Marrying him meant an elevation in status, money, a noble name, and constant invitations to the king's castle for every festivity.

"Perhaps the Taokiris are the ones who have approached your parents," I suggested.

She glanced at me sharply. "You think that is why they are keeping it a secret?" Her dimples deepened as she smiled fully.

"Maybe," I said, giving her a teasing smile.

She squealed in excitement, catching Imoni's attention.

"Enough gossiping," Imoni snapped. "You will train like you came here to."

We had arrived at the clearing where Imoni kept the targets for our practice. She'd set them up several feet ahead, planting the posts firmly in the ground, and adjusted the straws bundled together that surrounded each of them.

She pointed to Tumelo and Burye to my left. "Remember what I taught you," she told them while the rest of us stood behind, observing.

The two girls got into position facing the targets and raised their bows.

"How can someone be so excited about something and yet dread it too?" Chipo asked me quietly as Imoni critiqued the girls' stances.

"You mean the rite of passage?"

"Yes. What else?" she scoffed. "I am excited about showing my worth as a woman. I eagerly await the festivities. The hunt itself? Not so much."

"In the words of Imoni, it is tradition and it must obeyed."

She nodded. "But tradition can be changed, can it not?"

"Yes, it can. But it's not so easy."

"Why not?" She seemed genuinely angry. "These traditions are made by men, not the other way around. Why should we women follow traditions we have no say in?"

This was why I was friends with Chipo. I was struck with the overwhelming urge to tell her everything about Moyo, about my forbidden skills, about my desire for escape. I bit back the words. I could not risk Chipo's future here by incriminating her in my plans. But I ached at the thought that I would leave her and hurt her, just as I would hurt Tega.

Imoni stopped behind Tumelo and gently tapped her raised right elbow. She lowered it. It was easy to see that the girl was tense. She and Burye both let go of the arrows simultaneously, narrowly missing their targets.

Tumelo groaned and let the bow fall from her hand. "Let us go back to rabbits. This is frustrating."

"Very," Burye echoed, hand on her waist.

"Very, very," I muttered to myself.

"Is that what everyone wants?" said Imoni. "To go back to the rabbit holes?"

"Yes," the majority answered.

Imoni was not having any of it. She wanted us to be excited about every part of our rites of passage.

"Well, too bad. You will continue with archery. I'd like to actually eat something other than rabbit stew this year." She threw a look our way. "Chipo, Naborhi, you are next."

Chipo grumbled as we made our way to Imoni. She readied her bow, frowning. I raised my bow, aiming just left of the center of the straw bundles. I held my torso straight, my arm bent evenly parallel to my collarbone.

As one, Chipo and I let our arrows loose. They both thunked into the center of the targets.

Imoni only nodded at us and called for the next girls. But her eyes were lit with pride.

5

A FEW DAYS BEFORE MY HUNT, I DECIDED TO GO TO MOYO'S.

Tega was hanging wrappers on the wooden rail that lined the stairs to the roof when I bid her goodbye.

"I am going to see if the old man is all right," I said to her.

What I meant was that I was going to have a bout with him. I did not want to become lazy and let my skills become stale. And I needed that rush in my head to cloud whatever thoughts I had of the rite-of-passage ceremony. I had imagined I would not be in Kokori when the ceremony came.

She asked dryly, "Are you going to come back with a sprained ankle again?"

"That was before I knew how to ride a horse. Moyo has taught me well. I will not fall off again."

"If you say so."

It was hard to miss the reprimanding tone behind her words.

"Tega, I will be fine."

I was halfway to his house, daydreaming of sailing my father's ships, when I felt a cold wind at the back of my neck.

Zuberi appeared beside me in a swirl of fog. It was the first time I was seeing the spirit in days. It was almost as tall as me now.

I looked into its eyes. "Are you a spirit of nature?" I asked. It merely blinked at me and did not reply. "Are you lost? Oron is that way." I pointed far out to the east.

Zuberi simply bounded into the trees, scaring off some doves. Playing, I realized.

"Perhaps you'll accompany me to Moyo's?" I asked with a fond laugh.

Zuberi purred in agreement.

When we arrived, Moyo was definitely ready to teach me a lesson or two. We walked to the clearing in his bento-bean field. Zuberi lay in the sun, asleep.

"Do you feel well enough to spar?" Moyo asked.

"I do," I told him, tying my fists with the pieces of cloth he provided. He straightened up and immediately looked ten years younger. I moved toward my left while watching him. He followed me a few steps, then stopped.

I put up both fists. Left arm and leg outstretched toward my right. Right leg behind and right fist aiming for my left shoulder.

This fighting style was called Eguaya, the Dance of War. Moyo had learned it from his time in the Egor clan. The dance avoided wasting one's strength at close-range fights. It required bodily control, flexibility, and knowledge of one's opponent.

With a sharp turn I attacked first, alternating with high kicks and short bursts of hand jabs aimed at his stomach. He pulled back, evading my movements easily, not wanting to counterattack. He angled forward, using both hands to block my attack and shove me backward. I breathed out and balled my hands again, putting them back in formation.

I had to find his opening before he found mine. I lurched at him and tried to sweep his legs. He sidestepped to his left and got his opening when I placed one hand on the ground hoping to attempt a kick. He spun around, while I stood up and did a somersault toward him.

"Ahhhhh!"

My voice was swallowed by the rustling stalks as I jumped toward him and spun. He grabbed my leg in midair and smiled. I tilted my body, using the other leg to strike. He let go of me and I fell, barely catching myself before my face hit the ground. I wasted no time in going back for another attack.

Taking a deep breath, I decided to get in closer. Hand-to-hand, body-to-body contact. He swung his left hand and I dodged, doing a split, and succeeded in kicking his right leg. He stumbled but steadied himself quickly to catch my successive punches.

And that was it.

With one quick move of his hands to my jaw, the fight stopped with me on the ground with a cut on my lower lip. I opened my mouth and moved my jaw to regain feeling there.

With a quick push, I was on my feet again ready for combat.

He raised a finger and I stopped.

"I am proud of how far you have come," he said, smiling broadly. "Take some time to rest. We will go at it again soon."

"I don't want to rest," I told him. "Let's keep going."

"If you are not tired, I am," he said, going to sit on the chair outside his house. Zuberi finally stirred awake and trailed him.

I tried to charge Moyo from behind, but he dodged quickly.

"What has gotten into you?" he demanded.

"I want to keep fighting," I said, even though my legs hurt.

"Why?"

I abandoned my fighting stance and stood straight.

Moyo cocked his head and smiled weakly, knowing what was awaiting me in three days' time. "Fighting me won't change anything."

"It will distract me," I replied.

"And then what?"

I could not find a decent answer to his question. He beckoned me over.

"Come to the house. I'll find you something to drink and give you the new book I just got. That should be distraction enough."

I shoved down my anxiety and took his offer. We stayed outside his house reading and drinking milk tea until the sun started going down. Zuberi played in the bean field, chasing birds and insects and its own tail. Zuberi disappeared just as the sun dipped below the tree line.

As I limped back home that evening, thoughts about the rite of passage crept back into my mind. My mother had told me all about hers. She had been so excited for it, and was eager to learn how to catch rabbits. She went into her rite and her quick marriage to my father with elation. I was more excited about sparring with Moyo.

When the timekeeper rang the bell for the fifth hour three days later, I was already awake and in the courtyard. Across my body was my quiver of arrows, and I held my bow in my left hand. I had my Assegai twin daggers strapped to my hip and thigh, and my tools for rabbit snares in a fabric bag over my shoulders. I tied my hair back with a white scarf, as would all the other girls. White was the color of Uwevwin, a symbol of purity and chastity.

I stood with a silver shell in my hand in front of the statue of Uwevwin, tucked into the corner of our courtyard, far from Egbesu and his Ọkan. "*Beautiful and wise goddess, keeper of the home, this is my offering to you. Guide my hands and feet today. Let your words be my words. Let your sight be mine.*" I kissed the coin and placed it at her feet.

The door to Tega's room opened, and my sister came out yawning. She carried a metal lamp that she placed on the ground. She had worked late into the night preparing cachupa, a local delicacy made of chicken broth, spices, and cassava that took almost three days to make. It would be my treat when I passed.

"I am so excited and nervous, and it is not my rite of passage." Tega chuckled, clasping her hands in front of her. She yawned again. "How do you feel?"

"The same way. Only double."

"Do you want to eat?"

"No. I have to go or I will be late. Imoni will not tolerate lateness."

"Be careful," Tega told me as I walked toward the front gate. "See you later."

We assembled at the market square waiting for Imoni. It was a short walk from the square to Innuere Forest if we cut through the lumberyard and used the old stone bridge over the creek that fed into the Ethiope. We stood around the well in the middle of the square and watched the sun come up.

Imoni arrived soon after in an ancient hunting dress. Her bow and full quiver were slung over her right shoulder. She looked from one girl to the other without uttering a word. After her inspection, she beckoned for us to follow her.

Chipo found her way to my side and fell in step with me. "I could barely sleep last night," she whispered. "How about you?"

"I could not sleep at all. It was frustrating." I could not tell her it was for a different reason. All I could think of was my future fading away, of it being replaced by marriage and housekeeping. Moyo's voice echoed in my head, despite my best efforts.

"Have you considered leaving without your sister?"

Chipo's voice brought me back to where I was.

"I had such a strange dream. I was being chased by a bush dog. I struggled to shoot it with an arrow, but my hands kept disappearing. I had to wait for the animal to come closer, then I bit its neck." Her eyes widened with her lips slightly open. "I ate the bush dog whole."

I laughed so hard, my ribs hurt.

"I couldn't tell my mother about it because she would have some sort of interpretation for it and we would have to go to the temple for guidance."

"Over nothing," I said.

"Over nothing," she repeated, then asked softly, "What if we only bring back snails? Rabbits are at least a staple, but what if they run too fast?"

"I guess we just have to be faster. But you should not be worried. Your traps are good, even better than mine."

"Do not flatter me."

"The lizard that jumps from the high uloho tree to the ground tells everyone he can praise himself if no one else will," I said, reciting the proverb. "Praise yourself, Chipo, when you deserve it."

She smiled a little and she seemed to move more confidently.

Imoni took us deep into the Innuere Forest and stopped at a forked path. One branch led to Innuere, and the other was a circuitous route back to Kokori. The day was dawning and the forest came alive with the sun. Sweat beaded along my brow and down my back, but I wasn't sure if it was from the heat or anticipation.

Imoni said loud enough for us all to hear, "Your rites begin now. You have until sundown to bring your kills to the orosuen's compound." Her eyes landed on mine. "Remember your teachings."

Some of the girls went off in pairs, and some by themselves. Chipo looked at me and held out her hand.

"Together?" she asked.

I twined my fingers through hers. "Together." No matter our futures, no matter whether we brought home stags or snails, I could face it as long as I had her.

We walked through breadfruit trees full of birds' nests until we found a pond hidden away in a tight-knit grove. The water was so still, we could see ourselves and the trees and the sky reflected back at us, as though it were glass.

Chipo motioned silently at the ground several yards away from us. Birds sang and called to each other, a cacophony that hid the sound of our steps as we approached a near-hidden rabbit warren.

We moved quickly to locate all the holes, vegetable scraps and stalks near the openings. Then we set up our traps.

We waited for a long time for the rabbits to come out. I caught Chipo looking toward the pond, no doubt wondering if we'd need to resort to hunting for snails.

I was about to console her when a rabbit ran out of the warren, right into a trap.

Chipo moved quickly and quietly to remove the dead creature from the noose and reset the snare. She held the rabbit's body gently in her hands as we resumed our post. She'd always been sensitive when we'd caught rabbits before, but this time I, too, felt the weight of this death. Tears stung my eyes, and I placed a hand on Chipo's, over the incredible softness of the rabbit's ears.

We knew that the rabbit was not special, that it would not distinguish us as hunters. But we decided to make up for it with patience. By the time the sun crept beneath the trees, we had caught three rabbits each.

We disassembled our snares and carried the animals back to the orosuen's compound.

"And our rites are completed," Chipo murmured.

I hoped my answering smile hid my fear.

By sunset, we were all at the orosuen's estate. Most had brought rabbits, though none as many as Chipo and me. A girl named Leena, the best marksman in our group, brought an antelope back. The antelope was huge, and the three arrows she'd used to take it down were still in its side. Everyone wanted to see the animal, and they praised her for a good hunt.

Orosuen Jabali's estate was opulent and spacious. The house was three stories high and painted a blinding white that seemed to glow in the dimming light. Big pots on iron stilts were lined near the brick wall in the open-air kitchen at the back of the estate, away from the outer courtyard where we gathered, ready to cook the meat we had brought from our rites. Lit lanterns floated on a wide pool, fighting for space with pink and orange flowers bursting forth from the surface. Two stone statues of men stood on either side of the entrance to the grounds, each carrying a torch that was lit as soon as the drumming started, announcing our arrivals.

Hundreds of people milled about, dressed in their finest clothes and already drinking wine.

The boys who had just gone through their own rite of passage trooped in after us. They were stone-faced and proud, but I noticed a few cracked smiles of excitement.

Their rite of passage was carried out more discreetly than ours. They camped out in the farmland just outside Kokori with the captains of the Abavo. The boys went through all manner of tests that were never to be revealed to Kokori's women, even to their wives or mothers.

One of the Abavo, a man in ashy tumbras with a beefy bare chest, chanted the names of the boys as they entered the grounds, and each already gathered responded with "*We greet you.*"

The girls sat on cushions set up in a corner of the courtyard, shaded by long, colorful drapes.

Imoni and several older women carried over pots of elaborately prepared dyes made from red camwood and palm kernel oil. The strong smell tickled my nose as they painted the dye on our skin with their fingertips, decorating our bodies and faces until we looked exactly the way they wanted.

When we were all settled and the gates closed, Orosuen Jabali emerged from his house. He stood at the top of the front steps and waved his horsetail. We all stood and bowed. His first wife joined him. They wore matching outfits made of a beautiful purple fabric, and she'd put up her hair in a matching wrap to accentuate the beauty of her round face.

They both descended the stairs and met with Imoni and the three Abavo captains. They conferred for a short while, and I knew that they were discussing the names of those who had just passed their rites.

Orosuen Jabali stepped forward then and raised his horsetail. "Siwo, siwo!" he cried.

"Siwo!" we all shouted in reply, and the drumming increased. We had all passed our rites of passage. I was a woman now, just like my mother, just like Imoni, and I actually felt proud of myself.

I hugged Chipo, who hugged me back just as tight.

Imoni came over to us with a statue of Uwevwin in her hands. The goddess was in a kneeling position, her head down, humble, as we all were supposed to be from then on. On her left hand was a four-ring mark every married woman in Kokori had—three rings branded on her after her rite of passage, and a final one after the rites of a wedding ceremony were completed.

Imoni went around to each of us, blessing our future homes with the statue. When she finished, she chanted, "*Siwo, siwo*," and broke into song.

We joined her in singing and dancing.

I had never been good at the traditional dances, but I danced as well as I could, side by side with Chipo. And just for a short while, I forgot about my worries.

The animals we brought were skinned and cut by the boys.

Some of the older women took the meat and proceeded to the

open kitchen. We joined them to prepare the food while the boys drank, danced, and sang.

"You did well," Imoni whispered to me as I tended my fire. The wood let out small sparks that floated in front of my eyes.

"You taught me well." I straightened up and looked at her.

"You learned nothing from me," she said, and smiled.

"The praise is yours to take."

"Do not let it boil over," she said, pointing at the pot. I quickly took apart some of the firewood and watched the fire dim.

"Your mind is far from here." Imoni's voice was soft, not accusatory.

"It is not so far."

"You are not the first one to be afraid of what might happen next," she murmured, touching my shoulder. I could smell her lavender oil, and for some reason the scent made me want to cry. "You will be a good wife. You do not have to worry."

If only I were worried about that.

"Let me see how the other pots are doing. Smile, Naborhi. You will be married soon."

I forced a smile, my face straining under the weight of the pretense.

The celebrations went on all night, until first light, when we all made our way to the clan's temple up the hill from the orosuen's estate. By then, some of the men were so drunk they needed help walking.

As the sun rose over the horizon and lit up the old stones, the boys knelt on the ground outside the temple while their faces were painted and then washed clean, signifying they had let go of their boyhood and were now men. Men who were free to do whatever they wanted to.

Then it was our turn.

We lined up in single file, Chipo ahead of me, and headed inside the grand temple. Imoni walked in front of all of us, holding a white chicken as an offering, and some of the girls carried food we had prepared for the priests.

The men and the others who had followed us stayed outside, forbidden to enter.

The old temple was made up of several edifices with sharp peaked roofs connected by short bridges. Cashew and black almond trees grew rampant, lending a fruity scent to the grounds.

We were led through the main prayer hall, which held an impressive terracotta statue of Egbesu in a long robe looking up, an Ọkan above him. Beneath the statue was a glistening pool, where we dropped coins after prayers. Cold air wafted in through the big round windows and nearly blew out the candles mounted on the arched pillars surrounding us. The dome-shaped roof was made of intricately carved stones, where birds now made their homes.

The hand-painted columns on both sides of a long passageway held smaller figures of Egbesu's brothers and sisters, the gods and goddesses and spirits that have the destiny of man in their hands. There was Udi, the wine god, with a goblet in his hand, and Okunovu, the spirit of the waters. There was also Emedjo, who brings his blessings when the Ethiope reaches its highest level, and Edjokpa, who brings a bountiful harvest of palm every year. I prayed to each one of them as we walked, asking for strength.

We crossed another bridge to get to Uvwewin's pavilion, set separate from the other buildings, on higher ground, facing the rising sun. In the middle the chamber was a statue of a pregnant Uvwewin, the crown on her head signifying the home being a crowning achievement of a woman. She blessed any woman who paid homage to her with children and a good home. I kept my prayers to myself in this room.

Standing next to the statue was the odede, Kokori's oldest woman, with the ceremonial branding iron and bucket of hot coals. Her wispy gray hair ruffled in the slight wind.

We gathered around her.

Imoni placed the chicken underneath the statue and faced us. "I am happy to see you all here. Your mothers and your mothers' mothers have walked this path before you. This is the final step. In the eyes of the goddess that protects our families, you are all blessed. Your homes will be full of happiness, and you will bear strong boys."

Our group's resulting smiles were wide and even Chipo giggled. I imagined Imoni in my place, and my mother only two years after her. What had they been thinking? Did it ever cross their minds that they did not want to bear children just yet? Did they ever think about all the places they had never seen?

The odede did not waste time with words. Maybe it was because she looked about ready to sit down on the grass and take a nap. With Imoni's help, she burned a three-ring mark on the back of our left hands.

When it was my turn, Imoni gripped my hand tightly before the odede marked me. She held my gaze as my skin seared, and I refused to cry.

When we were done, Imoni shouted "Siwo!" again, and we responded in kind.

Chipo spread her arms wide to hug me. She had tearstains on her cheeks from the branding.

"We've done it, Naborhi," she cried. "Together."

I squeezed her back, her *Together* ringing in my ears.

When we emerged from the temple, the crowd cheered, and men put us on special chairs they had brought. We were lifted up and paraded around for all to see, marching down the hill, in the streets, into the market, to the banks of the Ethiope.

They returned us to our families after the sun was fully up. Tega and Tamunor were waiting at our gate, smiling wide. Tamunor whooped in excitement and Tega bounded over to me, laughing and crying and hugging me tightly.

When she let me go, Imoni took my hands carefully, avoiding the painful mark. "Fynn is so lucky to have you as wife," she proclaimed. "I am proud of you."

Though the day had just begun, we retreated into the house. Tega crawled into bed with me, and I told her everything that had happened, down to the smallest detail. When she dozed off, I rolled so my back was to her, the weight of everything bearing down on me, and I finally let myself cry.

6

A FEW DAYS AFTER THE RITE, UNIKA BROUGHT THE ULOHO wood he wanted to take to Okpara directly to our house. With a little coaxing from Imoni he agreed to let me accompany him to the boatyard. I was ecstatic, my heart soaring in excitement, but Unika brought news that dampened my joy.

"In two months, you will marry Fynn. His father has journeyed to Oring Island for salt, so we have to wait until he comes back. Otherwise, you would be married already."

Thank you, Sayo Goredenna.

By the time he returned, I was sure I would have come up with at least enough money to get to Iga. I would have to cut down on spending even further and save every coin provided by Unika for new clothes and supplies, and I might still have no choice but to borrow from Moyo. I didn't want to do that. I'd wanted to start my new life owing no one. But now, it seemed less likely.

The money to settle down in Iga was another thing. We would have to work for it. Me and Tega.

If Tega agrees to come along, said a voice in my head.

She will, I said to myself. *She has to.*

"I will sleep here tonight, and we will leave before the sun rises in the morning," Unika told me.

I knew what that meant. Instead of assigning the cleaning to Tega, I decided to do it myself. I took a broom and a small bucket of water and a rag to the room that once used to be my parents' bedroom. The room was slightly musty, a strong contrast to how it used to smell. My mother had loved her scents. She would haggle for a bargain over everything but her perfumes. She especially loved wild dagga. She would lather it on her neck and on her temples and that smell would linger, sweet, dewy. Alive.

I opened the only window in the room and sunlight flooded in, dust particles floating in the beam. Above the bed, the tapestry of flowering highlands remained untouched by time. Unika had painted it using charcoal, the Kokori way. It had been a wedding gift to my parents. Unika was talented as an artist but he refused to pursue it seriously. Instead, he joined my father in whatever business he'd wanted to do.

I was sweeping under the bed when I heard something scrape along the floor. I bent down, peering under the bed, and spotted something. I reached for it.

It was a cowrie bracelet. My heart stuttered in recognition.

"What is that?"

I looked up to see Tega peering down at me from the door.

I showed it to her. "It was Mother's. One of her favorites."

"It is beautiful," she said, coming closer to inspect it.

"Give me your hand."

She stretched out her right arm and I clasped the bracelet around her wrist.

"Are you sure you don't want it?" she asked, doe-eyed.

"She would have wanted you to have it. Your wrists are so delicate."

"Thank you," she whispered. "I miss her so much."

I squeezed her hand. "I know. I do too."

"I forget sometimes," she said quietly. "I forget what she looked like, what she smelled like, the sound of her laughter. Not for long, but just enough that it frightens me."

Her words cut deep into my soul, where the same fear of forgetting resided.

"I know what you mean," I told her. "I'm afraid one day I'll wake up and never again remember the exact color of her eyes."

Tega nodded at me, tears gathering in her beautiful dark eyes. Our father's eyes, same as mine. Even Imoni did not have our mother's unique amber irises.

Tega joined me in cleaning the room without me asking.

The next morning, Unika and I woke before the sun.

"Do you have all that you need?" Unika asked as we settled into the half-covered cart full of uloho logs. The shaved bark was still a little green.

"Yes, I do."

He nodded once and snapped the reins of the horses, urging them forward. The cart rocked from side to side as we began the journey through the fields to Okpara.

Unika did not look so much like my father. His skin was fairer, like milk after it had been boiled. He had a small mouth that was constantly chewing gworo and a straight face pulled together by thick eyebrows.

He was also unlike Okota in other ways. He smiled occasionally and spoke quietly. The only way he showed his anger was to spit out his gworo and walk away. He would return when he was calm. It was a wonder to me how two such different people could come from one place.

After an hour of riding in silence, Unika spat out some of his thoroughly chewed gworo. "I regret not being there during your rite of passage. I would have loved to see you carried about."

"And to eat all the food that we cooked," I teased.

He laughed out loud. "Yes, that too."

"You were in Burutu and busy. It is no one's fault. You did not miss anything interesting."

"You speak as if you did not enjoy yourself." He swatted flies away from his face as we passed grazing land. The cattle on it were fat and healthy. White egrets flew in from the river and settled on their bodies.

I responded with a half shrug. "Maybe a little. But I was more tense than relaxed."

"I know," he declared, scratching his chin.

How could he possibly know?

"What do you mean?" I dared to ask.

"It would be unnatural if you did not feel anxious. You are entering into another phase of your life. An important one. You will marry, start your own family, and raise your children." Unika looked at me meaningfully. "And that means setting aside the dreams you have had in this old phase of your life in preparation for the reality of your new one."

I adjusted the long scarf atop my head, which spread around my shoulders. My body shook in response to something other than the cold wind.

He unwrapped the banana leaf that held some agidi. He broke off a piece and handed it to me. I sniffed the scent of the congealed delicacy that had perfectly blended with the tangy smell of the leaf and took a bite.

"Are the logs for one of our boats?" I asked with my mouth full, turning slightly to glance at the wood.

"No. For another's ship. The man who needs it will come for it tomorrow. Some men still have it in their heads for sailing far beyond the Bitter Sea." He shook his head.

"Why?" I thought of all the stories about the dangerous waves beyond the Bitter Sea that swallowed up boats.

"Pride, I think. For the glory of it all."

"And what if they meet their death?"

"They will go to their ancestors. My only job is to make sure they sail boats with good wood on their journeys. And to collect my money."

I sighed at the thought of these headstrong men. Were they fearless or just plain foolish? But I thought the same could also be asked of me. Was I foolish to think I could achieve my dreams of independence? So far nothing had gone the way I wanted.

I shook my head clear of my doubts. I would be going far beyond my home, into uncharted waters. I was not fearless, but I was not foolish. I just knew what I wanted and I was willing to fight for it.

"How many men work at the boatyard now?"

The cart shook as we went over a small bridge, a small stream flowing lazily beneath us.

"Twenty men work for me now. They are good men," he said, looking up at the fast-moving clouds.

"Are you happy as a boat-maker?" I asked, hoping he would not find offense in my question.

He smiled, leaning to his side to elbow me. "You are not going to give up, are you?"

I shook my head. "I want to know. You used to paint before you started working with my father, and then you took over his business. Did you ever want to be a painter instead?"

"Yes, I used to. I was not very good. I knew I would not make much from it. Shipbuilding gives me the fulfillment and the money I require to live a decent life. So, to answer your question, I am happy to be a boat-maker."

"I see."

He chuckled. "What do you see?"

"Nothing," I answered truthfully, looking down at the stony ground. We were getting close to Okpara.

"But I do miss painting sometimes," Unika murmured softly after a moment. "It also made me happy."

I stared at him, at this man who was more a father to me than my own had been, a man who was kind and gentle and hardworking, and realized that he hid so much of himself from me, from the world. That his hands, so strong and capable from heaving uloho logs and sanding hulls, craved to hold a brush. "I really liked your paintings," I tell him gently.

"You remember them?" he asks, surprised—and delighted.

I nodded, smiling. "I remember the one with the woman in a ball of light. It is unforgettable."

Unika smiled back at me, his eyes lit in a way I had not seen in years, and I swallowed against the sudden emotion rising in my throat.

We arrived at the massive stone bridge outside Okpara just as the sun began to set. Unika had to pay the Abavo on duty a merchant-tax fee before we were allowed to set foot in the capital.

Unika took us through a wide street and down a slope that was host to many breweries and food stalls. The smell was intoxicating.

We were not far from the docks when a small crowd brought our cart to a halt.

Unika got down in one quick movement to check the cause of the delay.

"Stay here," he told me firmly. "I'll be right back."

When he did not return within a few moments, I too got down

to find out what was happening. I tied the horses to a post on the side of the road and pushed through the crowd toward a wailing sound. A girl was on the ground, her skirt rumpled and her tunic torn. She couldn't have been much older than me. She had a small cut on her lower lip and looked up at the crowd with wide, pleading eyes.

A stout man with a thin mustache shouted at the crowd. His voice, despite his small stature, was loud and commanded attention. He pointed at the girl. "She has lost her innocence. She has lost her pride. Who will marry a broken thing like her? Not any man in his right senses."

Some of the women and young girls in the crowd shook their heads and muttered to themselves.

"She seduced Chacha, our favorite brewer-in-training." The stout man pointed at a handsome boy who was standing against the corner of a nearby brewery, looking more amused than anything else.

"I did not seduce him!" the girl exploded. She turned to the young man, who seemed to have a problem with looking at her directly. "Chacha, tell them I did not seduce you," she sobbed. "Tell them!"

Chacha ignored her, examining his fingernails. My blood heated at his dismissiveness.

"She is a disgrace to her mother," the stout man went on, pulling out a cow-tail whip. "To other girls and wives-to-be. Let her feel the burden of the shame she shall bear."

The girl scrambled toward the man. "Father, please, do not do this. I am sorry for what I did." She eyed Chacha, who soon turned to go back inside the brewery. "I have learned my lesson."

"Beat some sense into her!" someone shouted.

I looked around at the angry, jeering faces and realized just how many people wanted to see the girl's blood. Chacha had gone free, leaving her to take the humiliation and beating. He did not even have the decency to beg for her. I balled my fists and ground my teeth.

I took a few steps toward them, ready to plead on her behalf, not minding what came after.

A hand grabbed my elbow, yanking me backward. Unika's alarmed face looked down at me.

"What do you think you are doing?" he demanded.

"I can't just do *nothing*."

"I feel for her too," he said, glancing back to the crowd. "But there's nothing we can do."

The sound of the whip cracking on flesh made me flinch.

"Crowds can turn on anyone at a moment's notice. It is best we start moving again."

My heart screamed at me to go save the girl, to shout at her father, to drag Chacha outside and let him feel the lash of the whip himself.

Instead, I allowed Unika to guide me back to the cart, the horses shuffling nervously as they sensed the crowd's fervor.

Mamuzo and Oghale were longtime friends of Unika. They sheltered us in their home for the night. The house had been colorfully designed in an Emevor style. There was hardly a surface that didn't have a splash of vibrant paint on it.

Oghale wore Emevoran traditional attire: a bright-orange top wrapper lined with beads, an equally eye-catching stiff skirt, brass rings on her neck, feet, and arms, and a beaded headband. Her hair was threaded into several parts that met at the middle.

She handed her baby to her maid and asked her to prepare the guest rooms after she put the baby down. She then asked for my help preparing the evening meal.

"He who brings gworo brings good health with him," I heard Unika say boisterously to Mamuzo as I followed Oghale to the kitchen. From the ingredients lying around, I could tell she was making crayfish soup. But there were additional ingredients that were not part of any recipe I knew.

"You have gone through your rite of passage," she stated, looking at the three-ring mark on my hand as she gave me a carving knife.

"Yes."

"And do you have a suitor yet?" she asked, passing me a cocoyam.

I set about peeling it. "I think I do."

"That is a strange answer."

I sighed, giving her a weak smile. "His name is Fynn. And I do not like him at all. But he comes from a good and well-respected family."

"That is important. But if you are not sure, then your family should not receive any wine from them." She added broth to the pot and added in a mound of vegetables.

"We have already received wine."

"Well . . ." She did not finish her sentence. I wondered if she understood what it meant to be bound to someone you detested.

She took a spoon to the pot and stirred. Steam drifted from the pot, and the delicious smell of the soup filled the room. My stomach rumbled.

"I had a Fynn once," she murmured while she stirred. "Hated the very sight of him. I was lucky to have met my husband. He is the complete opposite of that man."

Oghale poured some of the soup on her palm and tasted. She added ugbore, which was unusual, and tasted again. From the pocket of her skirt she took out a small book with thick pages and a writing brush. She dipped the brush in an ink jar on the counter and began scribbling in the book.

I abandoned my chopping, staring at her until she looked up at me.

She arched a brow at me, putting the book back in her skirt pocket.

I looked around, picturing an Abavo bursting in through the door and catching her so openly writing into a book.

"How?"

She chuckled. "My husband taught me to write."

"What?" My voice was high, shocked.

"I know you will not believe me." She laughed. "Like I said, the total opposite of my Fynn. I like cooking very much. Mamuzo taught me so I can make my own recipes and write them down to give to my daughters. They too can make their own recipes and hand them down to their daughters."

She brought out a smaller pot and poured some water into it.

"What if someone finds out? What if I go out there and tell the Abavo?"

She stopped unwrapping the sack of flour on the table and grabbed my right hand, peering between my fingers. She let go of my hand with a small laugh. "Then I will take the thrashing. A small price to pay, don't you think?"

I looked in between my fingers at the ink marks there.

"My husband holds the pen like you do." She chuckled knowingly. "I will keep your secret if you keep mine."

I admired her courage. I admired her husband, too, and could not help but watch him while we ate to see what made him different from other men. There was nothing obvious. He spoke with a slight stammer, chewed gworo like Unika, and was just as tall. Whatever made him different was deep inside where no one could see.

That night, before I slept, I watched as the older woman wrote in her book by candlelight, her baby cooing by her side.

Could this be my life if I married someone like her husband? I would have a family of my own and I would have some sort of freedom in the confines of my home.

I knew it would never be enough.

The next day we made our way to the boatyard, sprawled along the northern shore with the city behind it.

Unika led me to his ships. They were arched and shapely, and compartments were being built beneath the upper set of wood to accommodate people and goods. The sides bore a drawing of Egbesu's sword for good fortune. All the boats stood on stilts leading right up to the water, which crashed against the shore violently.

The men came toward Unika and me as we approached.

"Egwo," I greeted them when they were all gathered, waiting for Unika's orders.

"Vren," they responded.

Unika pointed at two of the men in front. "You and you, I have the wood in the cart, at the top of the docks."

They nodded and hastily went about getting the logs of wood.

"Wedia, show me," he said to a man stripped to his waist. The other men returned to work, shaving wood and mounting sails.

Meanwhile Unika and Wedia examined a finished boat, smaller than the rest but pristine. I assumed it was a fishing boat or one of those trawlers that plied the Ethiope, carrying crayfish down to Emevor. I looked around, taking in the cloudless blue sky and the salty air.

I watched five women sitting on the dazzling white sands sewing a sail with expert fingers and two men loading crates onto a ship a few docks away.

I remembered the last time I was here. My mother had brought Tega and me when I was ten. It was one of the few times I had been happy around my father. We sat underneath the coconut trees and watched him work. We ate kpokpo garri and roasted edible worm and drank palm wine sold by the men who had come from Burutu. The thought of such a simpler time made me smile.

"Naborhi!" Unika called from the end of the dock. He gestured to the hut nestled between coconut trees that served as his office. Wedia had disappeared somewhere.

Inside the hut was cool and smelled of coconuts and wood. Spread out on the table were sketches and drawings of boats. One diagram showed a massive ship with five sails and extra ropes.

"What are all these?" I asked, peering at the drawings as my uncle entered the hut.

"I have been working on this for some time now," Unika said, using the tip of his finger to make circular motions around parts of the ship.

"We are going to change this, and this," he said excitedly. "The sails will be tricky but we will get them where we want them. The ship will go faster with these."

"I guess you do get to be an artist, in some way," I said, smiling.

His head snapped up and he laughed. "You are right. Though slightly more involved." His eyes went distant for a moment. "It is why I have always wanted a boy of my own. To teach him all that I know."

"But you are not married."

"I am not," he said, placing one hand on his hip and leaning toward the table.

"Why not?"

"Because I am waiting."

"We are ready!" Wedia shouted from outside.

"Let us go," Unika told me, moving to the door, ignoring me.

"Where?"

"So many questions." He laughed again, fondness in his eyes. "Just trust me."

Moments later I found myself aboard the new boat, gliding over the water, my heart racing. It felt like a dream. The blue-green water rushed past us and birds hovered above, their cries triumphant. Wedia stood at the helm, steering us out to open water, and the wind took up the sails. I closed my eyes, imagining I was a member of the crew, hauling ropes and climbing the mast.

I turned round to find Unika examining the ship, making sure everything worked the way he wanted.

The boat ran into a wave, and I held on to the edge as water splashed my face and shoulders. I laughed, dabbing my face with the edge of my scarf.

Unika came to stand by my side. "What do you think?"

"Anyone can see it is a marvelous ship."

He gave a slight nod of appreciation. "This will go on to be one of the fastest fishing boats in Agbon. Its hull bears a new design I came up with to increase its speed."

The boat angled to the right, edging closer to the city. We passed under the stone bridge where Unika had paid his merchant tax and steered toward the other end of the city, where we could almost see the palace of King Brumeh.

I lifted both arms wide as a strong wind pushed the boat forward a little faster. I closed my eyes and let myself be in that moment. I imagined I had left Agbon for good and was now sailing on a ship on the Northern Sea, heading to the most remote islands. Perhaps the island where Moyo had come from. I would write to him all about my time with his home clan.

And I would have Tega with me.

"Head back to the docks," Unika called to Wedia, and I opened my eyes, my reverie shattered. I was reminded of where I was and what awaited me when we returned home.

Unika was watching me carefully. But he simply said, "Do not forget to buy your sister some chalwa."

7

THE DAY UNIKA AND I RETURNED TO KOKORI, IMONI ANNOUNCED Sayo Goredenna was coming home earlier than planned. Her face lit up as she spoke, and I felt a huge lump in my throat.

Desperation seared through me, and I went to Moyo's. I was ready to ask him for some money so Tega and I could make the trip to Iga.

As I walked, all I could think of was Imoni's face. The joy she got from thinking about my marriage was something I did not want to put out. I wanted her to be happy. I wished I could make her that happy in some other way. By all accounts she was doing what she thought was best for me. She had taken on the role of mother for me and Tega, and I would always be indebted to her.

I calculated and planned. Even if I got the money from Moyo, there was still Tega's reluctance to join me. I had not asked her about it since that day at Moyo's, but I still couldn't imagine leaving without her. My head spun just thinking about it.

Suddenly, I looked up in the middle of the tall grasses outside the Oron Forest. I did not know how I had gotten here.

The preceding cold gave me goose bumps and Zuberi showed itself once again. It was bigger this time, several feet taller than me. It looked at me, then looked at the forest.

"I can't go with you. I am not allowed to. No one from here"—I pointed at Kokori—"is allowed to."

Oron was a no-go area. I did not think they would permit one person from Agbon into their queendom, even one who entered by mistake. And I doubted they would excuse me for following a spirit creature no one but me could see.

Zuberi's look seemed to tell me I could go on. That I needed to follow it.

It started walking toward the border.

I shook my head and was turning around to go home when a wall of roaring flame swept across the grass in front of me. I felt its searing heat, but it did not burn a single blade of grass. I turned around to look at the spirit.

Zuberi cocked its head at me.

The message was clear. I needed to follow it, and I had no choice.

I took a deep breath and followed the spirit.

As I got closer to the forest, I looked far into the semi-dark woods, scanning for archers. Zuberi purred, and it sounded coaxing, comforting. It looked back at me once again before going through two trees that stood like a gateway into the queendom.

I squared my shoulders. There was nothing on me except my daggers, but I felt that was enough.

So I walked into Oron.

The trees seemed alive with each step I took. Their creaking limbs made me draw out my daggers. I walked slowly over fallen leaves and branches that cracked with every step.

Zuberi kept moving forward deeper into the forest, seeming to have a destination in mind. I wondered why it wanted me here. What it wanted me to see. I wanted to turn back.

We soon came upon a clearing filled with sunlight. A bony woman in silky robes and a dress as dark as night picked herbs into a basket she carried on her left arm. Her braided hair was as white as the clouds on a sunny day, and the coral beads around her neck bounced and clattered as she moved. Armed men stood around her, helping her spot the herbs she was looking for, and she rewarded them with a toothy smile.

Suddenly, the woman snapped up from the plant she'd been plucking and stared toward where Zuberi and I stood, hidden in the trees. Her eyes widened, darting from me to Zuberi and then back to me again.

It was clear she could see Zuberi too.

She dropped to her knees and bowed. She quickly said something to the men, who did the same thing as her even though they could not see Zuberi.

Zuberi walked into the clearing, and the woman slowly stood up, her eyes locking with Zuberi's before falling back to me again. She said something else to the men.

With the way they stood up and charged forward, my instinct told me to turn and run. My legs felt heavier than normal, and I tripped over them as I raced back.

I was not moving fast enough. Had I forgotten how to run?

Something pierced my shoulder and I went down hard as the world faded out.

When I awoke, I was in a spacious carriage, the strange old woman sitting opposite me. The walls and seats were heavily padded, the cushions embroidered with butterfly patterns.

I squeezed my eyes shut as a headache plagued me. I went to rub my temples and realized my hands were tied behind my back.

"Sorry about the sleeping dart. My men assured me it was safer to have you come with us this way. Less chance of you running or putting up a fight. Don't move too much, you'll only make the headache worse," the bony woman said in fluent Iagbon. I stared at her, slack-jawed. Her features were too prominent for her small face. She could not be older than Imoni, judging by the faint wrinkles on her skin, but she seemed ancient.

"How can you speak Iagbon?" I asked.

"I learned," she replied simply.

I vainly tried to get out of the ropes again. "Let me go, please. I promise I'll return home and never come back here again."

"I will eventually free you. You just need to come with me for a little while."

"Untie me then," I begged.

To my surprise, she did. I flexed my wrists and hands to ease the ache left from the bindings.

"Where are we going?" I asked.

"The capital city, Mbiabong. We're almost there."

My curiosity got the better of me and I put my head out the carriage window. The sun had already dipped far down west. How long had we been on the road?

We were speeding through a wide bridge over a large river that disappeared into the horizon as we headed for the capital city of Oron.

My breath hitched at the sight.

I stared at the people walking on the bridge. Apart from how well-dressed they all seemed to be, adorned in colorful beads and scarves, they did not look so different from anyone in Kokori.

I could not believe I was really there, breathing the same air as Oroni people.

We went through the outer gates of the city, then a second set and a third. The closer we got to the palace, the grander the houses became. They were significantly taller than even the houses in Okpara, with flowering trees on every street, covering the city with a deep shade of purple.

"What kind of tree is that?"

"It's the drava tree. It brings harmony and peace to wherever it is planted," the woman replied. "That is why it is planted everywhere."

"It's pretty."

"What's your name?" the woman asked.

"Naborhi. Naborhi Tanomare."

"The name reveals the person," she stated. I wasn't sure what to do with that. "How long have you been seeing the red fox?"

"Zuberi?"

"You named the creature?" she chuckled. "Interesting."

I told her how I came to find Zuberi, and she listened with rapt attention.

"I knew something was afoot," she declared, just as we neared the palace. "You have been touched by Obassi."

"Who is Obassi?" I asked her.

She did not answer me.

We were led into the palace by the guards at the gate. They wore high brass helmets and upper-body armor over billowy, ankle-length uniforms. Most of them carried spears.

A gigantic statue of the queen welcomed us into the courtyard of the magnificent palace. What seemed like a thousand songbirds flittered from drava tree to drava tree, bringing vivid color to the stark white of the palace walls.

I looked around in awe. The building was massive, five stories high and seeming to stretch endlessly wide. I wondered how long it would take to walk around the palace, to visit every room and hall. One would surely get lost.

A guard helped me and the old woman out of the carriage.

I looked around me and thought briefly of escape. I saw no chance.

Would they believe me if I told them I had not meant to enter their land? That I had no choice?

The guard who helped us spoke in Anang, their native tongue, to the woman.

"Let's go," the woman said to me, walking briskly ahead.

We went straight toward the high, gold-embellished front doors, which groaned open, pulled by two palace guards. The air from inside smelled like lavender. It reminded me of Imoni.

I followed the woman inside, and the doors closed behind us.

The sheer size of the circular room made my head spin. I turned around to take it all in. The walls bore intricate carvings that looked to be made of brass, as did the large pool in the center of the detailed floor tiling.

The domed glass roof let in golden sunlight. The polished floor, the water, and the metal banister of the grand staircase reflected the light, dazzling me.

I followed the woman up the marble steps in to a larger room. There were elaborately designed windows high in every corner of the room and underneath each a palace guard. They were unmoving, like the statues carved into the room's pillars. A ten-tier chandelier made of carved horns hung from the arched ceiling.

But the most beautiful thing in the room was a white throne carved out of a live tree, holes in the ceiling letting its branches grow unimpeded. On either side of the throne, small flowering plants crept along the stone, twining around its base.

The sound of a door opening and closing echoed through the chamber and drew my attention to two women, who approached the throne from behind. They were both dressed in long, flowing dresses of red and gold. The rings of coral beads around their necks were too numerous to count, and they wore their hair braided and adorned with brass combs.

My companion took three paces back and bowed. I mimicked her movements.

The taller woman wore a bigger and more unique brass comb lodged in the top part of her hair. I suspected she was Obong Iniiemem, the queen of Oron, and she sat on the throne while the other stood beside her, her hands clasped in front of her. The standing woman glared at me, her gaze chilling me to my core.

The queen spoke to my companion in Anang. The woman reverently introduced herself to the queen. They talked for a while in their native tongue, the queen occasionally glancing at me curiously. The queen's companion never once removed her eyes from me, nor her hand from the pommel of her sword.

I could have listened to them speak for hours. Anang was so different from Iagbon, less sharp and more musical. The women's words rolled softly from their tongues.

My companion stopped talking.

Obong Iniiemem looked me over, her dark brows furrowed.

"The oracle tells me you are from Kokori," the queen said in Iagbon.

"I am," I replied.

The oracle spoke excitedly in Iagbon. "I have not seen the red fox since my teenage years. And there it was, standing next to this girl from Agbon. And she could see it too."

"What is your name?" the queen asked me gently.

"Naborhi Tanomare," I replied.

The oracle turned to the queen. "I will take her to the cave and find out why the red fox brought her here."

The queen leaned back.

The woman next to her whispered into her ear and the queen nodded.

"My sister makes a good point," the queen said, fixing her dark-brown eyes on me. "How can we trust you when we know nothing of you? You will go with Inemesit. Whatever she asks of you, do it. Tomorrow you will both come back and we will decide where to go from there."

Inemesit bowed again and I bowed alongside her.

The queen sent two palace guards to accompany us out while she and her sister disappeared the way they had entered.

I could not hold back my questions anymore.

"Who are you?" I asked my companion.

"Inemesit is my name. I am the oracle of Obassi."

"What is the red fox?"

"The spirit of Oron, the messenger of Obassi."

We passed by a group of men loitering at the entrance of the palace. They turned to stare at me. Did I really stick out that much?

"Who is Obassi?"

This time she answered, "He is the patron god of Oron, the protector of our queendom and its people."

"But I am not a part of your people. I do not know if my ancestors may have been related to your people, so why did Obassi send me Zuberi?"

She chuckled to herself. "I will find out why you are here. No need to look so worried."

Was it that obvious how scared I was? "How will you do that?"

"I'm the oracle. Obassi speaks to me. And he has had more to say lately."

"What has he been telling you?"

"He has been showing me things. Signs that make me believe that your presence here is going to stir things up. There is always a reason for the things Obassi does. Have faith. He brought you here; he will tell us why."

We entered the carriage with our escorts, who kept a watchful eye on me. We left the palace grounds slower than when we had arrived.

I realized that Mbiabong was smaller than Okpara as I took in the views again. I caught the faint smell of flowers, bread, and woodsmoke from myriad street-food stalls.

We exited the innermost gate and the carriage took a sharp right, riding through the narrow, busy streets until we reached a street carved down the middle with a long row of drava trees. The houses on either side of the street were jammed wall-to-wall, their browned bricks surely faded from a bright red. Their slanted roofs were made out of the same rocks used on the street.

Carriages rode in and out of the adjoining street, most heading for the public house at the end of the road. I had never seen so many carriages in one place.

We stopped in front of one of the houses, a fluffy cat sleeping on the front steps.

We got out of the carriage and Inemesit told the driver to wait for us. The guards stayed behind with him.

Inemesit led me up the steps, treading lightly to avoid the cat, and opened the front door to reveal stairs illuminated by ornate red lanterns. "Up you go," she told me briskly.

On the second floor, she pushed open a round door and we entered a room with long, curtained windows. Vases of growing plants dotted the windowsills, an unmade bed stood against the wall, and there were embroidered wooden chairs and more red lanterns filled the space. An upper, lofted landing could be accessed by winding stairs, and it had plants growing along the rails.

"Welcome to our home."

A boy with a bare, heavily tattooed torso came down the stairs. His skin was a gorgeous patchwork mosaic of luminous white and deep, dark brown. His loose tan trousers swept around his bare feet like a skirt. He looked to be the same age as me.

A girl was behind him on the stairs. She was very pretty, with narrow eyes and smooth brown skin. The gold jewelry on her fingers and toes glistened, and the beads bounced off her chest as she walked. She could not be more than twenty years old.

"These are my children, Atai and Edem," she said in Iagbon.

The woman spoke to them in Anang. I heard her mention my name and Kokori.

"I can speak the Traveler's Tongue," I offered.

"Oh, that makes things easier then," Edem said, smiling widely. She did not look like her mother, apart from her eyes.

Inemesit invited me to sit on one of the chairs next to the fire pit, where a small fire crackled.

I noticed the books stacked on the side table and took the one on top. It was a compilation of old lore written by an Iduni and translated into the Traveler's Tongue. "I have read this," I said, surprised. "It is one of my favorites."

"How can you read? You are from Kokori, are you not? Unless your laws have changed . . . ?" Atai asked curiously.

"No," I answered. "They have not. I learned in secret."

"That is brave," Edem said.

"Very brave," her brother agreed.

"Edem, please get her something to eat before we leave."

"Yes, Mother," Edem replied, and went to a door almost hidden behind the staircase.

During a quick but delicious meal of vegetables, sweet-and-sour yams, and smoked fish, Inemesit answered all her children's questions about how I came to be in Oron.

"Atai will come with us to the cave. He is to succeed me," the woman explained to me. "He is going to be a fine oracle," she added proudly.

She changed to an all-white dress with tight sleeves, and gave me a similar white dress to change into.

"Get dressed," she said. "I will wait for you in the street."

I changed in Edem's quaint room. The dress was a little loose, and Edem tied a white sash around my waist to give the dress a more fitted look.

"Now it's gorgeous," she said, beaming.

I came out of her room to see that Atai had put on a long white tunic over white trousers. He held back his long hair with a white scarf, and beaded shoes covered his large feet.

"Let's go," he said, leading the way.

Unlike Kokori, which had streetlamps on posts, the lamps here were hung on the drava tree branches, giving our walk a soothing, lavender glow.

The oracle was already in the carriage with the guards, and I joined them. Atai sat with the driver in the front of the carriage.

On the way, I soaked up every sight, every quaint home and stunning boulevard. I was blown away by the beauty and tranquility of this city, so unexpected.

The carriage stopped at the foot of a rocky hill, one of many among the fields of grass and grains. A silvery haze descended as the clouds cleared, allowing the moon to come out. There were lanterns hanging on poles in the fields, and Atai explained that farmers in Oron often worked late into the night, when it was cooler. In Kokori, farmers left their farms at sundown and went back at sunup.

The carriage driver gave a lamp to Atai and another to the oracle, but they were hardly necessary. The moonlight was bright on our path as the oracle led the way up the steep, rocky hill, Atai beside me.

I looked up at the night sky. I reckoned Tega had gone to Imoni by now. They must be so anxious, wondering where I was and what had happened to me. I wished I could tell them I was fine, that I was not so far away.

A small, frightening part of me did not wish to return.

"Are you all right?" Atai asked. He looked genuinely concerned.

"I was thinking about my family, that they must be worried about me."

"You'll be back with them soon," Atai assured me. "What is your family like?"

"Like any other family, I would say. Nosy and meddlesome and loud."

"Do you get into trouble often?"

I smiled indulgently at him as we crossed a small, trickling stream. "Something like that. I am very stubborn, my aunt says. Trying to do things I should not."

"Like learning to read in secret," he said, smiling, and I grinned back.

"That is why my aunt wants me married quickly. To get a husband that will teach me humility and keep me out of trouble."

"But you do not want to get married." He was not asking.

"No."

"What do you want?"

I thought it might be the first time someone had ever asked me the question so plainly.

"Dangerous things unbecoming of an Agbon woman." I sighed. "I cannot believe I am really here."

"I can't imagine the kinds of stories you'd been told, but I promise you are safe."

I don't know why, but I believed him.

"Tell me more about Obassi," I said, changing the subject.

He cleared his throat, but before he could speak, his mother answered me instead, her voice steady despite the steep incline. "We came from the Lost Lands, wandering for a long time with no place to call our own. Then Obassi sent the red fox to the first oracle, and his cleansing fire guided the oracle and our people to where Mbiabong now stands. With Obassi's power, she sprouted the Oron Forest while our ancestors built the city. While we no longer see Obassi's fire, we know it is still there, safeguarding our future."

"And now Obassi's red fox has led me here."

Atai smiled. "It has. You are lucky. What I would give to see the red fox. To be blessed by Obassi."

"You don't have to sound so glum, my son." Inemesit chuckled. "You will see it when it is time."

I looked up at the sky again just as a star streaked across it. Then another. And another.

"We are close," the oracle said when we reached a stream flowing steadily downhill.

Soon we came face-to-face with the mouth of the cave. The entrance was narrow and looked like it could fit only one person at a time.

Inemesit asked us to take off our shoes before we entered.

Atai went in first and I followed. There were smooth rocks protruding from the walls, and the floor was rugged. Water flowed gently across my toes, cool on my aching feet. The air smelled musty and damp.

I followed Atai's lamp until the narrow cave gave way to a large opening, a breeze blasting my face, making me blink.

The cavern was vast and cold, with more protruding stones on the floors and the walls. The moldy smell was gone, replaced by clean, cool air that refreshed my lungs.

My breath caught at the tree growing in the center of the cave, the ceiling carved wide open above it. Moonlight beamed into the cavern, illuminating the small waterfall tumbling from the opening and pooling around the tree's roots. The tree itself was a vivid, glistening scarlet, from its oval leaves to its branches to its trunk to the pool at its roots.

I stood aside to let the oracle walk toward the tree, her hands up in the air. The guards knelt on the cold, wet floor. Atai stayed by my side, and I felt his eyes on me.

The oracle washed her face with the water, but it did not stain her. She stood up and started singing, walking slowly around the tree. The song was uplifting and her ethereal voice echoed around the cave, captivating me wholly.

Watching and listening to her made me feel weightless, peaceful, and warm, even though a cold wind came ripping through the chamber. It felt like someone was giving me a hug I badly needed.

As Inemesit continued to sing, Zuberi appeared from behind

the tree. It towered above us, its head almost touching the cave roof. It looked directly at me, and I was overwhelmed with emotion. I felt the power its presence brought, and I did not realize I was bowing until my knees touched the cave floor.

Inemesit continued her song, and I realized it was how she was communicating with the fox, with Obassi. As she moved, as Zuberi's eyes followed her, and as the magnificent tree swayed and rustled in the wind, I finally felt the magnitude of my situation.

The gods had something planned for me, and I only hoped I was enough for them.

8

THAT NIGHT, I SLEPT AT INEMESIT'S HOUSE, ON A SPARE mattress by the fire. The oracle had retired as soon as we returned home, her energy drained from communing with the gods. Edem had already gone to bed.

Atai and I ate a light meal and sat in the chairs, watching the flames dance across the logs.

"You are to be the next oracle, correct?" I asked him, trying to appear casual.

"Yes, when the time comes."

I hesitated. "Could you hear what was spoken tonight?"

Atai stared at me a long while, his hazel eyes seeming to peer into the depths of my soul. The attention raised goose bumps on my arms.

"Yes," he replied simply, "I could."

I knew from his tone that he would not tell me. I exhaled a

laugh, but there was no bitterness in it. They had their rules and customs, and I would not ask him to bend them when I would hear the news tomorrow in front of the queen.

I changed the subject then, asking him about his childhood, his sister, their traditions. He told me about his friends, his schooling, his dreams.

By the time the fire burned low, I felt an ease, a comfort with him that I had not felt with anyone but Tega and Chipo.

I yawned, exhausted from this day that did not seem to want to end. Atai smiled and rose, stretching. I tried not to stare at the expanse of bare torso the movement revealed.

"Get some sleep, Naborhi," he murmured. I liked the sound of my name in his mouth far too much for my own good. The way his accent rounded the vowels turned it into a melody. "You've had a long day, and you deserve rest."

I smiled gently at him. "Good night. And thank you, for everything you and your family have done for me."

He grinned back at me and nodded once before heading upstairs.

I burrowed into the blankets on the mattress, letting the warmth from the fire and our conversations lull me into a deep, dreamless sleep.

The oracle was quite sure of what she had heard from her god.

"Obong Iniiemem," she said with a bow toward the queen.

We were back in the throne room. The queen was seated in her imposing chair, her sister beside her and armed to the teeth. To their left, ministers and advisors sat at a grand marble table, each dressed colorfully but distinctly. I had a feeling there was more meaning to their clothing than met my eyes.

"There is only one reason for this girl's presence here," Inemesit went on. "Obassi wants peace between Agbon and Oron. The animosity has gone on long enough, and he knows that if it is left to continue, our relations will be irreparably damaged."

There were frenzied whispers and glances between the courtiers, but one glare from the queen's sister silenced them.

"Are you sure, Inemesit?" Obong Iniiemem asked.

"Yes. The message was very clear."

"Check again!" The queen's sister's voice boomed across the room, making me jump. Atai touched my shoulder gently, steadying me.

The oracle was not fazed by the woman's terrifying gaze.

"Kehina," the oracle began, and the name clanged through my mind, realization dawning at last.

Kehina.

This angry, fierce woman before me was the Oroni princess who was snubbed and betrayed by King Brumeh. It was his breaking of their engagement that had started all this discord.

"There is no mistake in what Obassi has told me. Or are you doubting me?" *Are you doubting* him? I could hear the insinuation in the oracle's meaningful silence.

Kehina looked around wildly, catching herself. "No . . . no . . ." she said quickly. I watched her swallow her anger and put on an expression of forced humility. "I just want us to be sure. She is from Agbon, after all." She pointed at me with murder in her eyes. Instinct screamed at me to get out of that room, out of Oron, and never look back. She was a predator about to pounce on its prey. Goose bumps sprang on my arms.

"The word of the red fox is law," Atai said, loud and firm, before I could flee. "Obassi has spoken. We *all* must obey."

Kehina's expression turned stormy.

"After the humiliation . . ." she started to say, but shook her head. Once again she met my gaze, a dark, vengeful smile on her lips. I swallowed the weight that was lodged in my throat. I needed to get far away from this woman.

"Kehina," the queen chided softly.

"Excuse me," her sister said abruptly, balling her hands into fists. "I seem to have come down with something."

She hedged a bow to her sister that bordered on insulting, and all but stormed out.

"She will learn to live with it," the queen said, exhaustion lacing her voice. "We have held a grudge for far too long. Obassi is right—if I let this continue, we may never recover what has been lost."

She turned her attention to me. "Naborhi Tanomare, you are free to return to your clan." Her eyes drifted to my hair, to the sunset-red streak still visible. "Something tells me this will not be the last we see of each other. I hope that you will return to us often, and that you will not hesitate to seek our oracle should Obassi . . . come calling."

Her words sent a chill down my spine, but I nodded and bowed to her.

The queen ordered escorts to take me back to the Kokori border.

Inemesit led me outside to a carriage, and Atai helped me up. It was smaller than the oracle's had been, but was still quite comfortable. The oracle held my hand through the window before the carriage could move.

"You should be back home by nightfall. He will take the fastest routes," she said glancing at the carriage driver. Her voice lowered to a whisper, "There was more to Obassi's message. This is not the end."

Alarm flooded through me. "What?"

She shook her head, eyes on the guards now entering the carriage with me. "Wait for the red fox."

I glanced at Atai, but he looked as confused as I was.

Before I could say anything, the driver snapped the reins and the horses took off, the carriage lurching forward. Inemesit held my gaze for as long as possible, and Atai waved goodbye.

The oracle's words turned my blood to ice water. What else was there? Why was this god not through with me? What else did I have to do? I'd hoped my mission from Obassi had been complete, with a truce forged between our territories.

I knew then that this had been a foolish hope.

We traveled all day, going down rolling hills and through rocky paths near creeks and streams. I didn't see any clans or settlements as we stopped for brief moments to stretch our legs.

By sunset, we left the carriage, and two guards guided me through the forest toward the edge of Oron. I recognized the path I had taken yesterday—had it only been a day? It was nearly twilight when we arrived on the other side of the forest. I stepped out into the field, my heart aching strangely. I turned around for a final goodbye but they had disappeared. I thought I saw a streak of sunset red, a flash of a fox's tail, but the forest was empty and silent.

I turned back toward Kokori and began the walk home.

Tega and Imoni were sitting in the courtyard looking worried and worn-out when I arrived just after dark. With the number of cups lying around, I was sure there had been others who had joined them, perhaps inquiring after me.

Imoni cried out when I stepped through the gate, lurching to her feet and hugging me so tight I thought I would faint.

"When we could not find you at Moyo's we feared the worst," she said, touching my face to confirm I was really there. "Tamunor and his father just left. They'd been searching the woods with the Abavo all day."

Tega squeezed me from behind, and I felt a surge of love for these two women, my anchors through it all.

"Imoni sent a message to Unika," Tega said into my back. I thought I felt wetness on my shirt. "He is coming to join the search party."

Imoni stepped back and brushed her hands down my arms, taking my hands in hers.

"Where did you go?" Imoni asked me. Tega curled into my side.

I took a deep, bracing breath. "Oron," I answered.

Imoni gasped and Tega jumped back from me, her eyes wide in shock.

"What were you doing in Oron?"

"Zuberi wanted me there."

"Who is Zuberi?"

"The spirit I've been seeing," I replied, not trying to hide my excitement. "Zuberi is a messenger of the Oron god, Obassi." I thought I might trip over my words I was hurrying to say them so quickly. "I was actually in Oron. I met the queen and her sister and their oracle. And Mbiabong, their capital, is so gorgeous. It's beautiful and clean and so different from anything I've ever seen."

I told them everything. In doing so I was able to realize just how incredible it all was. And how lucky I was that I had not been harmed in such a risky and unknown land.

"I can't believe this," Tega whispered. "It's incredible, Naborhi. You've done so much, and entirely on your own." There was something else hidden in her words, but I couldn't quite parse it out.

"There is more," I murmured, lowering my voice. "The queen wants to end the feud between Oron and Agbon."

Tega's eyes were so wide I could see their whites all the way around.

"Do you really think they will open their borders to us again?" Imoni asked.

She got her answer the next day. Word spread like wildfire that Obong Iniiemem was on her way to Okpara to meet with King Brumeh. She rode with white banners, the color of peace.

9

WAIT FOR THE RED FOX.

I waited for days, but Zuberi did not reappear.

Instead, I started hearing a voice.

The day after I returned home, I awoke to the faint sound of whispers, so quiet they were unintelligible. My bedroom was empty, and no matter how hard I tried to escape the sounds I couldn't.

Tega found me in my room, curled in a ball beside my bed, and the whispers vanished.

The next day, as I was helping cut vegetables for dinner, the voice came back, causing me to nearly slice my finger off. I could hear the words clearly, if quietly.

Help me.

It was a boy's frightened voice, high-pitched and breathy.

Each day, the voice got louder, but the words stayed the same, eventually becoming so loud it was like he was yelling into my ears.

He would call out to me at random, never at the same time of day. I could not ignore it even if I wanted to. It began disrupting my chores, my training with Moyo, my sleep.

Then the voice turned to visions.

I found myself tied up, lying on a bumpy floor. My back ached and my wrists were sore. I propped myself up with my shoulder and stood up. I was in a room completely devoid of light apart from the faint beams coming through the three narrow cracks in the walls. I peered through one and saw a tall building with circular markings on the side. I tried to scream, but all that came out was a ragged gasp.

My vision tilted and I had the indescribable feeling of *tearing* before I found myself on the other side of the room. I could make out the silhouette of the boy against the dim light behind him, but I could not see his face.

"Help me," he begged. "Please."

I came back to reality in a pool of sweat.

I was lying on the ground of the courtyard, Tega hovering above me, her expression worried.

"Naborhi, what is happening?" she asked me, and I could hear the fear in her voice.

"I don't know," I whispered. "I keep hearing this boy, crying out for help. And just now I swear I *was* him, could see what he was seeing and where he was captured."

She wiped sweat from my forehead. "Do you think this is a sign from that god?"

I closed my eyes. Was this what Obassi wanted? For me to help this boy?

"I don't know," I said again.

That night, Chipo joined us for dinner. I filled her in on my journey to Oron, and she nearly fainted. But to my surprise, she asked questions about Mbiabong and the queen and even the geography of the countryside as I'd hiked to the cave.

It was the first time I realized Chipo hungered for knowledge about the world beyond Agbon, perhaps just as much as me. I was ashamed I had not seen it sooner.

But perhaps that hunger was not enough.

"I have good news," she announced while we ate. She was hiding a smile behind her bamboo cup of wine. And in that moment, I knew. My heart plummeted.

"What is it?" Tega asked excitedly.

"The Taokiri family have asked for my hand," she cried, throwing her arms wide and nearly spilling her wine. "I am betrothed to Birungi!"

Imoni cheered, dancing in her seat, and Tega whooped with joy.

"I am so thrilled for you, Chipo," I gushed, squeezing her free hand. "I know how much you'd hoped for this."

My eyes burned, and I hoped Chipo thought they were tears of happiness.

Imoni got more wine, and the four of us celebrated and sang

and danced. My best friend, my other sister, was going to marry a wealthy man whom she had been desperate to have. I'd heard kind things about the Taokiri heir, but I could only hope that he would be worthy of a woman like Chipo.

That night, after she had left and we had all gone to bed, buzzing and warm from the wine, I lay in bed, tears streaming past my temples and onto my pillow.

I loved Chipo, and was so happy that her dreams were coming true, and my chest ached with the knowledge that our dreams would not intertwine. She would marry Birungi and they would build a family here in Kokori, or perhaps Okpara. And they would always be her priority.

And I would be gone, or worse, trapped in my marriage to Fynn Goredenna. And the days where we were each other's partners, each other's mirrors, would be a distant memory.

I felt like I stood at the edge of a cliff, poised on my toes. I was fighting to stay upright, to not tumble over into the abyss. But I could not fight the wind—it was pushing, prodding, without a care for my desires. Sooner or later I would lose the ground beneath my feet.

"Naborhi, you have a visitor!" Imoni's voice woke me late the next morning.

I groaned softly, rolling to avoid the sunlight streaming into the room. It must have been nearly midday.

"He says it's important!" she called after a moment.

He?

I hurried to get dressed and ran out into the courtyard.

Atai stood with Imoni by the gates. Imoni was looking between us suspiciously, no doubt wondering if his presence signaled doom for my engagement to Fynn. But I was preoccupied by the strange, harried look in Atai's eyes, even with the wide smile he had plastered on.

"It is good to see you," he murmured. "You look well."

Tega popped up out of nowhere, beaming. "Would you like something to drink? We were just going to sit down." I wanted to roll my eyes at her obvious meddling.

Atai glanced at me as if seeking permission, and I smiled. "Please, it would be lovely to have you, right Imoni?"

My aunt shot me a look but nodded gently. "Of course. Join us."

She welcomed him in warmly and offered him some wine.

"Thank you, but I cannot drink wine," he explained. "It is taboo for both me and my mother."

"I understand," I told him, swirling my bamboo cup full of the glistening liquid. "We do not eat the meat of pigs, as Egbesu forbids it. But we can drink as much as we want and to me that is much better." I smiled and downed my drink. It left a tangy taste on my lips.

Imoni smiled warmly as she handed Atai a cup of red spice tea instead.

We chatted for a while, Tega delivering an endless stream of questions to Atai about every aspect of Oron. Even Imoni seemed charmed by him as he spoke.

Finally, Tega asked Imoni to help her look at a torn dress in her room. Imoni gave me a meaningful, warning look as she passed. *Behave.*

"My reason for coming," Atai said when we were alone. "My mother and I . . . we wanted to know if you have been experiencing anything unusual. She would have been here, too, but she's resting at the public house in town. Our journey here triggered her leg pain."

I glanced at him sharply. "Unusual?"

He swallowed audibly, and his discomfort put me on edge. Atai did not seem to be someone who was easily rattled.

"Have you been seeing Zuberi?" he asked. And then, after a moment, "Have you been receiving any messages from Obassi?"

My pulse picked up its pace, my blood thick in my veins. "I haven't seen Zuberi since I left Oron, but I've been having these . . . visions."

Atai swallowed again, nodding. "Can you describe them to me?"

I told him everything, how they'd begun, the boy's words, what the room looked like.

Atai grew pale, and I found myself speaking faster and faster, panic clawing at the words as they left my throat.

"Thank you for trusting me with this," he murmured. "I worry that this is quite serious, if Obassi has involved himself."

Footsteps sounded down the stairs, and we quickly changed the subject as Imoni reappeared, offering refills. Atai politely declined, saying it was time he returned to Mbiabong, and Imoni sent him home with some of Tega's honey bread.

I walked Atai to the gates, out of my aunt's earshot.

"I think I need to help this boy," I ventured, turning to him, "but I don't know how. I don't even know where he's being kept. Those buildings are unlike those in any city I've been to. Not that I've been to many." I said the words with an edge of bitterness, but an idea bloomed in my mind, tentatively.

"I think you're right. I need to speak with my mother, to get her advice and see if she has heard anything while I've been gone."

I nodded, the idea taking root. "I'm going to ask Moyo if he recognizes the place. He's traveled the entirety of Otọrakpọ and knows more about it than anyone I know."

"He's the man who taught you to read and fight?" I nodded again, and Atai gave me an unreadable smile. "I would very much like to meet him. I will discuss this all with my mother and return to you. I fear that we need to move quickly."

Unease and something close to excitement fluttered in my chest. "How quickly?"

He hesitated only a moment. "Tomorrow. If Moyo does not recognize the location, we will need to find someone who will, and that may mean journeying to some other cities in Agbon."

Which could be dangerous for him, even with the newfound truce between the monarchies. There were some in Kokori who did not look kindly on the Oroni.

It would also mean delay, and even I knew that the boy's life hung precariously in the balance. Obassi was not subtle with his urgency.

"Moyo lives in the bento field just north of here, by the woods to Innuere. Meet me there by midday."

Atai nodded. "See you tomorrow. Good luck with . . . tonight."

My stomach panged as he smiled sadly and walked through the gates. I'd understood the true meaning in his words.

Good luck with saying goodbye.

10

THAT NIGHT, IMONI COULD NOT STOP TALKING ABOUT ANOTHER meeting with the Goredennas happening later that week to fix a date for the wedding. A priest of Egbesu would be called to determine an auspicious time.

"Things are moving forward so quickly, and still I cannot wait," she sang.

That wait would, unfortunately for her, be forever.

When she finally retired to bed, I wasted no time in dragging Tega up to my room.

We settled on my bed, and before I could even think how to begin this conversation, Tega asked, "You're leaving, aren't you?"

Her voice was small, and I felt tears prick my eyes almost immediately.

"Someone is in trouble and I have to help him."

"What about your wedding? We have already received the wine," she said frantically, and I cringed as she went on. "What about Imoni? And Unika? Will you not tell them where you are going?"

"I think it is best not to."

"They will be so hurt, Naborhi. And so worried."

"I know that. We owe both of them everything, but I cannot stay. Not even if I tried. Obassi is not yet done with me."

I told her what Atai had planned for us, and her shocked expression was replaced by one of concern.

I took a deep, steadying breath.

"This is it, Tega. I have to leave. *We* have to leave." I took her hands in mine. "Come with me. We will face the world together. I don't have a lot of money but I'll work for it. I'll protect us. And we will see and experience so much more than this."

She gently pulled her hands away.

"This is your journey, not mine."

"Come with me, Tega, please," I urged, desperation in my voice. "Please."

"I'm sorry, Naborhi. I haven't changed my mind," she whispered. "I'm staying."

"I don't . . . I don't . . ." My voice broke.

I didn't want to hear those words. I wanted her to say yes.

"I want to live here, and I want to build a family. I don't dream of far-off lands, or of great adventures on the high seas. That's always been you. And it's time for you to take a step toward that dream."

Tears streamed down both of our cheeks.

I could not drag her along. I had to let go, but I did not know how. I could no easier part with a limb; it was impossible to do without force. My heart ached terribly.

"I love you," I whispered, not knowing what else to say.

What does one say in such a situation?

Tega wrapped her arms around me.

She held back her sobs and said, "Come back if you can. Just so I can see you. Send messages to Moyo, so I know where you are. I'm sure he will read them to me."

"I promise. I would never abandon you."

Tega took deep, grounding breaths and pulled back. "You need to pack."

Just like that, she was all business. She quietly helped me gather supplies—a water skin, bread, peppered cured meat, dried fruits, preserved mushrooms for cuts and wounds, bandages, my knives, my bow and quiver of arrows, spare sets of clothes, cloths for my monthly cycle, my cloak.

After my bag was packed and hidden under the bed, Tega and I lay intertwined, talking softly about what awaited me, the endless possibilities of adventure and danger. She dozed off after a while, still gripping my hand, but I was restless throughout the night. I could not sleep.

I rose just as the sky began to lighten, and Tega stirred beside me.

After our prayers to Egbesu, we crept downstairs. Tega would cover for me with Imoni, so that she would not come looking before Atai and I had left.

I stared at the front door for a long while, my sister patient beside me.

This could be the last time I was in the home I grew up in, the home where my mother had braided my hair and sang to me, where Tega and I had fought and played and danced together. The house where my parents had died.

Obassi had put a test before me. I would help this boy in need, and I knew there was a chance I would not return.

"Tell Chipo I love her, and that I'm sorry I kept this from her. And tell her how truly happy I am for her and her future with Birungi."

Tega nodded squeezed my hand. "I will."

I exhaled slowly and hugged her tightly. "I love you. Tell Moyo if you ever need me. He'll get word to me."

She held me so hard I felt my ribs bending. "I love you, my sister. Be free."

I choked back a sob and headed out into the courtyard. I spared one final glance back at my home, my sister, my life. And I crossed through the gate.

Moyo was already awake and sitting on his porch when I arrived.

"It's a bit early for training, Naborhi," he said dryly.

"I have news."

I had already told him of my visit to Oron and the strange voice pleading for help. I didn't have much of a choice when the voice suddenly appeared while I was mounting Nour. I'd fallen off her and curled into a ball with my hands crushing my ears. Trying to escape it.

So I filled him in on Atai's visit.

"Come inside," he murmured, rising from his chair. "I want you to draw this vision."

I took time to draw out what I had seen and get it correctly, the exact shape of the strange tower, the layout of the room where the boy was being held.

Finally, as the sun broke over the horizon, Moyo examined the finished drawings and said, "This is the Tower of Ewuare."

Ewuare was the capital of Idu, the kingdom that occupied the cold mountains near the Northern Sea and the farthest reaches of our continent, Otọrakpọ.

"That is the Broken Barrel," he said, identifying my next scribble. I was impressed. Despite my horrible drawings, Moyo could make out the places. "It's a popular public house in Ewuare, right by the tower. And this building, that's Anchor's Forge. What you are looking for is right in the middle of these places."

"Why would Obassi want me in Ewuare? He is not an Iduni god."

The sound of hoofbeats caught my ear, and we both looked up sharply. Moyo opened the door, and Atai and Inemesit sat atop a white horse, waiting. The oracle was dressed the same as the last time I had seen her, in silken robes and a dark dress, coral beads wrapped around her throat. Atai wore a short, sleeveless shirt over wide-legged trousers with flat fabric shoes. He adjusted the scarf tied around his neck as we came closer. I tried not to notice how his tattoos shifted with the sculpted muscles in his arms, and failed.

"Atai, Oracle, Egwo."

"Vren. You look well, Naborhi," Inemesit said, getting down from the horse. Her gait was springy and her expression cheerful.

"You look well too. How is your leg?"

"It feels better, and I am ready for today's journey."

Inemesit came up to me and took my hands in hers. She regarded Moyo with a knowing gaze before turning her attention back to me. "Are you ready for this?"

I nodded, giving her what I hoped was a confident smile.

"Have your visions changed? Any new details arising?"

"No, nothing new. But we have discovered where the boy is being kept."

Inemesit smiled proudly. "Excellent."

"He is in Ewuare, by the tower," Moyo chimed in.

Something flickered in the oracle's gaze, but I couldn't read it.

"Then you'd better get moving. You have a long journey ahead of you, but Atai will accompany you," the oracle declared, turning to her son. "He will help you with whatever you need. Aren't you glad now that I made you pack that cloak?"

Atai rolled his eyes and dismounted from their horse. "Yes, Mother."

"I will join you as far as Orerokpe, before I need to return to Mbiabong."

Moyo said suddenly, "I will also accompany you to Orerokpe. I know you can then find your way to Ewuare from there."

Inemesit smiled. "That would be appreciated, Moyo."

There was a chance that Atai had told his mother Moyo's

name. But something in her tone made me think the two of them knew each other well.

"I just need to gather my supplies. Naborhi, will you help me?"

I followed him into the house, and he dug through his cabinet. He brought out a worn scroll and a small metal object. He unfurled the paper and spread it out over his table. It was a map of Otọrakpọ, and I was suddenly very thankful for his geography lessons. I recognized Ewuare all the way to the north, and the stretch of land between it and Kokori seemed insurmountable.

"This is my wayfinder. My father gave it to me when I was a boy. His father had gifted it to him, and his father before him."

I held the small device in my palms. Its dials spun slowly, adjusting to the new placement, before finding due north and settling. Its metal was worn smooth and shiny, but it was intricately carved with old symbols I couldn't interpret.

"Thank you," I murmured.

We reviewed the map, and as his hands slid over the Lost Lands, my breath caught.

"We will pass through Iga?"

"Yes. It's the fastest way."

I could not count how many times I had dreamt of Iga, of Tega and me living there, away from the constraints of our clan, free to do as we pleased. Now I was going to pass through it without her. The thought filled me with sadness.

He handed me a small coin purse. Inside it were silver shells and a few gold trellics.

"Thank you, Moyo."

"You do not have to thank me. I'm happy to help."

I grabbed the map and placed the money in my bag. Then I looked up at his shelf of books. "May I have that?" I pointed at a book of fables. "And that," I said, pointing at a history of Otọrakpọ.

He handed them to me, a small smile on his lips.

"Thank you," I said, putting them in my bag.

Moyo quickly packed spare clothes and extra food, and then I carried our bags outside, where Inemesit was gathering bento beans and Atai sat on the porch, soaking up the early morning sun, his hand clamped around Tamunor's arm.

"What are you doing here?" I gasped, and my cousin shot me a guilty smile, looking like a thief caught in the act.

"I caught this one snooping in the forest," Atai drawled, bored. "Says he knows you and Moyo." He released Tamunor and my cousin skittered away, wide-eyed.

"I had a message for Imoni from my father, but when Tega was so cagey about where you were, I figured you were here. What is going on, Naborhi? Are you leaving?"

"You don't need to know."

"Well, I am going with you to wherever it is you are clearly going."

"You most certainly will not," I snapped. "Go back home and forget you saw me."

"I will not go back home. I cannot see you leaving with strangers"—he gestured at Inemesit and an amused Atai—"and not come with you. You are my family."

"Restless feet will surely fall into a snake pit, Tamunor. Leave right now," I demanded.

"If I have to run after you, I will."

"By the gods, go home, Tamunor!"

He did not yield. He moved to stand by the carriage.

Atai walked to his mother's side and whispered to her. She chuckled at what he said.

"Let the boy join you," Inemesit called. "He is certainly not going to let us leave without him."

I gave in. "Fine. But you better not hold us back."

We waited while Moyo helped Tamunor pack a bag with some of his clothes that could fit him.

I held Moyo's wayfinder, examining it closely.

"An Oroni woman created the wayfinder you know." Atai's voice was proud, and I knew I wasn't imagining that he'd puffed up his chest a bit.

"Can you use one?"

"Of course."

"Good." I smiled innocently at him. "I'd hate to be the only one of use on this trip."

Atai laughed loudly, and something fluttered in my stomach.

When we were ready to go, Moyo brought out Nour from the stable. It was a tight squeeze, but she carried him, Tamunor, and me. We gave our bags to Atai and Inemesit to carry on their horse.

We set off at a brisk pace, and I forced myself to face forward, to not glance back toward the house, toward Kokori.

There was no going back now. I was on my way to Ewuare.

11

ORerokpe was the smallest clan in Agbon. It bordered the Lost Lands and was known for its constant rainfall and the safehouses that were built during the invasion of the Lost Lands. We decided to spend the night in a public house Moyo had previously visited.

Inemesit paid for the rooms.

"So what can I get you before you retire?" the bartender asked, herding us to a stump of a table to sit. A chandelier with five large candles hung above our head, illuminating the stains on his lower teeth.

A gust of wind from an open window made the candles flicker, but they did not go out. The place smelled of palm wine and wood ash. A man in a far corner played the udu, but not very well. By the way his neck was drooping, I could tell he was drunk.

"What do you have?" Atai asked, and the man listed the food options.

We all chose what we wanted, and the publican peered at me before he walked away.

So far nothing bad had happened, except for Tamunor's complaints about the hard chairs and a few locals who could not stop staring at us.

"Go back to Kokori if you are already so miserable," I told my cousin anytime he made a complaint.

He would stop talking and look offended. "I am here to protect you," he would reply. "I will go back when you do."

I could not stop worrying about him. What if something happened to him? What would I say to his father? Guilt tore at me. And I could not stop worrying about what lay ahead.

We waited for our dinner in silence, listening to the rain drumming on the roof as it transitioned from heavy to slight and back to heavy again.

Tamunor spoke first. "So," he started, "who is going to tell me where we are going to?"

He glanced at all of us around him.

He was already coming with us, so there was no need to hold anything back from him.

I told Tamunor about my visions and the boy being held in Ewuare.

Tamunor listened quietly, his arms folded across his chest. His brows went up when I stopped talking, and he tilted his head, considering. His eyes dashed from Atai to me to our older companions.

A flash of lightning lit up the room and thunder boomed.

Tamunor unfolded his arms and leaned against the table. He

seemed to have made up his mind about something. "What kind of trouble do you think he is in?"

"We do not know yet," I replied. "All we know is he needs my help."

His eyes narrowed and he looked like he wanted to ask more questions, but he was interrupted by the man placing our food and water on the table. The savory smell of ripe plantain mixed with palm oil, water leaves, pepper, and dried fish made Tamunor lick his lips.

I frowned when I saw the eggs on top of my food. I spooned them on to Tamunor's plate, and he smiled.

Tamunor explained, "One time she got really sick from a bad egg, and now she can barely stand the sight of them."

"Same thing happened to Atai when he was little." Inemesit chuckled. "Snails. He won't even look at one now."

Atai caught my eye and gave an impish grin.

"I don't mind eggs," Moyo mused, using his spoon to divide his egg. "It's bento beans I can't stand."

Tamunor and I laughed at that, and Moyo looked at us in surprise.

"You live on a bento-bean farm," Tamunor said.

"I like the way they look, and I love the smell on the field, but I can't stand the taste. That's why I give them away to the rest of the clan."

Atai and Tamunor began discussing their favorite ways of preparing roasted yams.

I was reminded of my mother and all the food she used to

make. She was an expert at making irhibo-otor, my favorite soup. She made it in the courtyard on rainy days. I would watch her make it in an evwere, adding pepper, roasted erhe, urhirien, and finally a roasted black fish on top. I used to long for rain just to eat the soup.

Inemesit dropped a few more silver shells on the table. "In case you want to eat some more."

Tamunor cried out in delight and snatched up the coins, rushing to the bar to order more food.

I drank my water, smiling softly.

Moyo ate slowly and silently. He looked worried.

His expression mirrored what I felt. I had never been so scared my entire life. Dreaming about something was quite different from actually doing it.

That night, I was so anxious I could not sleep. The next day, we would leave Moyo and Inemesit and venture into the Orerokpe Sands, the long stretch of desert leading through the Lost Lands.

I stared at the roof all night until morning came.

The butcher who delivered meat to the public house was a friend of Moyo's. He gave us directions that would take us near the border.

The five of us passed through a sea of moonflowers along the way. Their silver petals almost glowed in the early morning sun. Their crisp, clean scent filled my nostrils and eased the tightness in my chest. For a moment in that abundance of flowers, I almost forgot about my fears.

We crossed to the other side of the flower field, past a stream and over a small hill, and came upon the Orerokpe Sands.

It was an endless sea of reddish-brown dunes, as far as my eyes could see. It was beautiful in its severity, in its devastation.

"The Lost Lands," Atai announced, straightening up. He held a hand above his brow and stared into the desert as if trying to find something out there in the empty space.

"We have to go through this?" Tamunor grumbled.

"Yes," I told him, looking at the map. "Go home now if you want." This time, I said those words to myself too.

"This is where we part ways," Moyo said.

Inemesit and Atai stepped away from us. The oracle spoke quietly to her son, who nodded at her every word.

Tamunor shuffled away, giving us all the privacy for our good-byes. I turned to Moyo, his face etched in sadness and something eerily similar to love.

"How can I ever repay you, Moyo?" I asked, my voice cracking.

He smiled gently. "You already have." He took my hands, "In my clan, there is a mighty river called Iso-ao-natunya. Its name translates to the Smoke That Thunders. It moves rapidly through bends and cliffs, breaking past gigantic boulders. The river makes a thunderous, roaring sound as it flows, sending mist into the air around. Despite those obstacles, despite those boulders, the water moves fast and strong. It cannot be held back. It cannot be less than it is." His eyes welled, and I felt my heart ache. "That is how you are, Naborhi. Like the unstoppable waters. Ufi and I never had the chance to have children. We would have been lucky to have had a daughter like you. I am so very proud of you."

I blinked back tears and threw my arms around him. He hugged me fiercely.

"Go well, Naborhi," he said.

I nodded. "I will write to you. Please take care of Tega."

"I promise."

Inemesit and Atai stepped toward us, and Tamunor hurried closer.

"Your journey may be rough," said the oracle, "but everything will come full circle soon enough. Obassi does not make mistakes. He picks the person best suited for the time and the place." She gave me a reassuring smile and glanced at Atai.

"Obassi will protect you all," she said.

"I know," Atai replied.

"Be safe. And eat your vegetables where you can."

Tamunor howled a laugh as Atai blushed. I smiled.

"It's time," Moyo urged gently. "The midday heat has passed."

I looked out at the sands before us and took a deep breath. I could go back home, I thought. I could forget about my desire to be free, the drumming in my gut, the pain of the boy in my dreams. But his fear was bone-deep. And as much I was afraid of the unknown, it was nothing compared to his fear, to my fears of what awaited me if I turned back.

I stepped forward. Atai followed, Tamunor behind him. And our journey began.

12

WE WALKED THROUGH THE AFTERNOON AND INTO THE evening, sand merging and sliding beneath our feet until we no longer had strength. It was hot, and it felt like sand had crept into my lungs and throat, but we had to ration our water. We still had two days left in this barren wasteland.

Night finally descended and with it came a much-needed cold. We stopped to sleep under a small tree with almost no leaves. With the few sticks we found, Atai struck up a fire. We gathered around it and ate my dried fruit and the dried fish Atai had brought. I wrapped my cloak around myself, amazed at how many stars were out in the night sky. The desert looked serene in the darkness, the sands illuminated by the starlight and the faint glow of the crescent moon.

Atai and Tamunor were discussing the recent truce between Oron and Agbon. Apparently, despite the pleasant meeting between the queen and king, Kehina had been trying to sow discontent among the Oroni courtiers. Obong Iniiemem had ordered her out of Mbiabong on a temporary exile, but Kehina had already vanished.

I shuddered at the thought of Kehina loose, her sister's control over her obvious anger deteriorated. I took out the book of fables to distract myself.

"Naborhi, tell us a story? I feel you would have good stories to tell," Atai said, taking a bite of fish.

I kept my eyes on my page. "Why do you think I would have any good stories to tell?"

I saw him point at my book from the corner of my eye.

"Please eat your food and enjoy the silence," I replied, hoping I would not have to speak again anytime soon.

"She dislikes being interrupted when she is reading," Tamunor chuckled, and I glared up at his grinning face.

Atai spoke up again, humor dancing in his eyes. "If you do not tell a story, I will have Tamunor tell me stories of your childhood. The naughty ones."

"Oh, have I got stories to tell you," cried an eager Tamunor. "When we were but ignorant children, Naborhi went into a barn and—"

I quickly cut him short, slamming my book shut. "Fine. I will tell you a story."

Atai smiled, obviously cherishing his victory.

"I know a story from one of Moyo's collections. It is about a tree here in the Orerokpe Sands."

This got their full attention.

"The location of this tree is ever-changing, but always above it is a handlike cloud, never moving." I put up my hand and snapped it so my fingers faced the ground.

"This tree has faces for fruits. If you stare into the eyes of a face, you will swap places with that face and whoever was there will be freed. Until the next fool, eager to look into your eyes, comes along. The end," I said, picking up my book again.

"That is not a very good story," Atai stated grumpily. "Maybe I was wrong after all."

"Yes, you were," I replied, chuckling, and threw a date into my mouth.

Atai brought his legs closer to the fire. "I will tell you a story then. A story about Grasshopper and Toad. Grasshopper and Toad were very good friends for years, yet they had never eaten at each other's houses. One day, Toad said to Grasshopper, 'My friend, tomorrow come and dine at my house. My wife and I will prepare a special meal. We would love it if you came.'

"The next day, Grasshopper arrived at Toad's house. When they down to eat, Grasshopper reached for his food and it made a shrill noise. When Toad heard it, he said, 'Grasshopper, can you not leave your chirping behind? I cannot eat with that noise.'

"So Grasshopper tried to eat without rubbing his forelegs together, but it was impossible. Each time he gave a chirp, Toad complained and asked him to be quiet. Grasshopper was angry and could not eat. Finally, he said to Toad, 'Please come to my house for dinner tomorrow.' "

I closed my book to listen to Atai's story.

"The next day, Toad arrived at Grasshopper's home. As soon as the meal was ready, Grasshopper washed his forelegs and invited the Toad to do the same. Toad did so, and then hopped toward the food. 'You had better go back and wash again,' said Grasshopper. 'All that hopping in the dirt has made your forelegs dirty again.'

"Toad hopped back to the water jar, washed again, then hopped back to the table, and was ready to reach out for some food from one of the platters when Grasshopper stopped him. 'Please do not put your dirty legs into the food. Go and wash them again.' "

Tamunor started to laugh at this juncture, and I joined him, the image of Toad hopping up and down clear in my mind.

Atai continued, making faces as he spoke.

"Toad was furious. 'You just do not want me to eat with you!' he cried. 'You know very well that I must use my forelegs to hop about. I cannot help it if they get a bit dirty between the water jar and the table.'

"Grasshopper replied, 'You are the one who started it yesterday. You know I cannot rub my forelegs together without making noise.'

"From then on they were no longer friends."

"Now, that is a good story," Tamunor declared. "It is so funny." He continued laughing, tears coming out of his eyes.

"It is a good story," I agreed.

"Thank you," Atai replied. "My father used to tell my sister and me that story all the time."

"My father never told us any stories," I said without thinking. "The only consistent words from his mouth were the bride price my sister and I would fetch and how much he regretted marrying my mother."

Atai shared a startled glance with Tamunor, who shook his head slightly.

I had spoiled the mood and I felt terrible. "It is a good story," I repeated, parting my lips in a smile even I could feel was awkward.

Tamunor wrapped himself tighter with his cloak.

"Who taught you to fight?" I asked, pointing at Atai's sword.

He stood up and drew out his sword.

"My father," he replied, putting one foot in front of the other. He swung the sword smoothly with his right hand and fought an imaginary opponent as he spoke. His moves were graceful, well-trained. It reminded me a bit of Moyo.

"My father always said a man should be able to protect himself and his family. He was a great man and a great friend."

I blinked, surprised. "Your father was your friend?" I'd never heard of a boy being close with his father. Even Tamunor wasn't friends with his.

Atai stopped thrusting his sword forward. "Yes. He was a good friend. He taught me how to read a map and use a wayfinder."

"How lucky for you." I hoped I did not sound as jealous as I felt.

"What about your father?" Atai asked, sitting back down. "He must have been bearable sometimes?"

"Father was who he was. Nothing else."

He pointed at my daggers. "Moyo taught you to fight, did he not? And to read and write?"

"Yes. He is a good man."

He shrugged. "It seems to me like you had a good father after all."

I glanced at him sharply, but his gaze was open, gentle. Tamunor coughed and lay down, staring into the fire.

"What about your mother?" Atai asked after a while.

"She was a beautiful woman. Strong, funny, hardworking. She was my foundation. She was a good woman."

"You must miss her."

I did not want to talk about my mother anymore, so I remained quiet and stared into the fire. He did not prod further and I was relieved.

"I will take the first watch," Atai volunteered.

When my back hit the ground, I regretted speaking about my parents. A painful memory flooded through my mind.

My mother had returned home from the market one day distressed, talking to herself. She mumbled about how my father was going to marry a new wife. She had heard rumors. That day she had confirmed it. Strolling through the meat market, she had found him talking to the girl and her father.

"I am glad," she said to herself. "It is time someone gave him a boy."

I knew my mother mourned the two sons she had lost after they were born. She lamented the ones she could not give our father.

When he returned, she confronted him about what she had seen. He went into a mad rage. This was worse than any of the quarrels they had had before.

He raised his hand high in the air and struck her across her cheek. He shook her vigorously. "Why did I even marry you? Why?" He struck her again.

She tried to fight back, but that only made him angrier. He beat her right before our eyes without holding back. His kicks met her stomach, her face, her legs.

Tega whimpered behind me while I just stood there, shocked. I recovered quickly and without thinking, I leapt on his shoulders, my hands around his neck, squeezing as tight as I could, wishing with just one more squeeze he would drop dead.

He grabbed me by my dress and threw me to the ground. I fell on my back and agonizing pain shot up my spine. Tears flowed from my eyes as I watched him kick Mother again and again until she folded into herself. My vision blurred as I tried to stand up and I fell to the ground, my legs trembling.

When he was done, he simply walked out of the courtyard, leaving us battered on the ground.

I crawled toward my mother and gasped at the damage done to her face.

By the time Tega had fetched a physician, the pain in my back had subsided. He gave her medicine and stitched her wounds, and told us our mother needed rest.

Tega and I were left alone with our mother for a few days. She made us promise not to send for Imoni. She was ashamed, ashamed of her life and her choices and herself.

Something I swore to myself that day I would never be.

13

AFTER WALKING FOR A DAY AND A HALF, WE CAME ACROSS a statue almost entirely buried by the Orerokpe Sands. Only its outstretched fingers rose out of the ground, each as large as we were. It must have been massive before time dealt with it. According to Moyo's map, we were on the right track.

Tamunor ran up to it, touching one finger and laughing with incredulity. I laughed with him. It was a sight to behold.

I drew closer and touched the cracks in the stone. A piece fell off. And then another. Underneath was a smooth black surface.

Atai came up next to me to examine it.

"It's so cold," Atai said.

I was about to say something when a spurt of hot sand shot into the air just beyond the statue. I jumped and shared a worried look with Tamunor and Atai.

Several feet from us another spurt erupted, raining down sizzling sand. The wind blew it in our direction, and I hissed when some burned my face.

Tamunor jerked back and almost fell trying to dodge the spray.

"Quick, put your cloaks on!" Atai grabbed his from his pack and we followed suit, holding them above our heads as we raced past the spurts of hot sand.

We did not make it far before we heard a thunderous rumble. The ground beneath our feet shook wildly before splitting apart, an explosion of hot sand shooting up. The fissure grew wider and rapidly made its way in our direction.

There was only one thing left for us to do.

"Run!" I shouted.

We bolted straight ahead, constantly dodging the sting of the sand, trying to stay the course of the map in my head.

There was another rumble, and a spurt of sand shot up not a dozen paces ahead of us.

We banked sharply to avoid it, but the ground gave way suddenly and all three of us tumbled down a steep hill.

Sand grated against my skin and filled my mouth as I gasped in pain. When I finally rolled to a stop, it felt like I had been scraped raw.

We seemed to be stuck at the bottom of a ravine, the walls rising steeply around us. I groaned and tried to lift to my feet, but I couldn't get my footing. The ground seemed to suck me down further with each movement.

My blood froze just as Atai cried, "Sink sand!"

I watched Tamunor's face momentarily go slack with shock, mouth open and eyes vacant. He then burst into motion, his body lurching to stand only for his knees to give way, his body collapsing back deeper into the sand. "Help!" he shouted, though for whom I had no idea.

"If you keep struggling like that, you will only sink further," Atai warned, looking around desperately for a way out.

"Son of a rat!" Tamunor swore, his face shiny with sweat. "Is it getting hotter? Please tell me it's not getting hotter."

I ignored him, my eyes scanning the bottom of the ravine. There was nothing to grab on to, to pull ourselves out.

"This is how I die," Tamunor said, disbelieving. "This is how I die?"

"Tamunor, calm down," I snapped, my voice shrill with panic.

"I am trying. I really am."

He only resumed his shouting. The ground still shook from the spurts, and hot sand rolled down the hill toward us, burying us further.

Sand pooled around my waist and blew into my eyes, making them water. I had to think, had to get us out of here, but fear clouded my mind.

Atai shouted as he suddenly sank up to his chin, one arm flailing wildly.

"Atai!" I called out, moving without thinking. I sank even more but I had to pull him up, even if only so we could all drown together.

I thrust my hand toward him and he held on as I yanked him forward. I forced his head up and held him close. His beard was covered in sand, and he spat some from his mouth in disgust.

"Thank you," he rasped.

"Thank me if we get out."

Sweat poured down my face, and my weak hands trembled as I held on to him.

There was nowhere to go.

Tamunor had stopped shouting, staring blankly at the ravine wall. Atai was clearing sand away from himself with much effort, and I could think of no way to get us out of there.

This could not be where our journey ended. What sort of a god would lead us all the way out here to die?

Just then, shadows fell over us from the opposite bank of the ravine.

I looked up to see two men riding humpbacked creatures with hairy noses and short necks.

"Praise Egbesu!" Tamunor exclaimed, sounding like himself again.

The skinny men were dressed in blue-and-white sleeveless tunics that covered their wraparound skirts. They wore head wraps underneath wide-brimmed hats and cowrie jewelry around their necks. Their faces were painted with white and yellow streaks, their lips painted black. On their hips were short swords and water gourds.

One of the men got off his mount, and the other followed suit. They each retrieved a rope from their packs and tossed one end down to us. Atai and I lunged to grab them. With all the strength I could muster, I climbed along the rope, the sand still sucking me down, unwilling to let me go. When I finally made it up the wall and over the ledge, Atai began his climb. I tossed my rope back toward Tamunor, but his arms were so weak he barely budged. Atai and I together with the two men had to pull him up. His palms were blistered and he waved them around to ease the pain.

The tallest of the two men sized us up, contemplating something.

"Who are you and what are you doing here?" he asked in Traveler's Tongue.

I answered, relieved he could speak the language, "I am Naborhi. This is Atai and Tamunor."

"I am Rukaye; this is Metitiri." He pointed to his companion. I noticed Metitiri had a split lower lip.

"Come with us," Metitiri urged. "There is a dust storm approaching. We have shelter."

I was thankful they helped us, but I was wary of them. I looked at Atai and Tamunor for a decision.

"You will not survive the Sands in this state," Rukaye insisted.

Atai looked first at me and then at Tamunor, who shook his head.

"No, thank you," Atai said. "We will go on our own."

He dug into his pack to pull out the wayfinder, sand spilling from the bag. He frowned at it for a moment and then pointed to what seemed to be north. Tamunor and I turned to where he gestured and saw a crimson cloud on the horizon. It was so huge it seemed to me like a mountain, and it was moving toward us at an alarming speed.

The three of us exchanged nervous looks before glancing back at the men.

"We told you there was a dust storm," Rukaye said, his blackened lips parting in a sly grin.

I weighed our options. We were sore, battered, and tired. I wasn't sure yet whether we'd lost any of our supplies to the fall and the sink sand. We had already been low on water that morning, and I hated to think of what we'd face if we got caught in the storm.

"Thank you," I said at last, nodding begrudgingly. "We would be grateful for the shelter."

They made room for us on their mounts. I rode with Rukaye, and he chattered amicably at us the entire ride.

But I kept my hands on my daggers as a precaution. No one was going to take me unaware.

We were near their camp when the storm reached us. Thick clouds of dust rippled across the sand like waves, and the wind was whistling in my ears.

Their camp was small and shabby. Metitiri bundled the animals into a small tent that looked like it was moments away from losing its battle with the wind.

Rukaye guided us inside a bigger tent, where two girls were

resting on a mound of blankets and cushions on the floor. One of them was dressed more heavily than the other. Her white attire wrapped snugly around her head, arms, and legs so that only her face was showing.

They did not speak to us but continued their sewing.

Tamunor awkwardly smiled at the girl not fully covered, and she returned his gesture with a death stare. He looked away quickly.

"Please, sit." Rukaye gestured to the cushions, and we obeyed, settling in. I nearly groaned with relief at being off my feet.

Metitiri handed us cups of cool water.

"That's a peculiar mark." Metitiri observed my hand as he gave me my cup.

"It's nothing," I said, taking the water from him and hiding my hand under my arm. The way he stared at me made me uncomfortable.

The men refilled our cups before sitting down next to us. Rukaye brought out a jar from a goatskin bag. He poured the contents into a cup, then from the pocket of his tunic he revealed a small vial of a colorless liquid. He put a few drops into the cup, and a distinct, strange odor wafted my way. It smelled sweet, like the first rain after the dry season mixed with burning leaves.

"What is that?" I asked.

"It is poison from the newkel root," he answered, pouring more of the liquid into the cup without batting an eyelid.

"Why are you drinking poison?" Tamunor asked, looking about ready to snatch the cup away from him.

Atai fidgeted where he sat.

"Why would anyone do that?" I asked, not able to take my eyes off the cup. Wouldn't he die from it?

"To develop a tolerance."

Rukaye emptied the cup down his throat and belched satisfactorily.

Tamunor let out a bleat of surprise. I balled my fists, watching for signs of the poison settling in.

But nothing happened to him. Rukaye cleared his throat and leaned back against the pillows. He handed the vial of newkel root to Metitiri.

Tamunor glanced at me and then at Atai as Metitiri poured his own toxic mixture. "How does one take poison and not die?" he asked.

"We consume small, nonlethal doses of a poison and build immunity to it over time."

"Very helpful, should we encounter any enemies," Rukaye added, tossing a too-knowing look my way.

Metitiri brought out a pipe and filled it with pungent leaves before lighting it. The smoke smelled sweet and tangy, unlike any of the herbs the men in Kokori smoked. He passed it to Rukaye for a drag.

Outside, the dust storm raged and the wind howled shrilly, the walls of the tent snapping sharply.

Tamunor kept staring at the veiled woman, so I kicked his

leg. He grimaced and looked away, but not before Metitiri spotted him.

"That is Uki," he explained, disdain lacing his voice. "She is one of the few who has the Ewen. She cannot go outside, as sunlight burns her skin, so she has to dress like that."

"Oh," Tamunor said, nodding. I watched Uki shrink in on herself and felt a surge of empathy and anger course through me. Why were these men belittling her for a disease she had no control over? It was clear that Uki lived a constricted life, and my heart ached for her to be able to break free.

"So where are you all headed?" Rukaye asked.

Atai replied cautiously, "Ewuare. We have an urgent message to deliver."

"This message requires three of you?" Rukaye laughed boisterously, and Metitiri joined in.

Atai stiffened. "Yes," he gritted out.

"It must be a very important one."

It was an unspoken question, a desire to know more. Rukaye waited for Atai to elaborate, but Atai just stared back.

The men obviously did not believe him, but Rukaye did not ask any more questions. He took a long drag from the pipe and let out the smoke in small rings.

"Have you ever had liwa?" Rukaye asked when he caught Tamunor staring.

Tamunor shook his head, and Rukaye passed him the pipe. Tamunor placed it in his mouth, inhaling deeply. He began to choke almost immediately.

“Not for me,” Tamunor said in between fitful coughs, hurriedly passing the pipe back to Rukaye. “I think I am going to die,” he wheezed.

I couldn’t help but laugh at his twisted face, the whites of his eyes turned a pale green. Atai rapped him on his back.

“Not everyone can handle liwa,” Rukaye told him, chuckling.

For some reason, that nagged at my pride. “I will partake,” I said. Rukaye eyed me disbelievingly, but he handed me the pipe.

The liwa was strong, whatever it was. It took all my willpower not to cough. I continued to take drags, and with every breath it became easier. Then the tent began to fold up.

I panicked and grabbed on to Atai. His hands melted. What was happening? I looked at everyone in the room. They all had blurry faces.

“Are you all right?” Atai asked in a strange voice. He sounded very far away.

“She is fine,” Rukaye answered. “The liwa is working.”

A bird walked into the tent. Its feathers were in varying shades of green, yellow, and black. It ruffled its feathers.

“I can see a bird,” I said, my voice sounding like the ringing of a bell.

Rukaye came closer, his giant face next to mine. “Naborhi, follow the bird. Follow it.”

“What?”

“Follow the bird.” His voice sounded like Moyo’s.

I faced the bird. It walked like it had never flown a day in its life. I followed it out into the Orerokpe Sands. The tent vanished and with it everyone inside. The sun was gone and the moon had taken over. I looked up. The stars had never looked more beautiful.

I suddenly appeared at home. My father was there. So was my mother. He lifted his hands slowly and pushed my mother, then hit her in the face. I took out my daggers without thinking and lunged at him, but he faded into a cloud of smoke before I could get to him. I fell to the ground and glanced up to see Moyo. Only, he looked much younger.

I stood up, and my hands held a bow and arrow.

I fixed my eyes on a target swinging from a tree in front of me. I nocked my bow and lifted it just above my shoulders, my arms quivering slightly. Moyo looked ahead without speaking, but he touched my quivering arm. I stopped trembling.

"The wind can be your friend or your enemy. You must study it if you want your arrow to arrive home," he said.

When I thought the time was right I let go. And missed.

"I will do better," I told him, lifting the bow higher. I thought of my mother, of my father's fists pounding against her head. I needed to know how to fight, how to protect myself and others, how to stop people like my father from hurting everyone.

But before I could say any of that, Moyo disappeared in a cloud of smoke.

"Wait!" I shouted, but he was gone. My bones began to ache as if I had a fever. I squeezed my eyes shut, and when I opened them, Tamunor and Atai were staring back. Curiosity and worry merged on their faces.

I quickly looked around me, my head clearing. I had never left the tent.

"What happened?" I asked groggily.

Tamunor raised a brow. "You went mad." He laughed a little, but it was hollow.

Atai still gripped my clammy hand. I clenched my jaw and raised a brow at Rukaye.

"What was that?" I asked him.

"Liwa," he answered. "The first time is always tough. What did you see?"

The wind still howled outside. The storm, it seemed, was not going to stop soon.

"Nothing. I saw nothing."

Rukaye broke into a smile. He seemed amused by my answer. "It is fine if you do not want to tell me."

Even if I had wanted to tell him what I saw, I would not know where to begin.

While the storm raged on, we went to sleep. I kept my hands curled around one of my daggers, tucked under my pillow.

Someone shook me awake violently, and I was surprised to see Uki standing above me. The other girl and the men were no longer in the tent. I rubbed my tired eyes.

"You need to leave now," she said in the Traveler's Tongue.

"Why? What is happening?" I became alert at the urgent tone of her voice.

She gestured at my mark and for me to look outside while she woke up Tamunor and Atai. I peeked through the opening of the tent. Far in the distance, I saw a group of men and a woman. It was hard to distinguish who each man was, until suddenly I saw moonlight flash on the breastplates of two of the men. My heart thudded against my chest.

Abavo.

I cursed loudly. Did Rukaye and Metitiri call them because of me? Did they really know the meaning of the mark on my hand? Was this the end of my journey?

I stopped my wandering mind and focused on escaping.

"We have to leave," I said, and turned to Uki. "Is there another way out of here?"

"What's happening?" Tamunor asked, worried.

"Those sons of a rat called the Abavo. They're on their way here."

"Metitiri has spent time in Agbon," Uki said quickly. She was helping us gather our supplies, and even offered us some of their own. "He knows that mark means he will be rewarded for returning you to your family, to your fiancé."

Atai swore, and my stomach churned.

Uki gestured for us to follow her to the back of the tent. She moved a stack of boxes and tore open a rough stitch in the tent wall.

"Hurry," she said in a small voice.

Atai and Tamunor squeezed through the opening, but I lingered.

"Come with us," I urged, but she shook her head.

"I will not last long in the Sands without the shelter these men provide."

"You'll be punished for helping us," I rasped. "Please, let us try to protect you."

She smiled sadly. "The time will come for my escape. Until then, I will endure what I must."

My throat tightened at her bravery, her sacrifice. "Thank you, Uki."

She squeezed my hand and shoved me through the opening.

Atai was waiting for me, and he snatched my hand as we raced after Tamunor.

Once again, we were back in the Orerokpe Sands.

14

TRUST NOBODY.

That was the only the only thing on my mind as we silently marched on through the Orerokpe Sands, the sun beating down our heads. I had been suspicious of those men from the start, but I never thought they would have helped us only to call the Abavo on me. The only person who had proven to be decent was Uki.

I hoped she was all right. What would Rukaye and Metitiri do to her when they found out she had helped us? It hurt my heart just thinking about it.

I had to be more careful and cover the mark on my hand. I stripped a bit of fabric from my cloak and laced it tightly around my palm.

We walked all morning until it was too hot, and we stopped to eat and rest. We didn't speak, and I got the sense that the boys were leaving me to my thoughts. I wiped beads of sweat from my brow as the sun continued to pelt down heat. I was glad we would soon be out of this desert.

We reached the rolling Wolfden Hills just as the sun was setting, the sky a mix of soft pinks and oranges. Finally, there was some respite from the heat. Tamunor cried out in relief and threw his hands in the air before collapsing on the lush grass of a little knoll.

He breathed in deeply. "I never want to see a speck of sand ever again," he groaned.

I looked out at the green hills in front of us and the illuminated dunes behind us. The sun was gilding everything, and I had to admit that the Sands were beautiful, when you weren't fighting for your life within them.

A shepherd was herding his flock on the hill closest to us. They were unlike any sheep I had seen in Kokori, with thick, white wool and four sharp horns, two at the top of their heads and two curled up at the sides. The shepherd waved to us and I waved back, some of my anxiety easing.

We journeyed on for a little while and bought some fruits from a seller by the roadside. They were pinkish red, rough and scaly on the outside but soft on the inside. The juicy flesh was sweet but the seeds were tangy.

We chatted mildly and cautiously with the seller, a small and elderly man, as he packed up his stand. We found out his house was farther along the road, and he offered to give us a ride since it was on our way.

Sitting on the back of that horse-drawn wagon, seeing the

undulating, verdant hills before me with wild horses grazing and running across them, feeling the fresh breeze on my face, and watching the clouds change shape and color as the sun slowly set, was the first time I felt I could breathe. It was the first time I truly felt free from Kokori and all that was expected of me.

I was in the world, and it was open wide, and I could go even farther if I pleased. I wanted to whoop with joy, but I settled for a smile instead.

The fruit seller brought us to the edge of a small forest and bid us goodbye and good luck before turning down a small path skirting the trees to journey home. Atai and I examined the map, and he pointed to Djone Forest, which separated us from the Djone River. Once we crossed the river, we would be on the outskirts of Iga, and we would be more than halfway to Ewuare. My heart stuttered with the knowledge of how close we were to the city I had been dreaming about for so long.

The main path in and out of the forest appeared simple, a little curved, but lined with weeping oak trees that would guide our way.

There was a small note scrawled on the map in Moyo's handwriting. *Only for carriages.* There were some badly drawn sketches along this path even Atai could not distinguish.

There was a longer, winding road that almost circuited the entire forest that Moyo had indicated would be best to do on foot. By my measure, the footpath would add a full day of travel.

"What do we do?" I murmured to Atai.

He shook his head. "I'm not sure. For Moyo to make this note, there must be something dangerous on the carriage path. But . . ."

"Do we have a full day to lose?" Tamunor asked us.

Atai held my gaze, deferring to my judgment. I stared at the forest. The sky was a pale blue in the dying sunlight, and the trees were beginning to be cloaked in darkness. It wasn't wise to enter them in the dark, but I wasn't sure we could afford a night without travel.

I shook my head, looking first at Tamunor and then Atai. "I don't think so. I haven't had any dreams since we left Kokori, and I'm not sure if that's a good thing."

"Then let's take the carriage path," Tamunor answered simply. "There's no time to lose, and I'm sure we can handle whatever danger is there. Besides," he added, grinning crookedly, "it's time we put Moyo's training to the test."

I rolled my eyes, but something still nagged in my gut. I refused to acknowledge it; the carriage path was short, and we would be out of the forest before full darkness settled in. There were three of us, and I trusted my training, and Atai's.

We made our way down the carriage path and into the trees, and I ignored the sensation that the forest was swallowing us. We walked side by side, close enough that my arm brushed Atai's with each step. Tamunor hummed a cheery tune, but it sounded forced even to my ears.

Suddenly, a carriage appeared ahead of us, hurtling toward

us at breakneck speed. We jumped to the side of the path and the carriage shot past us, leaving a cloud of dust.

"What's chasing them?" Tamunor laughed nervously, looking back at the cart.

He jerked his attention toward the trees behind us, staring up into the branches.

"What is it?" I asked quietly, my skin prickling. Atai's hand drifted toward the pommel of his sword.

Tamunor shook his head. "I thought I saw something, but I must have been mistaken." His voice was not entirely convincing.

I looked up. There was nothing there except rustling leaves.

"Let's keep moving," Atai urged. "And keep an eye out."

"Walk between us, Naborhi," Tamunor instructed as we continued on, our pace faster than before. "Just in case we need to protect you."

I rolled my eyes at him, laughing tinnily. "Sure. Like I'm the one needing protection."

"That's what I'm here for. I have had my fair share of fights."

"As if you can throw a punch."

"I'll have you know I've won several arm-wrestling matches—"

Mid-sentence, Tamunor yelped, his eyes bulging.

"What is it?" Atai demanded, unsheathing his sword.

"I feel something around me, like a rope."

I palmed my daggers, eyes darting over him. "Tamunor, there is nothing—"

He suddenly squeezed his eyes shut and winced. There was a

shrill sound and then he was yanked from the ground and up into the weeping oak trees.

"Naborhi!" he screamed.

I was not fast enough to catch him.

Dry leaves rained down on me and I could no longer see or hear him.

Oh, Egbesu.

My hands began to tremble, and I clenched my daggers tighter, panting.

Atai stepped closer to me, raising his sword. "What was that?"

The leaves rustled above us.

"I think we are about to find out," I told him, watching branches shake, movement traveling down the line of trees.

Atai and I sprinted after it, barely avoiding tripping on the undergrowth as we went deeper into the woods.

Fear clouded my mind as I ran, and I desperately tried to shove it aside. My heart pounded chaotically and I could barely breathe, my feet screaming in pain after the day's walking.

"Come on!" Atai shouted. "It changed direction. It's moving this way." He beckoned for me to hurry up.

We chased it until we hit a small clearing. The rustling stopped and so did we. Atai spun slowly, his eyes darting everywhere.

"Where did it go?" I panted, frustrated.

Dusk had fully settled in the forest now, and everything seemed more sinister, more dangerous. We stood, listening to the wind roaring through the boughs, until Atai's head snapped to our left.

"This way," Atai said, and I hurriedly followed him.

I dared to voice the fear that lay in my heart. "What if we don't find him?" I asked.

Atai turned back to me, a finger to his lips. "We have found him," he whispered, pointing past a cluster of trees.

Tamunor was bound to a tree, gagged, his hands and legs tied together. A bonfire had been lit beside him, and the flames illuminated the terror in his face.

There were dozens of creatures surrounding him. They were small and silver-haired, and I could barely make out their feet and hands. It was like they were invisible, blending into their surroundings. They had scattered bowls and knives and fruit on the ground, and many were dancing around the bonfire and releasing more of those shrill sounds. Tamunor grunted and squirmed, struggling to free himself.

"Ebo," Atai spat. "I thought they were a myth. They hunt by camouflaging themselves, like chameleons."

"Are they going to eat him?"

Atai nodded, his face ashen.

"Why would anything want to eat Tamunor? He is so thin." I don't know why the words came out of me, and I almost laughed at the absurdity of the situation.

One of the Ebo approached Tamunor and rubbed a red liquid all over his body while making that shrill sound. It sounded like it was laughing at Tamunor, but then it opened its mouth and threw up a brown paste all over him.

Tamunor screamed around his gag. He struggled again to free himself, but it was no use.

I tried to observe the creatures' weaknesses and strengths. As small as they were, if they could carry off Tamunor, then I did not want to rush into a fight with them. Only a fool would test the depths of a river with both feet.

"We need to distract them," Atai suggested.

I nodded. "But how?"

Atai began to fill his bag with stones. "Wait here. When you hear me whistling and tossing these stones, they'll chase after me and you'll free Tamunor and run. We're close to the Djone—I tracked us. Head that way." He pointed just beyond the scene before us. "We will meet at the river."

"Be careful," I said to him.

He smiled and squeezed my hand before running silently to the other side of the trees, disappearing into the darkness.

I waited, heart racing. The Ebo were shrieking and dancing around Tamunor, circling in closer and closer.

Atai's birdlike whistle was impressive. The Ebo stopped immediately, their heads snapping in the same direction to my right, where Atai had slipped between the trees.

A stone whistled through the air and smacked one of the Ebo on the head, knocking it to the ground. The other creatures screeched in alarm, just as another rock smacked into the tree where Tamunor was tied up. The Ebo let out another shill cry, enraged, and they all shot into the woods after Atai. I wasted no time and swiftly ran to where Tamunor was bound, slicing through his binds with one of my daggers.

"You have no idea how happy I am to see you," he said as he pushed the ropes away from his body.

"I think I have an idea," I told him. "We need to go."

We ran in the direction Atai had told me, racing to the river, not daring to look back. I wanted nothing more than to get out of that forest.

I swore I could almost hear the river when the swarm of Ebo caught up to us.

Their loud screeches hurt my ears, and I palmed my daggers, ready to fight.

"Tamunor, keep running!"

I kept glancing up to see them swing from tree to tree, fading in and out as they drew closer. A whole lot of them descended a few feet ahead of us, mouths wide open as their blood-curdling screeches rent the air. They blocked the path forward, and I veered to our left. An Ebo appeared right in front of me and lunged for me. I lashed out, slicing my dagger across its arm. It hissed, just as another slammed into my back, knocking me to the ground. I lurched to my feet, immediately taking my fighting stance. A group of them closed in, and out of the corner of my eye I saw Tamunor racing toward the river, a band of Ebo chasing him.

An Ebo shot out at me and I moved quickly, fluidly, knocking it away and slicing at it. The rest attacked. I didn't want to kill them, even if they were trying to kill me. I had never taken a life—my training with Moyo had been for protection and defense, not for death—and I had no intention of starting now. But they were fast, hungry, and near-invisible in the darkness, and they didn't seem to have such reservations. I was holding them off, but barely, and I could feel my body tiring, the day's journey sucking the strength from my limbs.

I needed to run, needed to find Tamunor and Atai and get out of this forest. I narrowly dodged the teeth of an Ebo and punched it hard in the face, knocking it back into one of its companions. It broke their formation and I sprinted toward the gap I'd created, hoping against all hope that I was headed in the right direction.

I burst out through the trees and nearly tumbled into the riverbed. I skidded to a stop and spun around to make sure the Ebo had not followed.

They hadn't. I was alone, and the realization clanged through me—Tamunor was not here.

Panic caused my limbs to go numb, and my stomach twisted. I fell to my knees. I felt hot and cold at the same time, the exhaustion and terror finally breaking me.

"Tamunor," I called, my mouth dry. Nothing. "Tamunor!" I called, a little louder this time, trying to stand up.

"Naborhi!"

"Oh, thank you, Egbesu," I cried when I saw him coming toward me from farther up the river, a ridiculous smile on his face. Strength returned to my legs and I bounded over to him.

"I went through another path to confuse them and it worked," he explained.

I snatched him close and hugged him tight for a brief moment before I pushed him away and slapped the back of his head.

"Ow! Why did you do that?" he cried, rubbing his head.

"Never frighten me like that again," I snarled, panting.

"I hear you. But your slap is painful, you know?" He shot me a rueful smile.

I looked back at the forest and then down the tree line, where the river cut close to the woods and formed a steep cliff. I was lucky to have burst out of the forest here; it would have been a deadly fall if I'd been any farther downstream. "We need to find Atai. He must be farther upstream. The river is too close for shelter down there."

"But what do we do if we run into those beasts again?" Tamunor asked, shuddering. "I really do not want to be eaten."

"We fight them, and if we can't, then we run together. No going off on your own."

"I understand."

We followed the river upstream for most of the night. My legs were aching, and my feet were so swollen and scraped I feared they were bleeding, but we didn't meet any more Ebo.

Just when I worried I would collapse, when I became convinced that Atai had not escaped the Ebo after all, I spotted a small campfire just ahead.

I let out a small cry, and Tamunor and I ran toward it. Atai rose from the ground, a relieved smile on his face, just as I barreled into him. He hugged me tightly, shuddering, and I pulled back to squeeze Tamunor's arm tightly. We had survived.

"I'm so glad you're all right," Atai and I said at the same time, and we both laughed.

"Come, I caught some dinner for us," he said, gesturing to the fire, where three fish were roasting over the flames. You must be starving."

We settled on the bank of the river, inhaling our food and filling each other in on what had happened.

After we'd eaten, Atai went toward the forest to relieve himself, and Tamunor and I stared at the fire. The moon was up, casting its silvery light on everything.

I took stock of our situation. I had lost my bag somewhere in the frenzy, which meant I had lost my food, money, the map, and my precious books. All I had left were my daggers.

I looked at Tamunor. His eyes were bloodshot, and he looked so small and scared.

I had had enough of the near-death experiences. What if something had happened to Tamunor? How would I live with myself? Were my freedom and this kidnapped boy so important that I could continue to put him in danger?

I murmured to Tamunor, "I give up. We are going back home."

"What?" Tamunor squeaked, glancing at me sharply.

"This was foolish. Let us go back home."

"Naborhi," Tamunor said calmly.

"We can go back. We will just take the correct path."

My gaze moved from the fire to the flowing water, pale and shimmering in the moonlight.

"Naborhi," Tamunor murmured. He had come to my side, and when I looked back at him, his eyes were filled with worry. "We have come so far. We cannot turn back now."

Atai returned and glanced sharply at us.

"Is everything all right?" he asked, brow furrowing.

"No," I replied. "I was just telling Tamunor that we need to go home."

Atai's eyes grew wide. "We can't go back," he said, shocked.

"We are. For Tamunor's sake."

"We are here for a reason," Atai protested. "Obassi brought us here; he brought *you* here. We will be okay."

I stood up and gritted my teeth. "You can see why I am not inclined to believe that, given that we almost *died*. So I say we do the sane thing and get Tamunor back home."

He laughed in disbelief. "So you're giving up at the first sign of danger?"

"I'm not *giving up*," I snarled. "I'm being practical."

Atai shook his head.

"Obassi shouldn't have wasted his time on you." His voice darkened. "I will go alone if you are too much of a coward."

I stepped forward, clenching my fists.

"How dare you call me a coward!" I snapped, lunging for him.

Tamunor put himself between us, and I bared my teeth at him.

"Get out of my way so I can make him eat his words."

"Naborhi. Naborhi, listen to me," Tamunor urged, gripping my shoulders.

I shrugged him off and threw up my arms in frustration. "What are we doing? We don't even know what we're getting into! This was foolish, *I* was foolish."

Tamunor gripped my hands in his and spoke calmly. "You

are no fool, Naborhi Tanomare. And you are not a coward," he added, shaking his head. I did not miss Atai flinching at that. "You are doing something good for someone else, as you are always doing. You have always taken care of those who need it. You look after Tega, you are Chipo's biggest champion, and you've always helped me with my father. Plus, you are always giving me food."

"That is because you are so skinny."

"I will get bigger. Someday." He smiled.

Tamunor's words made me want to protect him even more.

I gripped his hands tighter. "Tamunor, we can go back now. I can get you home safely."

"No," he said, moving out of my reach. "I know I made a big deal out of coming with you. I said I was going to protect you, but I have not really done a good job of it."

"No, you have not." I couldn't help but smile at that.

"But look at where we are, Naborhi," he said, gesturing at our surroundings, the moonlight limning everything silver, and I finally caught sight of the walls and rooftops of Iga. "Did you ever think we would be so far from home?"

My breath caught in half a sob, and I shook my head.

"We have to keep going. That boy needs us, and we cannot give up on him. *You* are not going to give up. And I'm certainly not going to give up. I have to see this through. I am capable of that. I am."

I took a good look at him. He looked like a beaten-down squirrel, but he had a determination in his eyes I had never seen before. I breathed deeply and considered what he said. He was right. It would be foolish—and cowardly, I begrudgingly admitted to myself—to go back now.

"Tamunor, when did you become so wise?"

"Just before I was snatched up into the trees," he said, grinning.

I looked at Atai, sighing. His defiant expression had trickled down to one of remorse.

We quietly settled in for the night, lying down by the dying campfire. I shivered in the crisp evening air, wishing I had my cloak.

"Here," Atai murmured, offering his. I accepted it after a moment's hesitation, and he smiled softly.

"Thank you for saving my life," Tamunor said to my left as we stared into the endless expanse of starry sky.

"I had to," I replied simply. "What would I have told your father? I do not want your death on my hands."

"Thank you." He chuckled. "Nor do I."

I smiled to myself, so thankful that we were here, that we were alive.

"I am sorry I called you a coward," Atai said softly beside me, and he turned his head toward me, his eyes meeting mine. "I understand it's not easy, this task given to you, and I shouldn't have lost my temper at you. But I have faith in Obassi." Something in his eyes made my chest tighten. "And I have faith in you."

Maybe I was a bit of a coward. Maybe that was why when he had called me that I wanted to knock his teeth in. I had left Kokori without facing my aunt and uncle. I asked Tega to tell them why I had gone, why I would not be back.

And I had left my sister. I had left Tega.

Tears pooled in my eyes, but I blinked them back.

I looked him over and replied, "I am sorry I tried to hurt you for calling me that."

He smiled. "I guess I am lucky Tamunor was here to stop you."

"I guess you are." My answering smile snuck up on me.

"All I could think of was how I would taste," Tamunor confessed, jerking us back to the present. "I was so afraid I would never see my father again, and Iyo, and you guys, but the thought of how I would taste consumed my mind like ants on bean soup. Would I taste sweet? Would I be bitter? Just bland?"

"That is what fear does," Atai explained. "It makes you think and do strange things. Any one of us could have been taken as a meal. Who knows how I would have reacted?"

"I wish I could take medicine for it. Something that would make me never afraid again."

"Then you can relax when the Ebo try to eat you next time." I chuckled. "You will go down their throats with a brave smile on your face. It might even make you taste better."

"I would prefer that," he replied, grinning at me, and Atai laughed.

I fell asleep soon after, Tamunor's smile burning behind my eyelids and Atai's laugh ringing in my ears.

15

I WAS STARING AT IGA.

The place that once held such promise for me, and for Tega. I swallowed thickly. *How the future changes.*

Fog rolled down the far-off hills and disappeared into the cornfields on the other side of the Djone as we crossed the main footbridge over the river. We followed a wide dirt path damp with morning dew all the way to the city. The brown stone houses stood sturdy on carpets of grass, divided by perfectly manicured paths. Their angular roofs were elaborately painted in similar pale colors and their windows were small and elongated. Almost every house had a patch of vegetable garden.

The city was quiet in the early morning, the streets mainly empty apart from merchants and farmers. A man drove a cart full of split wood past us, toward a building bigger than any other around it. Smoke billowed out of the chimney with the smell of smoked fish.

It was a market of sorts, and it was busier than I'd expected. There were stalls selling everything from books and weapons to pickled vegetables and knit wraps. We bought some dried fruit, a loaf of thick, grainy bread, and a hunk of a salty, smelly cheese for breakfast. Almost everyone we passed had piercings on just about every visible body part.

Atai bought me a new cloak. It was a beautiful crimson, intricately embroidered and softer than anything I'd ever worn. I hugged him and thanked him profusely, and he actually blushed, the pale stretches of his skin almost as red as the scarf.

We were supposed to pass through Iga quickly, but I couldn't help but want to see what could have been for Tega and me.

"Let's stay," I said to Tamunor and Atai as we stood outside. The sun was high in the sky, but it was pleasantly warm, not like the fiery heat of the Sands. "Just for the night. We haven't had a good night's sleep in days, and we need to restock on supplies."

"Why do you want to stop traveling?" Atai asked. "It's not even midday yet."

I looked away from them.

"I'd just like to explore the city," I answered. "I don't want to say why."

Tamunor shared a look with Atai before shrugging. "Fine with me. We haven't bathed since we left Kokori, and my eyes are starting to water from your smell."

"Please," I murmured to Atai, ignoring Tamunor's joke, and he looked at me carefully before nodding.

We went to the nearest—the only—public house in Iga.

The owner welcomed us with a cool, sweet drink that we did not have to pay for. It was customary in Iga to give refreshment to strangers, he explained. He was old, older than Moyo, and he had a distinct nose ring that connected to a piercing in his left ear.

The hot, spicy food he served for lunch was delicious. I ate the first bowl quickly and requested another, as did Atai and Tamunor. He served Tamunor and me delicious tenenet, an alcoholic drink made from fermented goat milk and an assortment of herbs.

"I'm going outside for a bit," I announced after lunch, standing up from our table.

"Do you want me to come with you?" Tamunor asked.

"No. I'll be fine."

"Be careful," Atai said meaningfully, and I nodded.

I stood outside the public house, looking around. Three girls in brightly colored skirts and short blouses walked hand in hand. They talked in high-pitched voices, laughing as they passed by.

I went down the front steps of the public house and followed them all way to an open-air market at the settlement's center.

Despite the many people weaving in and out of stalls and the bush meat and fish being brought out of wagons, it smelled clean. Unlike the markets in Kokori that always reeked strongly of their wares and the people selling them.

The girls went over to the stalls that sold fresh produce. The potatoes, onions, and ginger roots still had sand on them. The girls rifled through a basket of corn still in their husks.

I caught myself staring at them, speculating about their lives.

Who were they and where had they come from? How much of their lives were theirs to live? Would Tega and I have come here to shop, dressed so beautifully and laughing so carefree?

I walked deeper into the market, shaking the thoughts free. It did me no good to obsess about what could have been.

One of the sellers shoved his wares in my face. The trinkets and jewelry he sold were lovely, with huge gems and finely crafted engravings. "Perfect for you," the seller said. "Perfect for your nose. You pay less if you let me do the piercing myself."

I shook my head and offered him a polite smile as I moved on. I knew Tega would want one, and the thought made me ache.

Everyone I encountered was warm, relaxed. I chatted for a long while with a woman selling fruits the size of my fist, gleaming like the jewels I'd passed earlier. She was from Okpara and had escaped a terrible marriage with the help of her husband's sister. They lived together here, peacefully and happily, and I noticed how her eyes lit up as she talked about her. The four-ringed mark on the back of her hand seemed faded, a faint memory of a nightmare.

The woman gave me a massive satchel of dried fruit for free, and I realized after I left her stall that somewhere on yesterday's journey, the wrap around my own mark had fallen off.

I exited the market and strolled down quaint, stunning streets, daydreaming all the while. Men and women alike gathered in gardens and restaurants, reading and playing games and drinking. I thought of how different my life would've been here had Tega and I made it. Had Tega and I had the same dreams.

By the time the sun was dipping toward the distant hills, I was exhausted from all I'd seen and all I'd wished for. I went back to the public house to take a nap. Tamunor and Atai had gathered a lively crowd with their arm-wrestling, and I waved to them before heading up to our small room.

As I lay in bed, my thoughts lingered on how happy the Igans seemed, how gentle this city was to its people. I began to doze off, and somewhere between sleep and wakefulness, the vision sucked me under.

The boy was sobbing, curled in a ball on the floor of the chamber, his cries so loud I felt them in my teeth. Fear and hunger ravaged me, and I stumbled backward, my back slamming into the wall behind me.

"Please," he cried, his face cloaked in shadow. "Please help me. I don't know how much longer I can do this."

I opened my mouth to speak when I heard the unmistakable sound of a sword being unsheathed.

The boy's sobs turned even more frantic, and my eyes darted around the dim room frantically, trying to see where the sound had come from.

"*Please!*" the boy screamed.

I jerked awake, bolting upright. My heart was pounding, my own terror coursing through my veins.

I felt suddenly ashamed for delaying us in Iga. The boy's life was in danger, and I was wasting precious time pining for an imaginary life.

I got out of bed and headed downstairs.

The public house had filled up for the evening meal. Luckily, Tamunor had kept a chair for me at our original table.

"Who won the arm-wrestling match?" I asked Tamunor.

"Who do you think?" he asked.

I tilted my head toward Atai, who grinned smugly.

Tamunor pouted. "No faith in me, I see."

I chuckled, sitting down with them.

"Yes, he won," he said, rolling his eyes. "He is really strong."

I looked around at the people drinking heavily and talking loudly.

The owner of the public house came to our table with bowls of what smelled like oghwevwri and some water. I let out a satisfied sigh when I ate my first bite. I felt that I could live in Iga just for the food.

"If I could have food like this every day, I would never leave here," Tamunor said, voicing my thoughts. I chuckled when he took a big spoonful of the food.

"How was your afternoon?" Atai asked when we finished eating. Tamunor had gone to relieve himself, and I was feeling full and sated and a bit unsure of myself.

"It was . . . interesting," I replied, and he raised his eyebrows at me.

"How so?"

I sighed. "I had always dreamed of running away with Tega and coming here." My voice was small, and Atai leaned closer. It did nothing to keep the tremor from my words. "I've always looked after her, even when our parents were alive. I love her so much, and feel so responsible for her, it was impossible to picture my life without her. But she did not want to leave Kokori, and I could not stay, and I left her."

It was the first time I'd said the words out loud, and I felt tears slip down my cheeks.

Atai reached for my hand and held it tightly. "I'm sorry you are hurting. I know how it feels to have a different fate from someone you love."

I glanced at him, and he gave me a sad smile. "When my mother dies, I become the Oracle of Mbiabong. My life will no longer belong to me, and I will be bound to the city and its queen. Edem wants a life away from the capital. She has friends in Ikot, a sleepy town by the sea, and she will move there once our mother dies. She's there half the month already, and each time she leaves, I know it's harder for her to return to us."

I squeezed his hand back, something loosening in my spine. "We are mirrors, you and I."

Atai gave me a curious look. "What do you mean?"

"I am desperate for a life bigger than Kokori, while all my sister wants is to put down roots there. You hunger for adventure, same as me, but you are the one who is rooted to your home. Your sister, the one with the freedom to live where she chooses, desires nothing more than a quiet life in a small village."

Atai stared at me, his gaze assessing, appreciative. My cheeks heat at the scrutiny, at the pressure of his fingers between mine.

"I am . . . very glad to have met you," he murmured.

Tamunor suddenly appeared beside us, and I jumped, pulling my hand back, my skin flaming hot.

"I come bearing free food!" he cried out triumphantly.

That night, the three of us crammed into the tiny bed, and I fell asleep with Atai's body curled around mine.

16

ONCE WE LEFT IGA, IT TOOK US TWO LONG DAYS BEFORE we saw another building. We passed people and carriages on the road, stopped at ramshackle stands, and camped beneath the stars, but the temple was the first solid structure we came across.

The temple was tucked between two hills, and its gateway was a rock with three heads looking to the north, east, and west. High up one of the hills, a towering statue of a crowned woman carrying a pot of spilling water loomed over us. All around her were trees bursting with blue flowers, and the grounds were dotted with small buildings, some open to the elements, like pavilions.

The temple was not marked on Moyo's map, or I would have remembered it. But we were tired from our days traveling through rocky terrain, and Tamunor had started groaning loudly whenever his stomach rumbled.

"Please, let's stop here for some rest," he begged.

Atai looked to me, and I sighed. "Just for a little while. We can't afford to lose any more time." I could still hear the boy's sobs ringing in my ears.

We made our way toward the temple. Women and young girls in big white skirts and short-sleeved red tunics picked up berries from the bushes nearby. Their hair was wrapped into golden hairpins and their feet were covered with red paint.

One of the younger girls directed us to an older woman sitting beneath one of the flowering trees.

Before we could even open our mouths, the woman asked us who we were.

"We are travelers," Atai was quick to say. "We wanted to rest here and gather our strength."

She was blind, but her milky eyes moved from Atai to me to Tamunor as though she could see us.

"I am Jenatra," the woman said, her voice clear and firm. "I am a Maguada, like the rest of the women here. We are priestesses of Iso, the sun goddess, ruler of light and sky."

We introduced ourselves, and I told her we were on a journey to deliver a message.

Tamunor chuckled at that, and Atai elbowed him.

The woman grabbed Tamunor's hand and felt his palm with her fingers. His eyes widened, looking from me to Atai.

"Come with me," she ordered, letting go of Tamunor and rising to her feet.

We followed her toward the front door to the temple. It creaked open when she pushed it to reveal a large hall. The walls were filled with paintings and carvings all the way to the ceiling. Candles were lit on every available surface, giving the room a soft glow despite the chill in the air.

She took us up a stairway and through a passageway lined with painted glass windows that reflected beautifully on the stone floor. We passed through a circular door and then we were out on a catwalk of sorts. More women walked around the grassy field below us. Underneath one pavilion a dozen women sat, legs folded and hands clasped above their heads.

"That is the meditation ground," Jenatra said as we crossed the catwalk. I had no idea how she managed to walk so surely.

We entered a small pavilion on the other end, at the center of which were a long table filled with food and comfortable-looking chairs. From a red-peaked pavilion nearby, a girl with two fans in her hands captured my attention. She danced to no music, swaying the fans gracefully. The movements of her legs were quick but delicate, and her arms moved fluidly, slicing through the air and coming to rest on her hips. The fans were like an extension of her body. She closed her eyes as she spun around with her feet rooted to one spot. She unfurled like the threads in a weaving loom.

"That is Tofe. She is beautiful, is she not?" Jenatra asked, lifting the lid on a big bowl of savory porridge.

"She dances very well," Atai said admiringly. He was looking at her the way many men look at beautiful women.

Tamunor was too busy scooping food into his mouth to pay attention to her. I smiled to myself.

"She dances to the music of the wind," Jenatra explained. "You cannot see the wind, but you know it is there when it raises dust, when it shakes the leaves of a tree, and when it moves the waters. So is its music."

I continued to stare at the girl as I ate. She was spectacular.

"The girls who are here," I started to ask the woman, "how do they come to be priestesses? Are they chosen?"

She shook her head. "They come on their own accord. They choose to have little contact with the outside world, to live a solitary life of spirituality."

I wanted to ask why. It was the same question I asked myself every time I thought of Tega. Of Chipo.

"And they are happy?" I dared to ask.

"Who's to say?" she replied. "Everyone knows what their own happiness means to them, and they either go after it or they don't."

I wanted Tega to be happy, but it was still jarring to think that what suffocated me offered her joy.

After we finished eating, we thanked Jenatra for the food and told her we needed to set off. She led us back into the main hall, and Atai and Tamunor bid her goodbye. I was just about to follow them out, but she held me back. I met her unseeing gaze and could not look away. Her hands reached for mine and she wrapped them together. Her palms were cracked but warm. She spoke to me, her voice solemn and soft.

"You seek happiness in the world, in yourself, and this is admirable. Though many know what their own happiness is, few have the courage to actually seek it."

"Thank you, Jenatra," I murmured, and she gave me a sad smile.

"The path to what you are meant to be is not an easy one," she intoned, and I thought of Moyo's words to me at the edge of the Orerokpe Sands. *The smoke that thunders. That is how you are, Naborhi. Like the unstoppable waters.*

Jenatra continued, "I will tell you this, though. Life is like shadow and mist; it passes by quickly and is no more. Live it fully, while you can."

Jenatra's words still circled in my head, mingling with Moyo's as we entered the Crooked Forest the next morning.

The forest was rumored to be the dwelling place of the Ikere, the all-female warrior tribe who—according to Moyo—could control *everything* in the forest, from the tallest tree to a tiny blade of grass. They were a peaceful people most of the time. Unless provoked.

Most of the trees were black oak trees and ancestor trees, but the top of their trunks and branches were bent and twisted, lending the forest its name. Perhaps it was something in the soil.

"I never wanted to set foot in another forest, and yet here we are." Tamunor shuddered.

"I could've done without another one," I agreed.

"This place reminds me of home," Atai confessed, looking up at the ancestor trees with fondness. The forest was heavy with shadows, but the path was clear and dappled with sunlight.

"I miss home too," Tamunor said, and Atai smiled at him.

We were close to our destination. After we passed through the

Crooked Forest, we would stay in Qua'i City for a day or two to earn money for the permits we needed to enter Ewuare.

A soft wind drifted through the trees and rustled some bell-shaped flowers hanging from needle-like stems on the sides of the path, emanating a shrill whistle. The stronger the wind, the louder the whistle. Atai whistled along, and Tamunor joined in. Even I hummed a tune and bobbed my head, enjoying the walk and the feel of the breeze.

It was so different from our time in the Djone Forest, and I felt myself relax slightly.

We stopped to rest around midday. We encountered several travelers and one fast-moving military procession, all dressed in purple and crimson.

"Are those soldiers from Idu?" Tamunor whispered while we lazed about beneath an ancestor tree. We were set back from the main path, and it was hard to make out details through the thick copse of trees in front of us.

I shrugged. "Possibly. Though I have no idea what they're doing down here."

We soon set off and came across no more strange groups. We had been walking for about an hour when Atai stepped off the beaten path to pick some berries from a bush with white and yellow flowers. Tamunor joined him while I sat on the ground, my back resting on a tree. They were laughing together as they ate, and I smiled to myself, my eyes drifting shut for a moment.

When I opened them again, they had moved deeper into the brush.

"Where are you both going?" I called.

"We saw something right over there," Tamunor said.

I stood up and hurried after them.

"What did you see?" I asked.

"A ball of light," Atai answered, placing his hands on his hips and looking around carefully. "It was glowing, but it's gone now."

The trees had gone silent, the whistling gone. I felt a sudden chill in the air that made the hair on my arms raise.

"Let's go back," I said.

Before we could move, a sound like a loud groan emanated from deep within the trees.

"*Now,*" I snarled.

The groan resounded again.

A figure dashed behind the bushes. I drew my daggers from their sheathes and Atai drew his sword. Another figure shrieked and ran behind the trees before I could make out what it was.

"What was that?" Tamunor asked, his voice trembling.

The forest answered him: an ominous, thunderous roar that echoed all around us.

I thought of the Ikere. Could it be them behind the trees? Had we done something to provoke them?

I pushed Tamunor behind me as the sound rang out again. Atai protected him from the other side. Every tree, every leaf, every branch was now an enemy.

For a long moment, there was a deathly silence that seemed to mock us. I could only hear my heartbeat pounding in my ears.

Then ropes came flying from the trees around us, ensnaring our bodies and sending us to the ground.

Tamunor and Atai landed heavily, groaning in pain. I landed on my shoulder, agony slicing up my neck. Swallowing back my cry, I slithered like a worm and rose to my knees with effort.

"Get up!" I rasped at the boys. "We have to run."

A dozen people emerged from behind the trees. I knew instantly that they could not be the Ikere—there was only one woman among them. She was tall, her face heavily scarred, and she had the most gorgeous head of curly hair.

They came closer, and I noticed that they were all armed. One of the men pushed me back to the ground as I tried to free myself. Two other men snatched up Atai's and Tamunor's packs, rifling through them. They spoke the Traveler's Tongue.

"They have nothing, less than nothing," the man who ruffled around in Tamunor's bag said to the woman. They threw the bags on the ground like they were rancid. Atai tried to get up, but the man closest to him kicked him back down. "Though that's a nice sword," the man sneered, picking up Atai's weapon. Atai snarled and lunged at him, but the man sidestepped him, laughing.

The woman walked closer to where I lay. "They will fetch a pretty price in Oring," she crooned, a nasty grin twisting her scars. *She must have been in a lot of fights to get scars like those*, I thought to myself. *And not fought well.*

One of the burlier men picked me up roughly and slung me over his shoulder.

Atai and Tamunor called out as they, too, were snatched up.

I struggled to free myself but it was no use. The ropes around my body were tight and the man's grip was strong as he carried me over to their wagon, several large crates waiting.

The man shoved me inside one that smelled like a wet dog. I fought to free myself, kicking and scratching at him. But he slammed me inside and locked me in. I screamed, raging against the walls of the crate, my lungs constricting with panic. I heard Tamunor and Atai being locked in their own crates, and I couldn't breathe, the walls closing in.

Suddenly, my mind was flooded by a memory that was not mine. A memory of the kidnapped boy.

He was with an older man who held his hand as they walked toward a carriage that shone brightly, as if it were made purely out of gold. Something glinted on the man's head, and the boy gripped his hand as tightly as possible.

The image changed to my own memory of Zuberi, when it was still small enough to fit in my hands.

Gentle warmth rose from my toes, getting hotter and hotter as it traveled up my body.

A raging fire burned around me within the crate, but I was not scalded. The flames roared and the ropes slithered off me.

I recognized the cleansing fire of Obassi. The one that had protected the Oroni for hundreds of years.

The crate burst open and the flames leapt away from me. I stood slowly, drawing my daggers, ready to pounce.

I heard the horses bay in alarm. The men moved away from the wagon, drawing their weapons, their eyes wide in fright as they stared at me. The woman shouted at them to hold their ground, but she looked stricken.

I heard a familiar growl.

Zuberi stepped out from behind me, baring its teeth. A burst of flames from its fur spread out in a raging inferno. The fire left no trace on the grass as it moved, but it caught the shoe of one of the men closest to me and his entire body was engulfed in flames. The smell of burning hair and clothing almost made me gag, but I raced toward the other crates just as the others turned and ran back into the trees, screaming. The flames did not stop, disappearing after them.

Something told me that they would not stop until they'd reached their targets.

I quickly unlatched Tamunor's crate, and he screamed before he saw it was me. I freed Atai next, slicing off his bonds, and he burst out, grabbing me in a fierce hug.

I looked back for Zuberi, but it was gone.

My tears flowed freely, and I started trembling from the shock of it all.

"Are they gone?" Tamunor asked. He was visibly shaking, still inside his crate.

"Yes," I replied.

I helped get the ropes off him and he crawled out. I knelt and hugged him tightly, then was limp with relief.

"How?" Atai asked, breathing hard.

"Zuberi. The red fox. It was here. It helped us."

Atai inhaled sharply. "Where is it now?" he asked urgently.

"It's gone," I said. "It disappeared after it sent fire after those thieves."

He bowed his head in reverence. "Obassi be praised," he said solemnly. "Now, let's get out of this gods-forsaken forest."

That night, after we'd finally emerged on the other side of the Crooked Forest, we camped just beyond the tree line among the knee-high grass. Insects that glowed a dazzling white hovered lazily around us, making the air shimmer.

Tamunor's hands still shook as we ate bread and the last of our fruit I had gotten in Iga. He had barely said ten words all afternoon. His silence was unnerving, disorienting. He hadn't even been so quiet when he was nearly eaten by the Ebo.

"Tamunor, you should sleep," I murmured. "I will take first watch."

"I am not tired," he replied, glancing at Atai and then at me. "You both should sleep."

"Are you sure?" Atai asked, his brow furrowed in concern.

Tamunor nodded distantly.

I tossed and turned, unable to get comfortable. Half-asleep and half-awake, the vision invaded my mind.

It was even more vivid this time, if that were somehow possible. I wondered if it was because I was getting closer to him, or whether his situation was getting more and more dangerous. I hoped it was the former, even though I suspected it was the latter.

I could not see the boy's face, but I could feel every one of his emotions as intensely as if they were my own. The fear, the anxiety, and the anger. His thirst, his exhaustion. Even the pain from the way his hands and legs were tied up resonated through me.

And worst of all, his hunger.

"Please hurry," he whispered. His voice was thin and rattling. "Please help me."

I jolted awake, my heartbeat thunderous. My stomach felt hollowed out from the boy's hunger, and I wolfed down some leftover bread.

Tamunor watched me as I ate and gulped down some water.

"Did you have another vision?" he asked quietly.

I shook my head and lay back down. I didn't want him to worry, on top of everything else on his mind.

I closed my eyes, desperate for rest. I felt Atai's hand brush my shoulder.

He'd seen, and he knew.

I let him.

17

I WAS HAPPY WHEN TAMUNOR BEGAN TALKING AGAIN THE next morning. We'd risen early and resumed our journey, and he'd chatted as we observed farmers gathering their crops in the muddy fields on the outskirts of Qua'i. They sang harvest songs while a group of young boys rang bells, the melody stirring us awake.

To get to the city, we needed a boat.

It was raining lightly when we arrived at the lake surrounding the city. Small fishing boats dotted the surface, and the docks were bustling despite the weather. We followed the signs for the ferry and boarded a spacious, roofed boat. The ferry captain was a sturdy, barrel-chested man with a warm smile. Atai gave him the last of our coins, hidden in the pocket of his trousers, and I felt a twinge of unease.

We were officially out of money.

I stared out at the water as we set sail, imagining the city currently hidden by fog. Qua'i, like its sister city, Qubi, was all-accepting. Everyone was welcome and treated with fairness. With the mix of people from all walks of life, it was only natural that they adopt the Traveler's Tongue as their primary language. I hoped we would be able to find work quickly, and that we would not face any trouble. I'd had enough hardship the past two weeks to last me a lifetime.

I looked at my rippling shadow on the water as the boat sailed toward the city. I was not the same person who had left home. And even if most of my experiences had been difficult, I was not going back to Kokori anytime soon. I'd seen too much of this devastating, beautiful world to return to a life so small.

The city came into view, its features tentatively creeping forth from the fog like stars appearing in the early night sky.

Qua'i was perched on the side of two adjoining mountains, the southernmost peaks of the Ewuare Mountains. Its tall buildings were jammed close to one another to accommodate the limited space and the bustling population. The buildings were mostly made of wood, with pointed roofs that seemed to stretch endlessly for the sky.

Our boat reached the docks and glided into an empty slip with the help of several dockhands. We disembarked and bid the captain goodbye before making our way toward the steep wooden ladder that would take us up to solid ground. There was an unlit lantern hanging from the bottom rung, and the wood was slick and mildewy as we climbed. The rain had finally stopped, but the fog was rolling back in from the water and sweeping onto shore.

"Where can we find the officials that will give us traveling permits?" Atai asked the dockmaster when we reached the main pier.

"Go up this way." She pointed at a set of wide steps at the end of the pier that fed into a narrow street. "Take the first road to your right. You will see the officials gathered next to the fruit sellers at the market. Can't miss them."

She was right—the bright purple color of the Iduni army uniforms could be spotted from miles away.

We approached one of the officials and he led us to the officers' main residences. There were a handful of people already gathered in the large, cool reception room. There were magnificent paintings on the wall, abstract and vibrant, and a soldier seated behind a desk stacked high with papers.

When it was our turn, we stepped up and introduced ourselves to the man.

"We need passage to Ewuare. How much for the permits?"

"Fifteen trellics," the man replied brusquely, not even looking up from his work.

My heart plummeted into my stomach, and Tamunor started to laugh.

"That is enough to build a new house in Kokori," he said in disbelief.

"Then perhaps you should return there," the soldier deadpanned. His dark eyes were flat and bored.

"That's too much," I said, glancing at Atai, his features pale. "We may not get to Ewuare on time."

"Do not bother trying to use fake permits," the man warned. "The kingdom is on high alert, and every border crossing is heavily guarded. You will only be sorry." He rolled up his sleeves and moved to go back to his work, but his features softened when his gaze fell on Tamunor's crestfallen face. "Look, if you really want to enter Ewuare, you can work."

"What work could give us that amount of money?"

"What can I say? King Ide has restricted access for anyone entering his kingdom. Security has tripled everywhere. He passed through Qua'i just the other day and gave us the orders himself." He huffed a bit at that. "He was certainly in a foul mood about something."

"What jobs are available in the city?" I pressed, trying to steer the man back to the matter at hand.

"You"—he pointed at me—"can work at the Red Tapestry. They only hire girls and women, but you will get paid enough."

"What is the Red Tapestry?" Tamunor asked him, his brow furrowing.

"It is a service house run by women."

"You want her to sell her body?" Tamunor blurted, wide-eyed.

The officer laughed. "The Red Tapestry is not like that. The women do not sell their bodies there. They sell their skills, their talents."

Against my will, my interest was piqued.

"It is a place for the elite," the man went on. "First of its kind! They support the artistic craft of young women. Poetry, painting, singing, dancing. It's just farther down the street." He turned to

Tamunor and Atai. "And then you young men can find work with the fishermen at the market. They are always looking for help. By my calculations, you could earn the money you all need to get a pass in five days."

Five days? What if something happened before then? What if we were too late?

But we had no other options.

We thanked the soldier and went outside. The sun had come out from behind the clouds, and the heat amplified the smell of fish that hung cloyingly in the air.

"What do you think we should do?" Tamunor asked, dodging an oncoming carriage.

"Get to work," I replied, watching the carriage until it disappeared. The streets were busier than before, people with all sorts of clothing and piercings and hairstyles hurrying past us. "I just have this feeling that if we do not get to Ewuare soon, something terrible will happen."

"So we make a lot of money as fast as we can," Atai said simply. He glanced at some men carrying bales of fabric past us. "Maybe we should meet back here tomorrow. See how we are all faring."

"I will be fine," I told him, hearing the concern hidden in his words.

"I know," he said quickly, blushing, and I smiled.

"Three days, then. We can calculate our earnings," I told them, sighing heavily. "Hopefully it will be enough."

Atai replied with a grim nod.

"I'd better find the Red Tapestry," I said, hesitating.

"And we'd better get to the market," Atai replied, not moving. His eyes held mine.

Tamunor put his hand on my shoulder. "Be careful."

"Be careful too," I murmured, hugging him tightly. "Do not make any trouble."

"I cannot promise you that." He grinned, winking.

Atai smiled softly at me. "Be safe, Naborhi. Find us if you need anything."

And then they were winding through the throng of people back toward the market. I stood there for a moment, taking in my surroundings. I wondered how we would fare in this strange city. Would we make enough money for the permits? I had no sure answer to quell my fears, but we had to try.

The Red Tapestry was a stately establishment walled in by tidy brick. The guard at the gate let me in after I told him I was looking for work. If he suspected I was a threat, he did not show it. He asked me my name before escorting me inside.

The compound reminded me of Orosuen Jabali's estate. It was large, with several courtyards opening up to each other. Between one large wooden house and the next were small gardens. The other brick buildings were connected by open passages of stone pillars with a few girls passing along them. The guard directed me to a smaller building with a round door with sculpted texts above it. There he said I would find the owner. I walked over and knocked.

"Enter," a voice commanded.

I pushed the door open to see a woman sitting on a beautiful rug a few feet away from me looking through books, a low table in front of her and two lanterns on either side. On the windowsill, incense burned and the smoke wafted up in a thin wisp. On the wall behind the woman was a dark-crimson tapestry depicting girls dancing and playing instruments.

She pointed at the woolen mat on my side of the table, and I sat.

She looked up and I could not miss the gentle spark of surprise in her dark oval eyes. Then she frowned. "You are not Qena," she said with a drawl.

"No, I am not."

Her long neck had a scar that looked like it was from a burn. She was very thin; her loose, lavish dress only enhanced how slender she was. The trinkets on her wrist looked like they could fall off at any moment.

"Who are you?"

"I am Naborhi Tanomare," I answered simply.

She gently placed the books on the table next to an ink bottle. "What do you want?"

"I am looking for temporary work. I need money for my papers into Ewuare, and I was told this place was hiring."

"Do you know what we do?"

"I am not so sure," I replied honestly, and she smiled softly.

"My girls hone their skills here. I am in the business of finding women with artistic talents and helping them make a living out of them. They are called Ziyas."

"That sounds . . . wonderful, really," I told her, and I could see that it pleased her. I thought I saw her eye flick to the mark on my hand, and I hid it in my lap.

"We do have work for you, if you are up for it," she said smoothly. "You would help two of my girls as their maid. You would help them clean, bring them their meals, do their laundry, and whatever else they need to make their lives easier as they focus on their training."

I nodded. I could do all that.

"Do you have a place to stay?" she asked.

I shook my head.

"You will be given a room here then."

"Does that mean I'm hired?" I asked with a hopeful smile.

"You are." She gave me a wide smile in return. "You may work here until you are ready to journey to Ewuare."

"Thank you, thank you so much, er—"

"You can call me La Hinan. I offer daily wages of ten shells. More if we have an event, like we do tonight."

She rose at that, and I stood along with her.

"I like people who are hardworking. If you do your job and listen well to instructions, you won't have a problem with me."

Just then the door opened and in walked a beautiful girl in a flowery white silk robe over a long skirt with several layers. Her short, dark-brown hair was braided on either side of her face like curtains. Her feet were covered in black painted swirls.

"Qena, you are finally here," La Hinan said.

"Apologies for my lateness, La Hinan." The girl bowed deeply.

The woman grumbled under her breath before introducing me. "This is Naborhi. She will be your and Enitan's new help. You will do whatever they need," she said to me, and I nodded.

"La Hinan, the guests have arrived," Qena said.

"Good. I will see to them right now. Please take Naborhi with you, and have Idia give her a change of clothes and help her get settled in her room and ready for work. She will serve the guests at tonight's event."

"Yes, La Hinan," Qena replied with a smile.

"Thank you, La Hinan," I said to the woman, bowing as Qena had.

"Where did you say you came from?" she asked me carefully.

"I did not."

She raised a brow, and I hesitated before answering.

"From Kokori. Agbon."

She looked me over slowly, nodding once before leaving the room without another word.

18

QENA GUIDED ME ACROSS ONE OF THE FOOTBRIDGES THAT connected one building to another, a lush garden beneath us. She was warm and welcoming, and I found myself relaxing a bit. We came across another person in the hall we entered, and she greeted us cheerily.

"I'm Idia," she introduced herself to me. She was the tallest girl I had ever seen—taller, even, than Imoni—with a sharp chin and sultry eyes.

I tried not to stare. "I'm Naborhi."

She gave me a friendly smile. "I'll show you to the bathhouse," she said. "You have some dirt on your face." She grabbed my hand without waiting for my answer. I quickly waved goodbye to Qena and hurried after Idia.

She took me across another walkway to another building that held a large bathing chamber, and she helped me get some water for my bath.

The water was warm and it felt divine to wash away the grime and dirt caked onto my skin from my journey.

When I was done, Idia handed me a robe and escorted me to my room.

"The girls you'll be attending to are perfecting their talents to become Ziyas. Do you plan on becoming one? Some helps around here have gone on to be Ziyas."

"I'm only here for a short while," I replied carefully.

"And where will you go from here?"

"Ewuare."

"Huh," she muttered, observing me.

"I never knew such a place like this existed," I said quickly, my eyes grazing over the compound. "It sounds too good to be true."

"It is the first of its kind. And La Hinan takes care of every girl here like we are her daughters."

Idia showed me to my room after pointing out Qena and Enitan's chamber right down the hall. It was small, but it had a comfortable bed and a sturdy dresser with some old books piled on top. She explained the room used to belong to a former maid who left the Red Tapestry to get married.

She handed me a bottle of perfumed oil that I rubbed on my skin. I soon smelled better than I had since I left Kokori. Then she handed me a long blue dress and an ivory waist-length wrap with long sleeves that I put on behind a small changing screen.

The dress was the softest thing I'd ever worn, and I could not stop touching it.

Idia looked me over approvingly when I came out from behind the screen.

Qena breezed into the room without knocking.

"You've changed. That was fast."

"Do you need anything?" Idia asked.

"Just the new girl," she said, stretching her hand out to me. "Come."

Idia tilted her head, a sign for me to follow Qena.

I followed the bubbly girl to the room she shared with the other girl I would be attending to, Enitan. Their room contained two large beds beneath veil-like canopies. It had two standing dressers and a plush rug in the middle. The windows were decorated with small carvings of birds. There was a mural on one wall of a girl with long, billowy hair. The colors were vibrant and I was captivated by the expression on the girl's face.

"Enitan painted that," Qena explained, gesturing for me to sit on the cane chair next to the open window.

Just then, another girl walked in, smiling, but her expression froze when she saw me. She was beautiful, too, though not in the delicate way Qena was. Hers was a bold beauty that would stand out in any crowd.

"Who is this?" she asked Qena curiously.

"This is Naborhi. She is our new maid."

"I am Enitan," the girl said, giving me a tentative smile.

"Naborhi," I introduced myself.

"I was just about to get Naborhi ready for the evening," Qena explained.

She picked up a small case from her dresser and pulled out a jar of kwali powder, peering at my eyes.

"Why do I have to put that on?" I asked warily.

Qena replied frankly, "Because you owe it to yourself to look your best."

"La Hinan's words," Enitan clarified. "She used to be a stylist for wealthy women before she founded the Red Tapestry."

Qena continued, "We are here because of our many talents, but we still have to look good. You earn a certain amount of respect that way."

I glanced at Enitan, who nodded.

"Do not blink," Qena said, applying the kwali underneath my eyes. "Enitan and I are Wazi," she explained. "It means we are almost ready to have ukẹchas. Then we will be Ziyas."

"Ukẹchas?" I asked.

"They support the Red Tapestry, mostly financially," Enitan cut in. "Usually, they pick one or two girls and pay for whatever they need to master their talents."

Qena explained further, "It means all I have to do is concentrate on doing what I love best without worrying about having to eat."

"How does one become a Wazi?"

Enitan answered. "To be one, you have to showcase your talent when La Hinan puts a call out. Then if La Hinan thinks you have talent, you will be trained so you can improve on that talent to snag an ukẹcha."

"And what is your talent?" I asked Qena, who was examining my eyebrows.

"*Talents*," she corrected with pride in her voice. "I can play the log drum and dance the Ekombi flawlessly. My mother is from Oron, and she taught me the traditional dance. Enitan plays the flute marvelously, so we usually train together. She also paints."

"How long have you both been here?"

She thought about her answer. "Shy of six months."

"Do you ever go home?" I asked.

"Occasionally. Enitan is here full-time, but she is often invited to paint portraits around the continent, and La Hinan escorts her."

"You are not from Qua'i, are you?" Enitan asked, peering at my hand.

"No," I admitted, fighting the urge to hide my mark. "Kokori."

Enitan gave me a conspiratorial smile. "I came from Uvwie."

"You two are like sisters then," Qena cried, beaming.

"We are," Enitan said, sitting down on the bed beside me. "But you don't look like an Agboni girl. They usually have this docile look in their eyes. Your eyes look more the opposite."

"Just like you," I said, and she laughed, squeezing my hand. I noticed she had a three-ringed mark branded on her skin, and I looked up at her. She had a hard, knowing glint in her gaze.

"I have seen my fair share of what life can spit in your face, and I have come out more beautiful than ever."

"Speaking of beautiful." Qena touched my hair. "You have such healthy, long hair. And this dash of red here, were you born this way?"

"Yes, I was," I lied.

"Exquisite," she approved. She doused the free ends of my hair with oil and combed it until she was satisfied.

"What about you, Qena?" I asked her. "Where are you from?"

"I was born here," Qena said. "I have never left Qua'i. I am always saying I should visit other places but have never once tried leaving."

"You should if you can," I said, trying not to move my mouth too much as she applied paint to my lips. "A roaring lion kills no game. Qubi is your sister city. And Ewuare is close by. You could start there, see the Rainbow Rocks I've heard so much about."

"Maybe," she said, smiling widely. "But I do not like the cold."

"Then Ewuare should not be on your list of places to visit," I said, and she laughed.

"You are right. Qubi is not so far away. I will start there. Perfect!" She pulled her brush away from my lips and nodded approvingly at her work.

Enitan peered over her shoulder and hummed in agreement. "Now you're ready."

I joined Idia and the other maids on duty in a large hall full of luxurious furnishings and dark, polished wood.

The ukẹchas sat on plush chairs drinking and talking among themselves in dignified tones. I served drinks while Qena and Enitan sat in a separate area with the other Wazi. La Hinan glided about, welcoming each guest with a warm smile.

During a lull, Idia gave me insight on what was going on.

"Those are the Ziyas performing today," she told me, pointing at about a dozen girls all dressed in patterned skirts and blouses sitting among the ukẹchas.

On a raised platform ahead of us, underneath a skylight, a woman emerged from behind the curtains. She had luminous white hair styled within an intricate metal headdress, and her eyelids were covered in blue and black paint. Her clothes, a tight-fitted, jewel-toned tunic that revealed her stomach and a long matching skirt, contrasted well with her smooth, honeyed skin. She was the most beautiful woman I had ever seen. She held a four-stringed instrument that she placed between her legs as she sat. She closed her eyes and strummed a few notes. The sound bounced off the walls and into my heart. It was a soft melody that stirred emotions. The entire hall was entranced.

Idia whispered. "That is Awalim. She is the most adored Ziya here. She was once the Ziya to the okao's right hand. But he got married and his wife would not let him near the Red Tapestry for fear he would be completely taken by Awalim."

I could see why she would fear that.

"She plays the rogu best. And Awalim's ukẹcha just passed away, so she is seeking another. After her performance, every interested person here will write their offer, and La Hinan will choose the highest bidder."

I saw La Hinan head toward the stage. One of the men closest to me raised a hand.

I was nearest, so I poured him a drink. He had a bush of a

beard, but his small, gentle eyes negated the fierceness his beard exuded. His fingers were adorned with gold and emerald rings. His robe was white with a gold inlay. His red hat was adorned with even more gold in the embroidery. His gaze never left Awalim. He took his newly filled cup and gulped it down.

Awalim finished her rendition, and her offers were passed on notes to La Hinan as she patrolled the tables.

She looked them over. "Gezan," La Hinan called, and the ukẹ-chas smiled toward the man with the bush beard. Gezan stood up and left with La Hinan, Awalim trailing behind them with her head raised high.

"Motukane is about to sing," Idia told me excitedly. "She has the loveliest voice."

Motukane was petite, with her hair braided in a magnificent crown atop her head. She stood on the raised stage and began to sing, her voice moving through the hall like a soothing cool breeze.

For a moment I was jealous of these girls. I wished I could sing extraordinarily, or dance, or play an instrument. But I had none of those talents. I could only admire those who had them.

The feast went on for another hour. More girls sang and danced and did acrobatics to entertain.

After the performances ended and all the guests left, I joined the other workers to clean up the hall.

La Hinan gathered us and paid us for the day when we were done.

"You did well today," she said to me as she handed me fifteen silver shells.

I hid the money in my pillowcase before I collapsed into bed.

I woke up the next day feeling energized.

After breakfast, I cleaned the girls' rooms and gathered their clothes that needed washing.

Idia showed me to the laundry house, a squat building adjacent to the kitchen. A natural stream flowed swiftly through the middle of the room. Idia demonstrated how the churning of the water washed the clothes.

I was able to get all the washing done quickly and had time to help take food to the kitchen for the night's dinner. Then I took the midday meal to the Wazi and Ziyas in the dining area.

That night, I sat with Qena and Enitan in their room, chatting while I braided Enitan's hair.

Her story broke my heart.

"I was once an obedient girl from a clan where men think they are kings and women are things to be ruled over. Then I fell in love with a boy who had come from a land far away. I thought that was my chance to be with someone who would treat me like a human being. I was barely sixteen, I had only just passed my rite and been betrothed to a loathsome man. I ran away with the boy I loved all the way to Qua'i, only for him to disappear into the night. I had no money and I knew no one here. I was hungry and homeless. Have you ever felt real hunger?"

I shook my head. "No," I admitted, finishing her hair and sitting beside her. Qena curled on her bed, gazing at Enitan sadly.

"Hunger like that changes people. Makes them see things that are not there. Well, I was in a hopeless situation until La Hinan took me under her care. I never could have guessed that playing the flute would be what saved me. Now I am safe and training to be a Ziya. People can be cruel and ignorant no matter where I am, but no one owns me here. I am free, free to be anything I want," she said, laughing softly, and collapsed back on the bed. "I could leave the Red Tapestry and set out to sea and that would be my decision," she said, and sat back up. "Rain can beat a leopard's skin, but it does not wash out her spots. My spots are still intact."

"How did you come to be here?" I asked Qena, and she smiled.

"My father. He is a physician. He wanted me to be one too. At first I enjoyed every bit of it—learning about plants, making tonics and potions, mending bones. But I liked dancing more. So when La Hinan did auditions, I showed her what I could offer, and here I am."

"What about your father? Is he not angry?"

"He wishes me well." Her expression grew fond. "He wants me to be happy, to do what brings me the most joy. He supports me no matter what."

I tried to imagine Unika and Imoni supporting me with whatever I decided, but I had to be realistic. They did not understand me—how could they support me?

Later, after I left them, I lay in my bed, dreaming of Imoni, Tega, and Unika. I was home with them, chatting with Chipo in our courtyard, and I was happy. But then the dream morphed into something more vivid, and I was trapped in the locked room with the boy.

My nose wrinkled at the strong smell of decay.

"Help me." His voice was a rasp, barely audible.

I tried to find him in the semi-darkness, but I could not. He sounded like he was close but anytime I tried to touch him, I ended up grabbing air instead.

I peered through one of the holes that let in the light, the tower illuminated by lamps in the street.

Something yanked at my leg and I fell face-first onto the floor.

The lights coming from the walls disappeared and the room fell into a choking darkness.

I jerked awake, my heart pounding. My ribs were sore, my eyes watering at the pain. As if my body had truly fallen.

I sat up carefully and could not get the urgency of the dream out of my mind.

Idia knocked on my door.

"Come in," I croaked.

"There are two very handsome young men looking for you at the gate," she said, her eyes twinkling mischievously.

Despite my sore ribs, I nearly ran outside. I had not known how much I had missed Atai and Tamunor until I saw then standing at the gate.

I hugged each of them fiercely.

"Both of you reek of fish" were my first words, and Tamunor barked a laugh.

"Naborhi, you look so different," Atai said. I saw that look in his eyes, the one he had given Tofe, the dancing Maguada. My heart stuttered a bit.

"Well, appreciate it while it lasts, because as soon as I earn the money we need, I'll be saying goodbye to these nice clothes."

"But you look so good in them," Tamunor protested.

"I know," I agreed. "But why are you here now? We weren't supposed to meet until tomorrow."

"We were worried about you," Atai answered softly, his eyes still boring into me.

"But need not have been," Tamunor added, touching the hem of my sleeve. "You seem to be in safe hands."

They told me all they had done at the docks to earn money.

"After the money we spent on food, this is what we have left."

Atai pulled out his coin pouch and poured the contents into his palm, revealing ten silver shells. My heart plummeted. That was only one trellic. And I had less than three trellics' worth of silver shells. We would need to work in Qua'i for weeks at this rate. The boy in my visions didn't have days to spare, let alone weeks.

A wagon carrying salted fish in a barrel rolled past us, heading toward the market.

"This isn't going to help us," I replied, fear leaching into my voice.

"Well, what else do we do? I hate the work," Tamunor said, and he made a face. "I will smell of fish till the day I sprout my gray hairs, but I've made up my mind to continue to sort fish until we have the money."

"Me too," Atai added. "We can try to take on more work, see if we can earn a few more shells a day."

"I will think of something," I said, trying to sound confident. My mind spun as I thought through our options. We needed help, but who would be willing to give us the money we needed? Who could I trust with the truth of our journey? What more could I do?

That evening, as I helped Enitan take her brushes and acrylics to the painting foundry, I noticed La Hinan walking out with one of the Wazi, a girl named Ekoi. Ekoi's cheeks were tearstained as they passed us and disappeared into La Hinan's office.

I asked Enitan later that night what had happened. We had seen Ekoi at dinner, and she seemed to be fine, smiling and laughing with the other Wazi.

"Ekoi was going to have to leave the Red Tapestry to take care of her ill mother, as no one in her family was willing to help. But La Hinan stepped in and hired a nurse for the mother so Ekoi could concentrate on mastering her painting skills.

La Hinan.

The girls were always talking about how good she was, and she had been nothing but kind to me. Maybe she could help us.

After bidding Qena and Enitan good night, I braced myself and made my way across the courtyard to La Hinan's office, where dim candlelight still glowed in her windows.

Obassi brought you here; he will help you. I heard Atai's voice in my head as I knocked on La Hinan's door.

"Enter," she called.

She was reading a large tome at her table, its language one I did not recognize.

"Naborhi," she greeted me, surprised. "Is everything all right? Do you need anything?"

I swallowed my anxiety, steeling myself. "I need your help."

She gestured for me to sit opposite her, and I obeyed.

I started at the beginning, from when I first met Zuberi.

She listened, occasionally nodding, until I got to my time at the Red Tapestry.

She sighed. "You and your companions have been through a lot to get here, and you still have your task ahead."

"You believe me?" I asked, unable to hide the hope from my voice.

She chuckled, the lines at the corners of her eyes doubling. "Who would make up such a story just to ask me for help getting permits into Ewuare? I believe you."

I let out a long sigh of relief. "Thank you, La Hinan."

"You will pay me back, of course—"

I nodded quickly. "Absolutely."

"By coming back here when you have completed the mission this god has set before you."

I stared at her, slack-jawed. "You want me to come back to the Red Tapestry?"

La Hinan smiled softly. "You have worked so hard to get here, Naborhi Tanomare. You have fought and sacrificed for your freedom and for your happiness as few people ever do. Not all my girls have experienced equal hardships, but all have the courage to seek their own destinies. It is what I respect about them most. It is what I respect about you."

I felt tears brimming in my eyes. "I could live here? You really mean it?"

"Yes, Naborhi," she murmured, gaze twinkling. "This is a formal offer of employment."

"Thank you," I whispered. "Thank you for all of this. I gladly accept your offer."

She nodded, then shifted into crisp professionalism. "I will have your money ready for you in the morning," she said. "Until then, get some rest. You will need it for this final leg of your journey."

That night, I lay in bed, unable to keep the smile off my face. We were so close to Ewuare, to the end of our journey. And when we'd rescued the boy, I could come back here and live freely, discovering my own talents alongside these wonderful women.

I ignored the small, wriggling doubt in my gut that reminded me of Tega, of the family I left behind, of Chipo—whom I had abandoned. I was going to be free.

I had to hope the price was worth it.

19

ON MY LAST MORNING AT THE RED TAPESTRY, I WATCHED Qena and Enitan practice in the courtyard, the soft sunlight gilding everything. Enitan played the flute while Qena danced the Ekombi. Qena had explained to me that the dance was meant to tell her story through graceful, symbolic movements. It was a way of honoring her past while keeping herself open and balanced for her future. Her swaying body was perfectly synchronized to Enitan's captivating flute music, so I could not tell whether it was Enitan's music that drove Qena's dancing, or if Enitan was simply giving sound to Qena's movements.

This space was important. There were so few places in this world where women could be safe to live and dance and paint and rejoice. The Red Tapestry protected these girls and their talents and in doing so set them free. They brought such beauty and joy into this world, and I felt suddenly overwhelmed with gratitude and respect for La Hinan, for Qena and Enitan and Idia and all the other girls here.

I could not wait to join their ranks.

A small crowd had gathered in the courtyard to admire Qena and Enitan, and when they finished, applause filled the early morning sky. I could not resist clapping the loudest.

Qena, Idia, and Enitan helped me pack the few things I had. Enitan gave me an old satchel she'd used when she'd journeyed to Qua'i, and Idia filled it with food, a new waterskin, some bandages, and a spare set of the Red Tapestry's beautiful uniform.

Qena lent me a gorgeous black fur cloak with ripples of white lining the edges and collar. It was much thicker and warmer than the one Atai had bought me, which would not offer much protection against the Ewuare climate.

"Make sure you return to give it back," she quipped, winking.

"Be safe, Naborhi," Enitan murmured, squeezing me tightly. "And come back to us."

"We'll miss you," Idia added, hugging me from behind. "I'll make sure we keep your room ready for when you return."

Qena sniffled. "If you don't come back here in one piece, I will personally come drag you out of Ewuare. I will finally have a good enough reason to leave Qua'i. That's my favorite cloak." We all laughed at that and opened our arms to her, and I had never felt so whole and loved. I suddenly missed Chipo fiercely—she would love it here, and love these girls.

La Hinan met us in the courtyard, smiling fondly at the four of us.

"Thank you for your work here, Naborhi," she murmured, handing me a small coin purse. "I wish you well on your journey, and look forward to receiving you when it is completed."

I bowed deeply to this woman who was a safe haven in and of herself. "Thank you for everything, La Hinan," I told her. "I very much look forward to returning your kindnesses."

She clasped my hands within her own before escorting me out of the gate. I waved goodbye to Enitan, Idia, and a tearful Qena, feeling my own eyes burn with tears.

Tamunor and Atai waited in the open wagon La Hinan had hired for our journey.

"Be well, Naborhi," she whispered, hugging me once. "Keep up your work."

I bid her goodbye, thanking her again. I hopped up into the carriage, greeting the boys, and settled in between them.

The carriage took off then, rolling down the street, La Hinan and her sanctuary disappearing from view. I hoped in a short time that I would be back here, carving out my own space in this world of opportunities.

The thought awoke something in me, fueling my determination to complete Obassi's mission.

After securing our documents from the Iduni guards, we soon left the bustle of the city behind and rode alongside the lakeshore, into the grassy plain at the base of the Ewuare Mountains.

We traveled on for a while, the air getting colder and the dry wind whipping at our hair as we ascended out of the plain and up the steep mountain paths. But as we got deeper into the mountains, the coldness started to fade. I was anxious about what we would discover in Ewuare, and it made me feel hot.

We arrived at a small plateau in the mountains, and we alighted from the wagon with our packs. Other travelers bustled about the space, some in carriages and some on foot.

There were Iduni soldiers *everywhere*. It was a sea of purple coats and hats, the occasional crimson uniform signifying a higher official.

"Well, that soldier did say that security had heightened," Atai said, and I could hear the anxiety in his voice.

"I wonder what's caused this," I mused. "Is it from the king's visit to Qua'i the other day?"

Tamunor shrugged. "Guess we'll find out in Ewuare."

We approached the side of the nearest mountain, where a line was forming behind a massive security checkpoint.

"Whoa," Tamunor gasped, staring up the sheer face of the mountain. I followed his gaze, and my jaw dropped.

The sun at our backs illuminated the extensive, interlocking system of pulleys, ropes, and carts that was carrying passengers up and over the mountainside.

"I've never seen anything like this," Atai murmured admiringly. "It looks ingenious."

"It looks chilly." Tamunor shuddered, pulling his cloak tighter around his shoulders as a stiff wind blew through the pass.

We waited in line, finally reaching the checkpoint, where we showed our permits to a soldier in a long coat of red and black, complete with a black belt around his waist and a black helmet with a red feather on his small head.

Even though I knew we had secured legal passage, my stomach still churned with fear while the soldier examined our documents for what felt like hours. He stared carefully at each of us, and I found myself sweating despite the brisk wind.

Finally, he nodded, stamping our passports and gesturing us onward. We were soon seated in one of the boxlike carts connected to ropes as thick as my thighs going up the steep side of the mountain.

We heard a thumping, juddering sound and then a loud noise like a tree snapping as it fell, and we started to move. It was slow and steady, and for nearly an hour we moved along the side of the mountain. Then we started our ascent.

Something about the air changed the higher we went. Every breath we took plumed out of our mouths, and the air thinned, our lungs straining a bit with the bite of the cold.

Something was stirring in me as we neared the mountain's peak. I looked out over the continent to our south, the sun bright in the sky. It felt like I could see all the way to the edge of the world. Qua'i was quaint and quiet beneath us, its lake molten in the sunlight. The Crooked Forest looked like no more than a patch of shrubs. And on the horizon, I swore I could see the reddish dunes of the Orerokpe Sands.

We had traveled across all that land. *I* had traveled across all that land. A kind of force within me grew as we crested the mountain's peak, and I caught my first glimpse of Ewuare.

It had all been worth it for that moment.

We gazed out over a cascading landscape of entangled snow-capped mountains, the city cradled in a cove between them. Stone buildings covered in climbing vines and flowers of vibrant reds, yellows, oranges, and greens met our eyes. The City of Colors truly lived up to its name.

Ewuare rolled down the edge of the mountainsides until it spilled into the port, where dozens of ships were docked and even more of them moored out in the bay. I took a deep breath of the crisp, clean air and relished the freshness. The city was more beautiful than I had ever dreamed.

We started to descend.

Tamunor rubbed his hands together and blew into them, his cheeks puffing. "I have never felt cold like this, not even on early mornings during dry season," he lamented.

"Once we get down, it will not be so cold," Atai said to him. "Though I wonder how those flowers stay alive in this climate," he mused, rubbing his palms together slowly.

I was not really sure what was going to happen once we left the cart. This wasn't a vacation; we were in Ewuare to save someone's life. I shuddered at the thought of failing. I hoped we were not too late.

Atai turned to me. "What do you think we are going to face down there?" he asked.

"Trouble." The word came out of me without thinking.

"Sounds about right," he said, smiling wryly. "Whatever happens," he added, squeezing my hand, "Obassi will see us through."

I half smiled.

Our cart lurched to a stop. Tamunor looked to me for an answer, and I turned to look out one of the small windows and observed some Iduni soldiers standing with the stern-looking men who worked the ropes and pulleys on the ground.

"What is going on down there?" Atai asked, carefully leaning over to look out too.

"It looks like they're questioning the people a few carts ahead of us."

The soldiers were confronting a small family, and they were repeatedly pointing at the dark-haired son. Something nagged at me, but then they allowed the family through and our cart jerked forward, resuming its descent.

We soon arrived at the drop-off point.

One of the men in control of the ropes opened the door to let us out, the cart still moving slowly. We swiftly leapt out of the carriage and had no sooner gotten out than an old man and his family of three rushed into the box cart and it began its ascent. It was an ingenious—though briefly stressful—way to move from one point to another.

We followed the crowd toward the Iduni soldiers posted at the monumental gates to the city.

We walked toward a lanky officer dressed in the same red-and-black uniform as the soldier we'd encountered on the other side of the mountain. His feathered helmet sat securely on his head, and he sported a trim, sparse mustache. He looked at our permits meticulously before he handed them back.

Then his questioning began.

He focused on Tamunor and Atai, effectively ignoring me.

"Where have you come from? Where are you heading? What business do you have in Ewuare?"

Atai replied smoothly. "We have come from Iga, and we are visiting Ewuare to deliver a message to our family."

"You came all the way from Iga to deliver a message?" The soldier's tone was flat, disbelieving.

"Yes," Atai replied firmly.

"Look," the man said, rolling his eyes, "those bureaucratic bastards have been on our backs for days. And all they bring us are piss-poor food and itchy cloaks. So my patience is thin and I need you to state why you are truly in Ewuare."

"We are here to see the Rainbow Rocks," I said. "We have heard so much about them, and we thought it would be worth delivering the message to our family in person so that we could spend time here. The city is so beautiful, and so well-run."

The man rolled his eyes at my obvious ploy to win him over. But he couldn't prove we were lying—the Rainbow Rocks to the north were Ewuare's finest tourist attraction. We weren't the only ones here claiming to be visiting them.

"Welcome to Ewuare," he grumbled, stamping each of our passports.

"Thank you," I said, taking back our documents and hoping

he would not notice Tamunor grinning smugly behind his hand. We walked down the gleaming stone road into the bustling city. I pulled my cloak tighter. It was significantly less cold than it had been at the top of the mountain, but it was still chilly. We saw more soldiers the deeper into the city we walked.

"The number of soldiers here is quite disturbing," Atai said, mirroring my own thoughts. "Something is definitely going on."

I wondered if it had anything to do with us coming to Ewuare. Surely no one knew who we were and why we were truly here. And word from Kokori could not have reached our destination before us. I shoved my worries aside and focused on the city bursting with life around me.

The streets were cleaner and wider than any I had ever seen, with tall arches at the ends of each one, forming beautiful intersections. Smoke came out of the vents on the domed roofs, blending with the white clouds above us. Children in sleek fur cloaks scampered underfoot, their parents chatting from adjacent doorsteps. The air was pure and faintly fragrant from the myriad flowers and vines covering almost every building we passed. From where we were, we could see the Ewuare Tower and we headed toward it.

We entered a wide avenue lined with houses completely covered in yellow flowering vines. We followed the road until we reached a carpet market full of bustling stalls and customers.

I approached a stall, greeting the weathered old man and the plump woman in a brown fur cloak behind him. Her gray eyes were heavily lined, which made them stand out. "Could you point us in the direction of the Ewuare Tower?"

The woman smiled widely. "Walk out that end of the market and you'll spot it—it's just a few blocks away. Can't miss it."

I thanked her and turned to leave before something made me pause. "Why are there so many soldiers around here?" I asked. "I never knew Ewuare was so heavily patrolled."

"King Ide went to Agbon for talks with King Brumeh, and this is the result," the old man hissed. "With these soldiers here interrogating everyone and clogging up traffic, our business is slow."

"You know King Ide is not there for talks," the woman interjected, chuckling. Her eyes gleamed with mischief. "It all has to do with Prince Senaga's disappearance."

"The prince is missing?" Tamunor asked, alarmed.

My hearing faded a bit, my heartbeat roaring in my ears. Atai gripped my shoulder, and I barely felt it.

Of course.

"Woman, stop saying nonsense!" the man scolded before turning back to us. "You did not hear anything about the prince," the man said, his eyes focusing on something behind us. "Do you want to buy a carpet?" His voice was loud and falsely inviting.

"We need to go," Atai murmured in my ear as a group of soldiers passed by.

We hurried out the other end of the market and onto the street, and I laid eyes on the tower just as everything clicked into place.

"Prince Senaga is the boy," I rasped, and Atai pulled me into a small side street, Tamunor ducking in after us.

"*What?*" Tamunor gasped.

I held my hand to my lips, trying to calm my breathing. "It all makes sense," I whispered, my gaze locked with Atai's. He had a look of grim resignation on his face that only fueled my panic. "The heightened security, the king's sudden trip to Agbon, that procession we passed on our way through the Crooked Forest. Prince Senaga is the boy I've been dreaming of. He's been kidnapped."

"But *why*? Who would do such a thing?"

"There are many people in this world who would, Tamunor," Atai replied, his voice almost a growl. He rubbed his hands over his face, taking a steadying breath. "The question is, why is the king on his way to Agbon? What does King Brumeh have to do with this plot?"

I shook my head, unable to answer that. "We need to find Senaga. *Now*."

Atai nodded his agreement, and we hurried back out onto the street, following the flow of traffic until we reached the Ewuare Tower.

It was even taller than it had appeared in my visions, and the polished stone reflected the sun, dazzling me and sending sunbeams glinting off the surrounding buildings. It had four sides, each with its own distinct markings: round, triangular, rectangular, and helix. In my dream, I saw circular and oblong markings, and I guided us around the crowd of tourists at the tower's base until we came to the side that bore the right etchings.

"Naborhi, look." Atai pointed at a tall, tidy public house to our left. Its sign read THE BROKEN BARREL.

"And there," Tamunor whispered, gesturing to a disheveled blacksmith's shop, the crooked sign reading ANCHOR'S FORGE.

Storm clouds gathered overhead, blocking out the sun, and the street around us darkened significantly. People hurried toward the Broken Barrel and other pubs nearby, seeking shelter before the storm could hit. Smoke wafted from the chimneys, conversation spilling out onto the street whenever someone opened a door.

"We're so close," I murmured, just as thunder cracked overhead. We were in the right spot, and the building we needed was nearby.

"Naborhi," Atai whispered.

He'd found it. The brick eaves were unmistakable. It had an arched entryway, and it was carved with peculiar patterns and what looked like handwritten symbols and fingerprints. The trimmings were lined with colorful stones that sparkled even in the dimming sunlight.

We had made it.

"Tamunor, go to the Broken Barrel," I ordered suddenly.

My cousin looked at me in shock. "What? Why?"

I shook my head. "I'm not discussing this. I can't focus on protecting Senaga if I'm focused on protecting you. Wait at the pub for us. If we don't come out within an hour, get help."

"Naborhi, I am not abandoning you." I had never heard him sound so fierce.

I gripped his hand. "I can't put you in danger. I do not like how tense these soldiers are. If anything happens to us in there, I would feel better knowing you are not in the middle of it, and that you can seek help for us, and the boy."

"But why not ask the guards for help now? Surely that's smarter than running in just the two of you!"

I shook my head. "And risk the chance of the guards incriminating us with whatever plot is in play? They might not believe our story, and we could get killed for simply *knowing* the prince is here."

He still did not look convinced, and I sighed, trying to back off a bit. "You are not abandoning me," I insisted. "Atai has my back in there. I need you out here in case something goes wrong."

I could practically see his heart breaking in his eyes, but he nodded after a moment. "Okay."

We gave him our bags with our money and documents, leaving us solely with our weapons.

"Be safe," he said forlornly. "And if you die, I will kill you."

"We will keep each other safe," Atai assured him, squeezing his shoulder.

I threw my arms around Tamunor, hugging him tightly. "I love you," I whispered, and took off with Atai, not allowing myself to look back.

We approached the semicircular doorway slowly and cautiously. The skies had opened up as soon as we'd left Tamunor, and with each step forward, the sinking feeling in my stomach deepened. But I kept moving. One foot in front of the other.

Atai tried the doorknob, and it was unlocked. My unease grew, and Atai gave me a wary glance before he gently pushed it open. I stepped inside, drawing my daggers, and he came in after me, sword at the ready.

The room was empty, dusty, and almost entirely dark, save for the faint streams of weak light coming from holes in the walls and roof.

It appeared to be an abandoned temple, statues and grand pillars crumbling in decay.

"If you encounter anyone who is hostile, disarm them and try to get information," I whispered to Atai, who nodded, his sword gleaming dimly in the watery light.

We passed through what looked like a small prayer hall. A pool of water had gathered on the floor, and a thick, musty smell enveloped the space. The arches overhead reminded me of my clan's old temple in Kokori. I thought of my rite and ceremony. How distant it seemed from my present.

We crept toward a dilapidated staircase and carefully ascended to a small landing. Gray light from the holes in the roof illuminated a door to my right, its hinges broken and the wood lopsided.

I carefully pushed the remaining part of the door open, the hinges groaning in protest. We were in a large, dark room. I could barely make out weathered pillars with tiny scrawls on them.

A sudden chill ran down my spine. *We're here.*

I took a step forward just as a knife flew at the side of my face.

20

IT WAS INSTINCT AND YEARS OF MOYO'S TRAINING THAT HAD me ducking, dodging the knife that would have stabbed me in the eye. The knife struck a pillar beside me, quivering with the force of the impact. I couldn't see who had thrown it, but I heard the shuffling of feet.

"Naborhi!" Atai cried, and I lurched to my feet.

"They're armed, and they're fast," I told him. "Stay on your guard."

We stood back-to-back, circling slowly. I saw a shadow dart from behind a pillar on my right to another, but I couldn't get a good look at who they were.

Someone slammed into Atai, knocking me forward and away from him. Atai instantly swung his sword, the clang of iron ringing out as his assailant fought back.

"Go!" he shouted at me as they shifted into shadow. "I've got this."

I was panting, eyes scanning for the original assailant as I crept toward where I had last seen them.

I saw the gleam of metal to my left before I felt the knife lodge in my upper arm. I gasped at the pain but lunged to the side to avoid the second knife being thrown at me.

They ran behind me then to a pillar to my right. Whoever they were, they had been well trained. Their movements were like lightning, silent and deadly.

I heard Atai cry out in pain, and I spun toward the sound.

The knives came at me again, this time from right in front of me. I dodged them, just barely.

The knife in my arm wobbled, blood dripping from the wound and onto my thighs. I swallowed back a sob and held my daggers tighter, my hands shaking.

Moyo had taught me how to incapacitate someone. I just needed to get close enough.

I breathed deeply, trying to calm my racing heart.

Despite those obstacles, despite those boulders, the water moves fast and strong. It cannot be held back. It cannot be less than it is.

I saw the figure dart behind the column next to me and I raced over, taking them by surprise. I spun behind the pillar and sliced low along their ribs. They hissed in pain and slammed their fist into me.

I cried out, dropping to the floor. The figure finally came out of the shadows, looming over me. She wore a stiff black sleeveless tunic over a knee-length black skirt with white spots, thigh-high boots disappearing beneath the hem. Her hair was tucked tightly into a red hair scarf.

She held one hand to her side, blood seeping through her fingers, the other lifting her next knife, ready to plunge it into my heart. I was lightheaded, but still grimly satisfied that my aim had been true. She would not quickly recover from that wound.

I scrambled to my feet, daggers up at the ready. She gave me a sinister grin.

"May your gods bless you," she snarled. But she was not quick enough.

A thunderous growl rang through the room, and Zuberi appeared at my side, his teeth bared. The woman's knife slipped from her hand in astonishment.

I wasted no time. I lunged forward and slashed her exactly where I needed to, low across her abdomen. She fell backward against the column, groaning in pain.

"My gods have already blessed me," I purred, looming over her.

She spoke a language I did not understand, pronouncing every word with a hiss.

If she moved even an inch, she would lose blood and eventually consciousness. She must have known this because she remained completely still aside from her heavy breathing, her eyes practically glowing in hatred.

Zuberi was quick to disappear the same way it had appeared. I ran toward the sound of Atai's battle.

He was fighting off another girl in the same attire as my attacker.

Atai had cuts on his arms and legs, and his lower lip bled. The girl was not looking too good, either, but she seemed to have the upper hand for the moment. She fought with a short sword, which

Atai succeeded in getting out of her grip while losing his own in the process. For a split second, it hit me how strange it was that our attackers were skilled with the very weapons we were most comfortable with. But then the woman kicked Atai full in the chest and he fell with a thud. He struggled to stand, groaning in pain, his breathing gasping and desperate.

I sized the woman up. She was considerably larger than me and certainly had the advantage of a larger weapon. I just had to use her strength against her. It was the only way a fighter of my size stood a chance.

She gave me a wicked smile, lifting her sword. "So eager to meet the same fate?" she crooned.

I looked down to observe her left leg was gently trembling, the same one she'd used to kick Atai. I felt a slow, wicked smile tug at my lips.

I struck first, swinging my daggers at her. She dodged my attacks easily and grabbed my wrists, bending them backward and forcing me to let go of my daggers.

Then she yanked the knife out of my arm, her other fist meeting my face with a brute force.

There had been no warning.

I fell back, feeling the pain settle on my jaw like an anchor, my arm on fire, leaking out fresh blood. She came at me again like a charging bull, kicking my curled body with her right leg. I took the first two hits and cried out in pain. Her left leg hesitated for a moment as she made to deal a heavier blow, weaker than her right. So my fist met her kneecap. The pain seared through my hand like it was on fire, but she buckled, nearly collapsing to the floor next to me before catching herself.

I jolted to my feet, flexing my right fist to alleviate the pain. It did not do much good. My left arm was burning and strangely numb, my skin sticky with blood. Atai was on his knees, hunched over and trying to rise.

The woman came after me again, leaping into the air to crash her fist onto me. I ducked and rolled to my right side, moving farther from her.

She landed hard on her bad leg, and her brow creased as she grunted. She roared and came at me, trying to grapple me and throw me to the ground. I twisted away from her grip and swept her left leg. She fell to the ground again but got up quickly, launching her left fist at me as fast as she could. I could not dodge it quick enough, and my face took the hit. I fell on my knees but got up hurriedly. Blood filled my mouth and I spat it out before I lunged and kicked her left knee again.

She held up her leg, hopping on her right. She then put it down but could not put weight on it. I maintained my fighting stance, one leg forward another back, fists up, observing her movements.

I could see the rage in her eyes blinding her. She would make me suffer if I let her get her hands on me.

We ran toward each other. She picked me up, lifting me into the air to throw me to the ground. I could hear Atai's scrambling to get up.

I twisted swiftly and wrapped my legs around her neck, elbowing her in the back of her head. She fell like a tree, bellowing like a wounded animal, but I refused to let go. My thighs tightened around her neck, her fingers clawing at me until she lost consciousness.

Relief flooded me, turning my body boneless. I stood up slowly, trembling, and looked at Atai. The room spun around me, but he limped toward me and caught me before I fell over.

"Thank you," I whispered into his neck. "You're okay."

"She didn't want me to go in there," Atai said breathlessly, pointing at a door across the room nearly hidden in the shadows.

We reclaimed our weapons, and with considerable effort, we walked toward it and dragged it open.

I recognized the room immediately. I'd been dreaming of it for weeks.

A weak, childlike voice said something in Iduni.

I recognized it and crept deeper into the room. There was a boy curled up in the corner, his hands bound by thick twine. I could barely make out his features, but he looked to be about ten—if I remembered Moyo's politics lessons correctly.

He looked exhausted. His hair was matted and greasy, and his clothes were stained and threadbare, hanging loosely on his skeletal frame.

"I'm Naborhi," I told him in the Traveler's Tongue. I approached him slowly and helped slice through his bindings. "This is Atai."

"Did my father send you?" he rasped, squinting at me.

"No," Atai answered, "we came by ourselves."

"How did you find me?" He finally took a good look at my face and blurted out, "You! I saw you in my dreams. Constantly."

"I dreamed of you too," I replied cautiously. "Who are you?" I both feared and sought his answer.

"I am Senaga," the boy answered. "Son of King Ide, Prince of Idu."

21

WE HELPED SENAGA INTO THE MAIN ROOM, HIS ARMS AROUND our shoulders.

The woman I had fought and stabbed had crawled toward the door to Senaga's cell. She lay on the floor, motionless, blood streaked on the floor marking her path.

I couldn't bring myself to check if she was still alive. I looked at Atai and he shrugged out of Senaga's embrace, kneeling by her head. He held a hand to her neck, checking for her pulse.

I didn't think too much about what it meant when he got up and moved toward the unconscious woman we had fought instead, binding her with fabric strips from his shirt.

Prince Senaga turned his gaze away from the women. "Who are they?"

"We have no idea," I confessed. "We've come all the way from Agbon to help you."

"Agbon?" he asked, shocked.

"Yes," Atai answered, rejoining us. "Obassi led us to you. He showed Naborhi you were in danger."

"Thank you for rescuing me. You will be highly compensated. I need to get back to my father. I need to let him know I am fine." I could hear the urgency in his voice, making him stumble over his words.

I held Atai's gaze. "We heard your father has journeyed to Agbon," I told the prince carefully.

He looked worried and pointed at the bound, unconscious woman. "She's who lured me away from my guards. She sometimes spoke Iduni to me, gloating about how easy it had been to deceive my father and how he was already on his way to Agbon. I did not know what she meant, but it cannot mean anything good."

I swallowed, my heartbeat quickening again. "We need to get you to safety. Is there anyone you trust?"

"I know a king's guard who plays competitive Ise at a tavern not far from here. I trust him with my life. He will help us."

Atai hesitated, looking back at me. I wasn't sure this guard would help us, but we had no choice.

"I will stay here and watch over these two," Atai murmured, gesturing to both women. "But take this," he added, removing his tattered tunic and hanging it to the prince. "You should wear it over your head, for disguise."

Senaga thanked him and wrapped it around his head. I took his hand and gingerly helped him downstairs and out of the temple.

The rain had let up, the sun peeking out from behind the gray clouds. The prince shielded his eyes from the brightness, and in the daylight it was easy to see the scrapes on his face and arms, the bruised, purple skin around his eyes, and the hollows of his cheeks. Why would anyone want to harm him?

"We have to get my cousin first," I told him, guiding him across the street and around the tower to the Broken Barrel.

The public house was crowded, people gathered near the large stone fireplace to fight off the cold. A large Iduni flag bearing its lightning bird symbol hung from the rafters. Wine barrels were stacked beneath the staircase that led to a lofted upper section. Several customers turned to stare at us, and I couldn't imagine what we looked like, so battered and bruised.

Tamunor sat next to the barrels, drinking from a jug, a bowl of untouched food in front of him. His anxiety was etched on his face.

He nearly toppled over the table when he saw me come in, a wide smile swallowing that anxiety when I put my arms round him.

"Are you all right?" he asked, looking me over.

"I'm fine."

"Is this the boy?" He eyed Prince Senaga warily.

"I am," Senaga replied, inching toward us. "Is this yours?" He pointed at the food.

When Tamunor nodded, Prince Senaga lunged forward and gulped down the water from the jug, then dug into the food. It felt like I had no sooner blinked than he finished the food. He looked at us meekly before rising. "Let us go now."

We followed him out of the pub and flanked him closely as we went past the tower, in the opposite direction, to the market. The prince kept looking over his shoulder, which was counterintuitive to our aim of not drawing attention to ourselves.

"Where are we going?" Tamunor asked.

I explained what I could, watching every face we passed by.

"So we find this guard. Then what?"

That question hit me. What then? Would I just go back the Red Tapestry? I had completed Obassi's mission; I had found Senaga and he was all right.

What was my next step?

We came across a shabby-looking tavern only a few blocks from the tower. Just as Senaga predicted, there was a group of king's guards playing Ise over a low table.

"That one," Senaga whispered to me, discreetly pointing out an older man with a graying beard and stern, steady eyes. "His name is Udoh. Tell him you seek a private word with Senaga's second-favorite guard. He'll know it's from me."

He and Atai slipped back outside, and I approached the table, clearing my throat.

"Captain Udoh?" I asked, hating how my voice trembled. The guards all looked up, one of them gasping at the state of me. "Could I speak with you? I need a word with Senaga's second-favorite guard."

The captain's expression was alarmed, but he rose and joined me outside. I tried to ignore the bustling murmurs of the guards he left behind, hoping we hadn't given away too much information.

"What is the meaning of this? Where is Senaga?" the captain demanded.

"Udoh," Senaga stepped out from under the tavern awning, and the captain bowed immediately before snatching him up in a fierce hug.

"I've been so worried, my boy," the man whispered, his shoulders shaking.

Senaga sagged in the man's arms, and I could see tears forming in his eyes.

"What happened? Where have you been?" Udoh asked urgently.

"We need you to come with us, sir," I cut in. "Bring your most trusted soldiers."

To his credit, the captain looked to the prince for confirmation, and he nodded firmly. "Please, Udoh."

The captain went inside and emerged with two women and a man. They fetched their horses and a carriage and escorted us back to the temple.

Atai was waiting for us where we'd left him, pacing restlessly.

The woman he and I had fought together was awake and furious, snarling at us as we arrived.

The captain hurried closer, the male guard flanking him with a sword raised at the snapping, feral girl. The captain grabbed her by the neck to still her movements. She screamed in his face, but he looked undisturbed. He yanked the scarf from her head and lifted her hair from the back of her neck, revealing a tattoo of a knife surrounded by flowers.

The look he gave her could have frozen the Sands. "She is from the Order of the Hidden Blade," he announced to us sharply.

"They are the most lethal band of assassins in the kingdom. We must get a confession out of her quickly. It will be difficult, but we have to try."

Prince Senaga gave a curt nod, and the two female guards clamped small sets of chains around the assassin's wrists.

"What of her accomplice?" Atai nodded toward the other woman's body, still sprawled across the floor.

"We will bring her with us and examine her body for evidence." The captain nodded at the third guard and he hurried to lift the woman from the ground, her body shockingly small in comparison to his bulk.

"You must come with us to the palace," Prince Senaga said as we made our way out onto the street once more. "You came all this way to rescue me, and we need to properly thank you for your help. Iyase Ohen will help us get word to my father. He will know what to do."

I looked at Tamunor and Atai. We were beaten and bloodied, and I wasn't sure we'd make the journey back to Qua'i in our current state, so I nodded. "We would be grateful for your hospitality, and we'd like to help with whatever your plans are."

Both assassins were loaded onto the carriage, the feral woman's limbs tied with ropes held tight by the two female guards.

We garnered glances and chatter from the small crowd as we made our way across the city toward the palace.

I had long lost feeling in my left arm, and each of the horse's steps sent my head spinning. Atai held me tightly around the waist, steadying me, but I knew even he must be fading quickly.

We headed downhill toward the harbor for a while before shifting back uphill on the opposite mountainside, heading toward the magnificent stone palace reigning over the northern end of the city.

I never imagined when I first saw Zuberi that I would end up in the palace of Idu, that I would have seen Oron, and crossed the Orerokpe Sands, and explored Iga, and still been mesmerized by the extravagant, gravity-defying palace before me.

The structure seemed to float above the city, built entirely into the mountain's sheer face. Our procession hurried along a steep bridge, nothing but air on either side of us as we crept higher and higher. We reached the gates, the guards stirring into action, a sort of frenzy of activity that set me on edge despite the sluggishness in my brain.

"Fetch the iyase," Udoh commanded from atop his horse. "We have brought Prince Senaga home."

We were ushered within to the main courtyard, and Udoh dismounted and helped us off our horses, ordering guards to bring the assassin and the body to the dungeons.

Tamunor leapt to the ground and reached for my hand, Atai helping me carefully slide off the horse. Senaga, frail and trembling, led us inside the palace, where a weathered, hunchbacked man in ornate robes awaited us.

"Iyase," Udoh greeted, bowing. Iyase Ohen was the right hand and trusted adviser to the king. I just hoped he could be trusted enough.

The iyase was too shocked when he saw Prince Senaga to do

or say anything at first. His eyes welled with tears, and his entire expression crumpled at the sight of the boy's beaten body. Then he threw his arms around him, like a father would his long-lost son. He found his tongue at last. "Oh, my boy," he wept. "We thought you were dead." His voice cracked, but he seemed to regain composure over himself at the sight of us. "We need to talk in private," he added, eyeing us suspiciously.

"These people journeyed across Otọrakpọ to save my life," Senaga assured him. "You can speak freely."

The old man sighed and continued, "Just five days ago, we were sent your bracelet and your heart. Or what we thought was your heart. A written message accompanied the package, claiming King Brumeh was behind your death."

My stomach seemed to be filled with stones, clarity hitting me just as the iyase rasped, "Your father left the next day, and he took his best soldiers and fastest horses. My dear boy, Ide did not go to Agbon for diplomatic talks; he went to avenge you. To kill King Brumeh."

I swayed on my feet, and Tamunor and Atai held my shoulders.

"But that is murder," Atai growled. "He has no proof. He can't just kill another king."

"He is going to invoke the rite of Oumouk Tangou, where one king fights another in the place of their armies," the iyase explained to us. "Whichever king wins brings victory for his people."

"But that would only start a full-scale war across the entire continent," Atai protested, his voice laced with agitation and something eerily close to panic. "I doubt very much that Agbon would simply let their king die with no repercussions. And with their new alliance, Oron would come to Agbon's aid. The Lost Lands would become a bloodbath."

"So Ide should just let the kidnapping of his son pass without conflict?" the iyase challenged.

"Nobody would be stupid enough to leave such a blatant calling card for war," Atai snapped. "Especially not a king recently engaged in peace talks with a queendom he'd been at odds with for thirty years."

I could see the iyase's temper rising, his face pinching as he opened his mouth to retort.

"If Brumeh was not responsible for your kidnapping, then who was?" I asked Senaga softly.

Everyone sat in silence for a moment.

"We will see what the Hidden Blade assassin has to say," Udoh offered weakly.

"And when she does not crack for days more?" Atai snarled. "What will you do then?"

Prince Senaga spoke up. "I do not believe King Brumeh had anything to do with my capture. We are at peace with each other, and have been for centuries. And even if he did, I am alive, and there is no reason to fight. War has no eyes. It will ravage the innocent and the guilty alike."

"Your father left four days ago. We have to send a message to King Brumeh. To anyone. Warning them about King Ide's intentions," Ohen said hurriedly. "I will send the fastest ship available."

"There is no time," Prince Senaga told him, his voice grave and meaningful.

They shared a look, and Ohen shook his head fiercely.

"No."

"But we have to stop them," Prince Senaga persisted. "They will start a war."

"It is too risky," Ohen responded.

"What choice do we have?" Senaga burst out. "We take the risk or we go to war."

"The pool has never been used to travel that far," the iyase warned, hesitating.

"The Azen will know what to do."

My ears pricked at the mention of the Azen, Moyo's stories surfacing in my mind. Prince Senaga's voice had authority, and there was a look of grim determination in his eyes. Whatever this risk, he was willing to take responsibility as crown prince to do what he thought was right. Ohen saw it, too, giving the boy a resigned nod.

"May I ask what this risk is?" I asked Prince Senaga.

He turned to me, the air about him a little different, more commanding. He had been raised for the throne, and well. "Come with us, and you will see."

I was hungry, half-broken, and tired, and so was Atai. Even Tamunor looked exhausted, but I knew I had to help. "I will come with you."

Atai agreed, and Tamunor too.

Udoh gathered the two female soldiers from before to escort

us. We mounted horses, two to a steed, and headed back out into the city, down the steep, staggering bridge.

The whole way, my feverish mind could focus only on the bloodshed we needed to prevent.

Could focus only on my family and Chipo, stuck in Kokori, caught in the bloodbath.

22

WE ARRIVED AT A GLASSWARE SHOP IN THE EASTERN quarter of the city, right by the waterfront.

Ohen and Udoh dismounted first and knocked at the apartment door next to the entrance to the shop. The door opened, but I couldn't make out who answered it before Ohen turned back to us and gestured us inside. The two soldiers stayed behind, guarding our backs.

"Any idea what we're getting into?" Tamunor asked, slipping off the horse in front of me and reaching out his hand.

"Not in the slightest," I replied, taking it and dismounting.

We headed inside and up a set of rickety stairs until we reached the main living space. Something smelled off about the place, which I suspected came from all the unique and unusual plants growing out of jars on every available flat surface and the boiling pot in an alcove whose steam was alternating from red to blue and back.

The women were almost indistinguishable, especially since they were wearing the same red dresses and beaded hats.

I suspected they were triplets.

They left their worktable to greet us. I noticed they did not bow to Senaga, but merely looked over him appraisingly.

"I told you he was not dead," one of the women said gleefully. She was tall, with luminous brown skin and shocking ice-blue eyes.

"You'll forgive my doubts. Your predictions have not always been accurate, sister," the squat woman with a mole on her face said with a chuckle. Her eyes were a deep bloodred.

"In fact," the third cackled, her golden eyes crinkling closed as she laughed, "they have caused more harm than good."

The blue-eyed sister scowled before turning back to us. "Why are you here, Prince?"

Senaga replied, "We need to use the pool to get to Okpara. We were hoping you would help us get that far." He turned to me then and said, "These are the Azen. They are almighty in this realm, and I have faith in their powers. Azen, this is Naborhi, Atai, and Tam—"

"Tamunor," my cousin squeaked out, eyeing the women nervously.

"Tamunor," Senaga finished. "They are the reason I am here before you."

As if on cue, the women looked past the prince and directly met my gaze. So these were the women who possessed magic that could be used by only King Ide. And his progeny, apparently.

I shifted uncomfortably under their scrutiny. Their gazes seemed to be burning through my soul.

"Risky," one of the women mused, and they started to speak among themselves.

"But with her we can do it."

"If we lend her our strength."

The golden-eyed one approached me, looking hard at the space around me. Her gaze snagged the red streak on my hair.

"Where did you come about your godly energy?" she murmured, thoughtful. I wasn't sure if it was a rhetorical question.

"She was visited by Obassi's red fox," Atai answered, a little too eagerly. *Protectively*. "He chose her for this mission to rescue the prince."

"We know of Obassi," the violet-eyed one intoned, "and his red fox." She turned and exchanged an unreadable glance with her sisters. "It could work."

"It could?" the iyase asked.

"What could?" Tamunor cut in.

"She could carry our message all the way to Okpara?" the prince asked hopefully.

The women nodded in unison. "She bears the god's power. It's the only thing that could protect her," the blue-eyed sister murmured.

The prince smiled timidly. I was surprised when he took my hands in his.

"Will you help me once again, Naborhi?" he asked me softly.

I thought once again of Tega, of Imoni and Unika, of Chipo cheerfully engaged to Birungi. I could do this. I could return to Agbon if it meant they were safe from war.

The women began gathering items from their shelves and putting out the candles dotting the room.

Then I looked back at the boy I had been dreaming about for weeks, who had been dreaming of me, the prince who was awaiting my answer on his kingdom's future.

"I will help you," I said.

"You need to heal her first," Atai barked immediately. "She's been injured and lost a lot of blood from the last time she *helped* you."

I blinked at the ferocity of his words. The prince nodded quickly. "Azen, could you help Naborhi? She has given so much and should not make the journey in this state."

The Azen nodded as one, and the red-eyed sister approached me with a small, oblong vial she seemed to pull from thin air. It hardly seemed like more than two sips of liquid, but when I uncorked it and brought it to my lips, I was surprised at how many gulps I had to take. The liquid was bitter and gritty, but I swallowed it all down.

Almost immediately, it felt like my veins were on fire. I could feel the medicine in my blood, and I watched as the knife wound in my left arm slowly knit back together, the scrape inside my mouth closing up, the dizziness receding.

"Better?" Senaga asked, smiling at my amazed expression.

"I'm still exhausted, but my injuries . . ."

"It heals injuries, not states. You have been through much, Naborhi Tanomare, and there is no cure for exhaustion other than rest," the golden-eyed sister replied.

"Which you have no time for," the blue-eyed one stated matter-of-factly. "Let us go."

I tried not to think too hard about why the sisters knew my full name.

The Azen led us to the ruins of an old lighthouse on a lonely peninsula at the farthest reaches of the city, jutting out into the icy-blue waters of the Northern Sea.

They ushered us into the crumbling ruins, but instead of heading up to the beacon, we crept down a crumbling set of stairs, the darkness so complete it felt alive.

I could hear our feet scuffing on the stones, and I forced myself to ignore how three sets of footsteps were missing from the cacophony.

"I don't like this," Tamunor whispered. I shivered as the damp chill seemed to sink into my bones.

We walked for what could have been minutes or days, until I noticed the darkness lightening slightly.

"We're nearly there," Senaga whispered assuredly.

Suddenly we stepped out into a small cavern dripping with stalactites. There was a raging stream bisecting the space, its water glowing an eerie, luminous turquoise. The room smelled damp and metallic, the stones slick from the river's spray as we carefully approached it.

"This is it," Senaga said softly.

"This is what?" I asked, confused and wary. There was something in the air that weighed on my bones. There was magic here; I just didn't know what kind.

"It is the final artery of Iso-ao-natunya," the red-eyed Azen stated.

My head snapped up and I stared at the woman in shock. "The smoke that thunders?"

Moyo's story echoed through my head, his words jolting something awake in me.

The red-eyed Azen smiled slowly and knowingly at me while the other two women began pouring the contents of the jars and vials they had brought into the water—plants, herbs, oils, even chunks of hair and fur.

"The river is old," the woman intoned, "and has many branches and channels, each with its own purpose. This is its easternmost artery, small in comparison to the others, but arguably one of the most powerful. It offers a way to travel, for short distances. You must focus on your destination, be it a person or a place, and the waters will transport you there. It is safe and we have guided many who needed it, but only within Ewuare. The river demands payment for its services, and traveling without the gods' protection—or our permission—will cost you dearly. The further you travel, the greater your cost."

I peered into the churning, glowing waters. I knew I had Obassi's protection—why else would I have been I brought here? why else was I alone able to see Zuberi?—but fear still tightened my throat.

"So think of Okpara, enter the river, and I would just appear there?" I asked.

The women gave a collective yes.

It seemed almost too simple.

I couldn't determine whether my fear was from the river itself or from having to return to Agbon.

I had seen so much of the world and I had learned so much about myself and I did not want to stop. I wanted more. I wanted to turn and run to Qua'i, to seek shelter with La Hinan and spend the rest of my days carefree. Instead, it felt like I was staring at the future I had worked so hard to escape, like running for hours only to realize I had not moved an inch.

"This is dangerous, though," Tamunor said abruptly. "Even with Obassi's protection and your permission, Naborhi could still be harmed?"

"There is always a cost, no matter how deep your pockets," the golden-eyed woman replied cryptically.

Atai tensed next to me, and I placed my hand on his arm. He turned to me with a worried expression on his face.

"We have no other choice," I murmured. "Every moment spent here is a moment closer to war."

I was afraid, but I had to do this. I could return to Agbon, I could stop King Ide, I could prevent a war.

"Naborhi—" Tamunor protested, but I turned to him, squeezing his hands.

"I have to do this," I murmured. "No one else can travel this way safely."

"You don't even know if you'll be safe!" he burst out, eyes wide.

"I will be fine," I told Tamunor. "I will just get to Kokori a few days before you do." I laughed, hoping he would laugh with me. He did not.

I swallowed against the knot in my throat. "I can do this," I tell him. "I trust myself. I need you both to trust me too."

Tamunor exhaled shakily, tears brimming in his eyes. Atai nodded to me.

"We believe in you, Naborhi."

Senaga turned to the iyase, who handed him something from a small pouch in his robes.

"Take this." Senaga held out a gold ring studded with emeralds. "Show this to my father and say these words: *the gods who were before rest in their tombs*. He will know I've sent you, and he will listen."

"You will stay here and wait for his return?"

Senaga nodded. "Thank you for saving my life, Naborhi Tanomare, and thank you for saving my kingdom. You will always have a friend and a home in Ewuare."

I smiled at him, his words making my heart ache.

I slid the ring onto my finger for safekeeping and approached the river's edge, crouching and making sure my daggers were secured in their holsters.

The Azen began to chant softly in a language I could not understand. Their voices were old and young, hauntingly synchronized.

"We will meet you back in Kokori," Atai said.

"I love you, Naborhi," Tamunor whispered, and I smiled at him.

"I love you."

I sat on the edge, letting my legs dip into the current. The water was somehow cold and hot at the same time. A silvery, mesmerizing song floated to my ears, coming from both the water and the Azen. It filled my heart with great sadness, and I fought back tears.

I sensed Atai, Tamunor, and Senaga standing behind me, watching.

"Obassi, who has brought you here, will see you through to the end," I heard Atai murmur.

I looked back at him, but it was not my friends who stood behind me but the Azen. Their song continued, getting louder, seeping through my senses and dulling out other sounds.

"You have to focus on your destination," one of the women said. "Focus on your king."

All I could hear now was their chanting. I closed my eyes and pictured Okpara, thought of the docks and Unika's ships and the bracing salty air blowing in from the Bitter Sea. I thought of the towering statue of Egbesu and the king's magnificent palace. I lingered on the palace, focusing on the pale marble I'd always admired from the boatyard, the lush trees in the forest surrounding the grounds.

I lowered myself into the river, keeping the vision of King Brumeh's castle at the front of my mind. I treaded water for a heartbeat, clutching the hand bearing Senaga's ring tightly to my chest.

Without warning, I was pulled under.

I was floating through emptiness. I was not in a body, not in any form of this world.

I tried thinking of anything, of anyone or any place. But there was nothing but nothingness.

Something shifted, something soft curling around me.

Zuberi appeared before me, larger than a mountain. His breathing filled the emptiness, slow and steady and never-ending.

He watched me, unblinking.

"Have I died?" I tried to ask, but I could not form the words, could not even feel my own lips.

Zuberi let out a low growl, his jaws opening wide, and he lunged for me.

Like a flash of lightning, I jolted into being, face down on the ground.

The whole thing had happened so fast I had to wait to get my body back. With a painful grunt I turned myself round to face the blaring blue sky.

It worked.

I could not believe it worked.

The ring was still on my right hand, my daggers still in their sheaths, but my shoes were missing. I checked myself. Nothing else seemed out of place. I knew who I was, I knew my task.

I also knew where I was. I was by one of the carved pillars of the palace walls in Okpara.

I needed to get inside.

My legs were all I had, so I ran, my breath sawing in my lungs. Once I neared the palace gates, I slowed down.

The gates were surrounded by soldiers—wearing both Agbon and Idu uniforms. The two groups stood opposite each other, as if they would begin fighting at the slightest sound.

King Ide had already arrived. I could only hope I was not too late.

Confronting the soldiers head-on could be a death sentence, so I took to the forest, hurrying through the trees, desperate for another way in. At the opposite corner from where I had arrived, in a tight-knit copse of tress overlooking the choppy surface of the Bitter Sea, I found my way in: an ancient oak, its thick branches an opaque canopy above me, stretching out across the palace wall.

I was so tired I could have fallen asleep on my feet, but I began to climb. Bark scraped my palms and my legs as I heaved myself up onto the branch and crawled along it.

The ground seemed miles beneath me, and I wobbled only once as I made my way across. When I finally reached the wall, I carefully dropped down onto the battlement and peered over the parapet until I could see the courtyard.

There were soldiers lining every available space against the walls, their eyes glued to the two kings at the center of the courtyard, dressed in their war apparel.

King Brumeh had his shield raised in a defensive position. It bore the sacred Ọkan symbol of Agbon and several deep gashes. His silver armor covered his legs and his torso, leaving his arms free—but exposed. His helmet had two antlers jutting out from each side. I frowned—Brumeh's armor was decorative, more ornamental than functional.

It was not aiding him against King Ide's onslaught, who was delivering blow after blow to Brumeh's shield with his ax. Brumeh swung his sword around and lunged at King Ide, who swiftly dodged the halfhearted attack and knocked the shield from Brumeh's hand.

Brumeh created some space between them. He looked on the verge of collapse, but I recognized that he was not trying to fight Ide. He was shouting something at him, but I couldn't make it out from this high up.

Whatever it was, King Ide did not leave Brumeh much breathing room. He roared, beating his bare chest with his free fist before bringing his ax down again and again on Brumeh, who was barely dodging the swings. The beads around Ide's waist rattled throughout the courtyard with each blow, his black trousers stained with what must have been Brumeh's blood—even though Ide wore no armor and no boots, there was barely a scratch on him.

I had to find a way to show myself. I needed an opening that would not get me killed or arrested.

King Ide roared again before charging toward King Brumeh. He turned from the weak slash of Brumeh's sword and used the butt of his ax to shove him away. The injured king fell to the ground, rolling toward the Iduni soldiers, who began to hit the ground with their spears, the metal ferrules at the base of the shafts slamming into the stones as they chanted in low voices. King Ide brought his ax down heavily on his opponent, but Brumeh rolled away and lurched unsteadily to his feet.

"*IDE, PLEASE!*" he bellowed in vain.

King Ide swung his ax against King Brumeh's sword, and he weakened him just enough for the sword to fall from Brumeh's hands. The chanting became louder.

Waiting for an opening was useless. It was now or never.

"No!" I shouted, running down the battlement until I was close to them. Before Ide could deal the final blow, I leapt into the air and landed awkwardly on his shoulder.

Ide grabbed me by my tunic and flung me away from him. I landed with a jolt on the ground between him and Brumeh.

All weapons were now aimed at me.

King Ide held up his hand to stop his soldiers from intervening.

"Wait!" I gasped, wobbling as I rose to my feet, "Stop fighting! Your son—"

King Ide did not wait for me to finish before charging at me.

I rolled over and picked up Brumeh's sword. King Ide swung his ax at me and I caught it with my sword, the impact jolting up my arm and burning in my shoulder. I cried out, losing my grip on the sword.

I immediately pulled out my daggers. They would be little help against Ide's ax, but they were *mine*, they had come from Moyo and they had served me well, and I would save this continent from war even if I died doing it.

The smoke that thunders.

The king closed the gap between us, and I sent a silent prayer to Egbesu, to Obassi, to my friends and family. The clash of his ax against my crossed daggers rang out, the collision so powerful it broke a few of my fingers in my right hand.

The ring. My grip had been sloppy with the ring on my finger, and my fingers had been nearly crushed.

The pain was sudden and fierce and the daggers fell from my hands. My heart beat furiously in my chest and cold sweat dripped down my back. He came at me again, but I jumped backward, tumbling to the ground, landing hard on my broken fingers. I swallowed back my scream, tears streaming down my face.

It was almost more than I could bear. But I had to show him. I fought through the agony and raised my broken fingers high for him to see as he loomed over me, ax poised to strike.

Senaga's ring gleamed in the sunlight, the emeralds shimmering around my swollen, purple finger. It stopped Ide in his tracks.

"The gods who were before rest in their tombs," I rasped, and passed out.

23

I WOKE IN MY BED IN KOKORI.

My head felt like it was full of lead and my lips were so dry they cracked when I opened them.

"Tega?" my voice was ragged.

I heard someone shift beside me, and a cool, soft hand closed around mine.

"Naborhi." My sister sighed in relief. She was seated beside my bed, her beautiful eyes bloodshot and her expression weary.

"What happened?" My pulse picked up speed as the memories flooded back to me. "How long have I been asleep? Did Ide kill Brumeh? Are we at war?"

"Hush, child." Imoni. She was sitting on my right side, and she laid a steady hand on my head. "All is well." She gave me a sad smile.

My throat constricted then, the gravity of my journey and my actions finally crushing down on me. I began to cry, hot tears slipping down my temples and into my hair.

Tega crawled into bed beside me, curling her body around mine delicately. Imoni shifted closer, stroking her hand along my hair.

I loved them, these impossible, incredible women. I had not realized how much I'd missed them, how much I had hated leaving them, until I was back and surrounded by their love.

Once I'd calmed a bit, they told me what had happened.

After my dramatic—but effective—interruption of the Oumouk Tangou, Ide had stopped his assault on Brumeh. Wedia, Unika's second-in-command, had been visiting the palace to get King Brumeh's approval on the designs for a new fleet of merchant ships. He'd recognized me when the kings brought my body into the main hall of the palace and had explained who I was.

Imoni came to a part that I remembered—when Brumeh's palace healers had stirred me awake long enough for me to tell everyone that Senaga was alive, he was safe in Ewuare with the iyase and Udoh, that Brumeh was being framed. The healers tended to my broken fingers, setting them straight, and I passed out again.

King Ide had swiftly made peace with King Brumeh, apologizing and promising further reparations, and returned home to see his son.

War had been averted.

Wedia had fetched Unika from the boatyard, and Unika had

immediately brought me home. That had been two days ago, and I had slept until now, my body utterly drained.

I had endured battles and a treacherous journey, and had stopped two kingdoms from going to war.

"There's something else," Tega said hesitantly, carefully. She handed me the small, handheld mirror from my dresser.

The red streak in my hair was gone.

I exhaled heavily, realization settling in.

That was my price, the toll that the Iso-ao-natunya had taken from me for using its powers. I no longer held Obassi's protection, would never again see Zuberi. My vision of the red fox had been my last.

I swallowed back my devastation. If the price of peace was that I was a regular human once more, I would pay it again and again.

A few days more passed, my body slowly recovering from its wear and injuries.

Chipo came to see me, even though her parents had forbidden her from having anything to do with me after the Goredennas came to take back their wine.

Her first words when she barged into my bedroom were "I can't believe you went off on this great adventure and you didn't even invite me!"

I laughed so hard I started to cry, and she held me tightly, demanding every detail about my trip. She was especially fascinated by the Red Tapestry and she actually gasped when I recounted what had happened when Tamunor was taken by the Ebo.

When I asked her about Birungi, she scoffed. "He's hardly as interesting as your journey." A sly grin spread across her lips. "Or as this Atai you talk so highly of."

I was mortified to find myself blushing. "We are friends, Chipo," I said firmly.

Still, the knowing glint in her eye remained.

"For now," she purred.

She visited every day while I was healing, bringing me gossip from the market and updates on the alliance being re-forged between Agbon and Idu. Apparently, King Ide still had not discovered who had hired the kidnappers, and I still felt uneasy knowing the culprit was still out there.

I glanced down at my right hand, where herbs were tied tightly around them to keep them straight. I could just make out Senaga's ring. A gift of sorts, perhaps. And a way to remain in the prince's sphere of influence.

Tega stayed by my side through it all, offering me whatever I needed and changing the herbs around my fingers every morning. My body healed quickly but my fingers still felt sore to touch.

Tega spoke to me easily and earnestly, as if I had only just returned from the market and not a journey from which she had never expected to see me again.

"How long are you here for?" she asked one night as we lay together in the darkness.

"I'm not sure," I answered truthfully. My old, familiar anxiety crawled back into my stomach, a toxic old friend I had been sure I'd cut off for good.

I knew Tamunor and Atai were on their way back, that they'd be here any day now. I could picture Tamunor's worried face as he hurried the sailors along and Atai trying to reassure him of my safety while masking his own fears.

"Imoni and Unika have not spoken of your future yet," she whispered.

My aunt and uncle had flitted in and out of the room, chatting about the weather and my healing and the price of fish at the small market. But they had not uttered a single word of true substance.

"I love them," I replied after a moment, "but they have no say in my future."

I knew that when I was ready to leave them again, I would need to do it to their faces. I wondered if they knew that.

On the sixth day, I was practicing lifting small items with my right hand and curling my fingers when Tega walked into my room, a grim look on her face.

"Unika and Imoni want you to meet them in the courtyard," she said solemnly.

I made my way downstairs, Tega helping me. Outside, Unika sat on a rug I had never seen before, Imoni by his side.

I knew right then I was going to get the talk I had been expecting. Tega stood at my back, her presence grounding me.

Imoni was the first to speak, and she did not hold back.

"We are furious with you, Naborhi," she said calmly. For some reason, it made her words more threatening. "What have your uncle and I not done for you? What did we do to deserve your abandonment of this family?"

A good Kokori child knows those kind of questions do not require an answer; it would be wiser to beg for forgiveness.

Unika looked on, his expression difficult to read.

"You go all the way to Idu—and with Tamunor, no less—and you do not inform us? You slip out in the night like a thief?"

"I had no choice," I said gently. "It was all the workings of Obassi. It was the reason Zuberi came to me."

She scoffed. "A god from another clan we know nothing about."

"Yes, and look at all that I have accomplished!" I snapped.

"You kept it from us!" Imoni cried. "You lied and abandoned us and you did not even *ask*!"

"Would you have let me go?"

Imoni hesitated, and I knew I had her then. Knew that this rage and indignation was covering a deep, bruising hurt that I had caused. Because I was right.

"Maybe," she answered meekly. "Or maybe after you had married Fynn, if he had given you permission."

"What would have happened to Senaga, to our kingdom, had you done that?"

She didn't answer, and I saw tears in her eyes.

It was now or never.

"I've been invited to live in Qua'i, by the owner of an establishment known as the Red Tapestry. The city is beautiful and the Tapestry is a haven for artists and scholars. For women. And I want to live there and discover my talents and live freely among my friends."

I could see the protest building in Imoni's expression, and I powered through it.

"It is what I desire more than anything, Imoni," I whispered. "I do not want to live in Agbon. I do not want to be married, especially not to Fynn. And I am so sorry that I hurt you." I turned to Unika, who was looking at me with pain on his face, and to Tega, who gave me a brave, watery smile. "I'm so sorry that I hurt you all by leaving you. I could not think of a way to include you in my plans when you were pushing me into a life I did not—could not—want. But I am asking you now to please let me go. Please let me choose my future for myself."

We remained in silence for a moment, the birds singing from the trees above us and the wind rustling the leaves.

Unika nodded once, shallowly. "I support you, Naborhi."

His words nearly toppled me over. Imoni looked at him sharply, her eyebrows raised.

"I have put aside my dreams for most of my life, and while I do not regret joining your father's business and providing for this family, I regret not being more honest with my own happiness, with what I wanted out of my life."

Tears slipped down my cheeks, and Unika gave me a sad, heartbreaking smile.

"I do not wish the same regret for you."

I returned his smile, hope swelling in my chest before I turned to my aunt.

Imoni shook her head and swallowed audibly. "I need to think about this, Naborhi," she murmured. "This is not the life I had wanted for you, but I recognize that it is the life you want. Please be patient with me."

"Of course, Imoni. Thank you," I whispered. "Thank you both for this."

They had given me so much in this world, and I loved them so much for it. I just hoped they could give me my freedom too.

That evening, Tamunor and Atai finally returned, their voices filling our courtyard. I turned to Tega, my excitement bursting through my chest and stretching a smile across my face.

She helped me down to the courtyard, where I was promptly swept up in their arms.

"Oh, thank Egbesu you succeeded," Tamunor cried. "I just knew I wouldn't survive a war. All that blood and battle?"

"And you're rotten at fighting." I laughed, tears of happiness blurring my vision.

I turned and introduced Atai to Tega, and they greeted each other warmly before Tamunor swooped her up in his arms, smothering her with kisses.

We went up onto the roof to catch up.

Atai handed me something from his tunic.

"Appreciation from the prince. He would have liked to have given you this himself, but he's confined to the palace until his kidnapper is identified."

Without even looking I knew it was money, enough to pay

back La Hinan and take care of myself for a long time. I placed it in the inner pocket of my skirt, feeling grateful.

"I heard you broke your fingers," Tamunor cut in.

I lifted both hands for him to see and wiggled my fingers. He laughed.

"I see you're healed."

"Thanks to Tega."

Tamunor smiled at Tega. "The most caring person we know. We could've used you on our trip!"

Tega laughed. "Something tells me you did just fine without me."

We chatted for a long while, the boys filling us in on their days at sea, which seemed even more relaxing than my days in bed.

As the sun drifted low over the Ethiope, gilding everything in its path, Atai turned to me.

"Naborhi," he said quietly. "What are you going to do now? Will you go back to Qua'i?"

I nodded. "I think so. Unika has given me his permission, but I am just waiting to hear what Imoni has to say."

Tamunor's eyes bulged. "They actually listened to you?"

Tega and I laughed. "Surprisingly," I replied. "And will you return to Mbiabong to continue your training?" I asked Atai.

He nodded. "Yes. I have to return to my mother and sister for a while. But I want you to know that if you ever need my help, I will gladly give it to you. I would not mind visiting Qua'i again, for such good company." He gave me a wide, earnest smile.

My eyes misted at his words. It felt good to have him in my corner, to begin to feel supported by my family.

"Thank you. I would not mind that either."

We spent the rest of the evening laughing and discussing our futures, the horrors and trials of the past few weeks behind us.

And I felt very free, indeed.

24

THE SUMMONS FROM KING BRUMEH ARRIVED THE NEXT DAY: an ornate scroll hand-delivered by a palace courier. I was to bring my family with me for a banquet being thrown in my honor in five days. And during the celebration, Atai, Tamunor, and I were to be given titles.

Tamunor stopped by that evening with the same invitation in his hand and a wide grin on his face.

"My father nearly fainted when he saw this," he chuckled. "So much for being a disappointment, eh?"

Five days later, my family, Tamunor, his father, and I made our way toward the capital in a carriage loaded with our luggage. Unika had called for it because Imoni wanted us to appear as a family of some substance.

We arrived at the palace before evening. The gates were thrown open and our carriage glided into the courtyard. I thought of the last time I'd been here, wounded and desperate, and I shivered.

Guards in forest green and white, holding spears far taller than themselves, were stationed at both sides of the giant uloho-wood doors. I gave them my name, and they bowed deeply to me, opening the doors to allow us inside.

We stepped into the airy antechamber and the doors closed behind us. White monkeys swung from the vines covering the walls and roof. The afternoon sun reflected the patterns of the high stained-glass windows onto the floor.

My eyes drank it all in, the finest of Agbon architecture. Crests of the royal ancestral insignia were etched on the pillars facing the doorway, and in the middle of the room was a gigantic boulder cut into a perfectly round sphere. Above it, hanging from the painted roof, was a chandelier that must have held two hundred candles.

To our left, palace workers climbed up and down the winding staircase and disappeared down hallways and into rooms.

A handmaid came to take our bags and showed us to our rooms.

The room I was to share with Tega was almost the size of our house. There was a large bamboo-frame bed in the middle of the room surrounded by floral curtains with green sheets and a dozen pillows atop it. The ceiling was a mosaic of matte, earth-toned colors.

A six-armed candelabra sat on a vanity with a bronze-framed oval mirror, perfectly arranged next to two folded wool blankets and a tray of fresh fruits.

The door to the balcony had been left open so the climbing plant from outside could grow freely, lending a hand in decorating that corner of the room. Opposite the bed was a standing dresser that was more than six feet wide and six feet tall and a washbasin half my size.

Imoni came into our room to check on us once we'd settled in. Tega had gone exploring with one of the handmaidens as her guide.

"And to think you have given me the most trouble, when you have brought me to the castle of the king."

I smiled softly at her and went out to the balcony. The sight of the cerulean sea and the expanse of rooftops gave me a sense of calm. Directly below me, guards brushed down horses in the stables surrounded by masquerade trees.

"Why do you look sad?" Imoni asked, coming to my side.

"I am not."

"Then what is it?"

I pushed myself away from the banister and sighed.

"You are going to be given a title," she murmured. "You're one of the few women with such a thing, and at such a young age."

Looking into her eyes I did not have the strength to say what I wanted to. I thought it would be easier to by now.

She held my hands in hers and brought my head to her chest. She was warm and smelled of her lavender perfume oil. I took in a deep breath and felt like I was home.

"You remind me so much of myself," she murmured.

I lifted my head and met her sad gaze.

"What do you mean?"

She smiled gently. "I was not always such a traditionalist, my niece. I used to resent my domestic fate, and wished for greatness and adventure just as you do."

"What changed, then?" I asked.

"Nothing changed." She laughed. "I shot that red deer during my rite, hoping it would grant me the privilege of choosing my own path forward. But all it did was increase my bride price. I was fortunate to have been betrothed to my husband—he was kind, and his family were welcoming and loving. But I knew my situation was not the norm, and when I saw how your mother's marriage fared, I became fearful for myself. And when my husband died . . . that fear took on a life of its own."

She pulled me closer, squeezing me. "I only ever wanted you to be taken care of, to marry a man who could offer you protection and stability like mine had, not like your father. I am sorry that my fears constrained you so, and that they isolated you from me. But I will support you in whatever you choose."

I hugged her back tightly. "I only want the freedom to live my life how I choose, and to honor this family with my actions, not my marriage."

"Being here is already an honor," she said, tilting my face up so she could look in my eyes. "You are favored by the gods, Naborhi. Their lights are shining on you. You have always been destined for greatness."

I felt tears prick my eyes, but I let Imoni clear them away.

25

TWO MAIDS BROUGHT IN DOZENS OF DRESSES FOR TEGA AND me to choose for the formal ceremony.

Tega rummaged through the reds and the greens while I went for the lone white option among them.

It was unlike anything I had ever seen. The sheer brightness of it was enough to catch anyone's attention. I put the dress on slowly and with care.

It had a sleeveless fitted lace top, cinched at the waist with a belt made entirely of feathers dyed a stunning copper, with a billowing skirt that stopped just at my knees.

I tried not to think about how much it would cost to make it.

The maid brought out a headdress made of the same copper-colored feathers and I put it on.

I looked at my reflection in the mirror and hardly recognized myself. I never wanted to take the dress off.

Tega went for a floor-length long-sleeved red dress with a tapered waist and a straight neckline.

The maids revealed simple, comfortable shoes for us to wear, and we accepted them gladly. Then they whisked away the clothes and disappeared.

I had not spoken to Atai properly since our return, and I went in search of him before we all needed to head to the ceremony. I found him wandering the south corridor, already dressed for the evening's festivities.

He wore an elegant black sleeveless tunic and trim, matching trousers. A thick, heavy-looking gold necklace circled his throat, and he bore matching gold bands around his biceps.

He startled when he saw me, his eyes wide in awe.

"You look magnificent, Naborhi," he gasped.

I smiled. "Thank you. You look very . . . refined," I added wryly.

He chuckled. "Who would have thought we would be here after all that happened?"

"Not me," I said, scoffing.

"But look at how things turned out. We helped save our people from a disaster. My queen and her sister are even here to honor Otọrakpọ's peace."

I glanced at him in surprise.

"Kehina is here? I thought she'd been missing since she was banished from court."

Atai shrugged. "I think the queen would rather appear as though all is well than present a chaotic front to her newfound ally."

I frowned. "I suppose so. Just seems strange that she has been forgiven for such a serious crime." I shook my head. "But that is why I am not a member of court." I laughed. "I don't have the head for politics."

He grinned at me, and I suddenly realized this may be the last I'd see him for quite some time.

"Atai, thank you for all your help," I murmured seriously. "I'm sure you will make a fine oracle when your time comes. And I hope I can see you even while you're training." I couldn't help but add slyly, "Maybe work on understanding those who don't have your staggering amount of faith in Obassi."

He laughed ruefully.

"I will. If you promise you will never, ever give up on what you really want out of this life. No matter how hard things get."

"I promise," I said, both to him and to myself.

He leaned close and brushed his lips against my cheek, the softest of kisses that sent my pulse pounding.

"I am very proud to know you, Naborhi Tanomare."

The banquet was held within the castle's water hall.

The room was dominated by a massive fountain carved with statues of every famed Agbon king. At the base of the fountain were two elevated thrones, where King Brumeh and his wife, Queen Nuru, sat, looming over the bustling crowd. I spotted Obong Iniiemem and Kehina, dressed resplendently in Oroni colors—the latter sporting more armor than fashion. The side glances were too obvious not to miss. Even I caught whispers, criticisms of Kehina's presence here, but the woman seemed aloof, disinterested, while her sister played the role of gracious royal guest perfectly.

Atai, Inemesit, and Edem kept close to the queen, if only to remind people that Atai had also helped in stopping the war, thus proving Oron was invested in peace. Something told me there would still be tension between Oron and the other kingdoms for a while.

The five orosuen of Agbon were also present.

I was talking with Orosuen Jabali's two daughters, Imoni by my side, when the servants went still and the music stopped. A man with a drum hanging from his neck strode out, beating it with aplomb. "King Brumeh, son of Sivwi. Chosen one of Egbesu. Crowned ruler of Agbon."

The king rose from his throne slowly, his injuries still affecting him. He wore elegant, flowing robes that made him look like he floated as he moved, and a headdress in the shape of a sun disc that reflected light in dazzling fragments across the room.

"Queen Nuru! Graceful queen of Agbon and all women."

Queen Nuru rose and joined her husband without taking her eyes off him. She wore a red sleeveless dress that grabbed her body, complete with a long, trailing robe and a gold headdress adorned with feathers. She appeared like a goddess who had come to grace us mere mortals with her presence.

"Let the festivities commence!" Brumeh cried, and we all cheered, the music picking back up and dancers in gold-embroidered dresses and gold accessories performing their famous belly dances. There was an abundance of wine, meat, bread, vegetables, and fruit. There were also ceaseless chatter and questions thrown at me and Tamunor, who did not leave my side.

"Were you not afraid?"

"How do you feel knowing you will be given a title despite your humble background?"

"When are you getting married?"

Imoni answered and fielded most of the questions diplomatically while I sipped my wine and watched the dances and acrobatic displays.

After about an hour, the servants and music paused again.

"Naborhi Tanomare!"

The king's shouting echoed through the room.

"Tamunor Paebi! Atai Mfoni!"

I carefully moved through the crowd until I stood before the king, Tamunor and Atai flanking me.

"For your bravery, for stopping a needless war that would have decimated our continent, you will each receive the title of Esivwo-re: Saviors of Agbon."

"You honor us," we replied in unison, bowing low.

"You honor yourselves."

The applause was thunderous, and the subsequent celebrating was even more frenetic than before. Tamunor's father kept looking at him with so much pride, bragging about him at every opportunity.

"That's my son," he kept saying to the person nearest to him.

Imoni cried as she put her arms round me, squeezing tight. "You honor your mother and your father," she said when she finally let go. "You honor us."

"Thank you, Imoni." I hugged her back just as tightly.

"I was just approached by Anon Masika," she whispered in my ear. "He deals in precious stones and he asked about your sister." She paused to hold back her excitement. "His son Xanda is almost of age and will need a wife. Look at the good luck you have brought Tega." Her grin was so wide, I feared for her mouth.

I couldn't help but give her a wry smile. My headstrong aunt, always scheming.

Imoni winked and dragged Tega and Unika along to meet the rest of the Masika family.

King Brumeh's approach saved me from the small crowd. We all bowed in his direction, but Brumeh seemed to have cast off his kingly aura and was simply enjoying himself at a splendid party.

"I am thankful for you both, and for your Oroni friend," Brumeh told Tamunor and me. "Naborhi, your bravery in the courtyard that day was remarkable. I know few individuals who could display that kind of courage and self-sacrifice."

"I must agree," a calm female voice said from behind me, and I turned to see that Obong Iniiemem and Kehina had joined us. The queen smiled warmly at me. "You have come very far from when we last met, Naborhi Tanomare."

I smiled back. "I hope I have proven my value."

The queen laughed. "You have indeed."

I realized then that Kehina was glaring at Brumeh, her eyes like chips of glass, primed to cut.

Brumeh looked wary but did not back away when the queen and Kehina stepped closer. I watched him fumble only once as

Kehina crossed to his side, his goblet nearly toppling as she shoved by him.

Tamunor and I exchanged an uneasy glance at this new development, but I forced a placid smile on my face.

"I propose a toast," Kehina surprised us all by saying. "To Naborhi's peace, and to the newfound peace between our kingdoms. May the past be forgotten as we move forward toward our future." Her voice was forced, brittle. I shivered at her words, not really knowing why.

"To peace," King Brumeh concurred after the briefest of hesitations.

He lifted his cup toward us, hand trembling slightly, a little wine sloshing out and onto my arm.

I caught a distinctly sweet scent. It reminded me of rain and dry leaves.

My reaction was instinctual, instantaneous. I smacked the king's cup away, wine splattering across all of us. The king's guard surrounded us at once, seeming to have appeared out of thin air, and pointed their weapons at me.

I lifted my hands quickly.

The music clamored to a stop, the mood in the hall darkening instantly. No one in our group moved.

"What is this all about?" King Brumeh barked at me, his tunic soaked with wine.

"Your drink was poisoned," I said with a squeaky voice, my hands slightly trembling.

"How do you know?"

"The smell. It's newkel root." Tamunor snapped his head toward me.

Out of the corner of my eye, I saw Kehina take the smallest step back. I wasn't sure she even knew she'd done it. Her eyes were blazing with such hatred, I had to do a double take.

I turned to look at her, realization slowly dawning on me.

"It was you," I whispered.

She took a defensive stance as all eyes fell on her.

"All of it was you!" I shouted, unable to hold myself back. She was responsible for *everything*: Senaga's kidnapping, the assassins—they'd known what weapons Atai and I would use. And now she'd turned to her last resort, killing Brumeh herself.

"Of course it was me, you foolish child," Kehina snarled.

"Kehina?" Obong Iniiemem whispered. "How could you do this?"

Kehina began trembling. "How could you forgive him? How could you do that to me?"

"The gods decreed this, Kehina. Obassi himself sent Naborhi to our kingdom so that we would begin to heal our old alliance."

"Damn the gods," Kehina snarled. "I am your sister. You saw what his actions did to me, the shame I carry with me every day. And you chose *him* over me."

Something shifted in the Oroni queen at that. She stiffened, seeming to raise herself to her full height.

"I chose our queendom over your pride," she intoned. "This was never about him."

Brumeh stood slack-jawed at the interaction, and somehow it made me want to throttle him.

Kehina gave an unnerving laugh at that, and raised her untouched glass to her sister, and to her former lover.

"May the gods curse your realms," she snarled, and tipped back her goblet.

I shouted, lunging for her, already knowing what her drink contained, but it was too late.

She threw the empty goblet onto the floor with a clang, the guards around us seizing her. She began coughing, blood dripping from her lips, and Obong Iniiemem cried out in alarm.

"Kehina!"

She merely gave us all a grisly, bloody smile before collapsing.

The room broke into chaos at that. Tamunor gripped my hand as he yanked us backward, out of the fray as Brumeh, Obong Iniiemem, and the guards swarmed Kehina's body.

Atai and his family appeared before me, my family behind them, and we stuck close to the door, standing as far away as we could without fleeing the scene altogether.

Eventually, the hall quietened, most of the guests having been dismissed or returned to their rooms in the palace. Inemesit and Obong Iniiemem were given Kehina's body to return to Oron. Brumeh seemed eager to put this entire affair behind him.

"Our truce still stands," he declared, then added cryptically, "Though its terms may be adjusted."

The Oroni queen gave him a regretful, knowing nod.

"I understand, Brumeh, and thank you for your graciousness."

She, Inemesit, and Edem were escorted out of the hall, several guards bearing Kehina's body.

It devastated me that Obong Iniiemem would carry the weight of both the loss of her sister and of her sister's unforgivable actions.

Atai squeezed my hand, and I could see him trying to hide his anxiety. "I must return to Oron with them, but I will write to you."

I nodded weakly. "I'll miss you," I murmured. "Thank you for everything, Atai."

"I'll miss you too. Perhaps you can make a stop in Mbiabong on your way back to Qua'i."

Something fluttered in my chest at that. "Perhaps I could."

He gave me a small smile, kissing the back of my hand. "Until then."

And then he was gone, bidding goodbye to my family and disappearing down the corridor.

The six of us remained, my family looking just as dazed and drained as I did.

Until Tega and Imoni gave me knowing, wicked smiles.

"What?" I asked, blinking.

"You know what." Tega chuckled. "Delaying your return to Qua'i by going out of the way to visit a boy in Oron? That hardly sounds like you."

"Depends on the boy," I sniffed, and Imoni's eyes twinkled with delight.

King Brumeh approached us then, and startled me by bowing. "Once again you have saved me, Naborhi Tanomare," he said. "I owe my life to you several times over. I will never repay this debt, but I will ensure this kingdom continues to try for as long as my blood sits on the throne."

I bowed back to him. "Thank you, my king."

"You and your family should return to your chambers to rest. I am sure you are all tired from the evening's events. We shall see each other before you leave tomorrow."

That night, we all drank wine and chatted for hours about Kehina, about my journey to save Senaga, even about the latest lumber prices for Unika's ships. It was the first time I could remember us all talking so freely, and so lovingly. And when Imoni and Unika hugged me good night, when Tamunor kissed the top of my head and then left with his arm slung around his father's shoulders, when Tega and I snuggled into our massive bed, curled tightly around each other, I knew we would be okay. I knew I could leave for Qua'i and still share my life with them. I would always have my roots in Kokori, but my family had allowed me to grow beyond its borders.

True to his word, the king personally bid us farewell the next morning as we all piled into another hired carriage.

I wasn't sure if he would keep his other promise, however. I knew I could not rely on kings to keep me safe, so I would not bet my life on it.

I would keep myself safe, and I would keep myself free.

26

ANON MASIKA CAME WITH HIS TWO BROTHERS A FEW DAYS later to start talks with Unika for Tega's betrothal to his youngest son, Xanda.

Xanda was tall and solidly built, but what should have been an intimidating physique was counteracted by his babylike face. He was clearly smitten with Tega; he could not stop staring at her and smiling at her comments. Eventually, he asked his father and Unika if he could speak to Tega alone.

Tega and Xanda went up to the roof, and by the way she was laughing so freely, it seemed his feelings were reciprocated.

Tega was all smiles after Xanda and his family left. She came over to my room and sat on the chair that faced my window. I was packing my things into the bags I would bring with me to Qua'i.

"Xanda is very handsome, right?"

It did not sound like a question. I smiled to myself as she continued.

"And he is so funny." She chuckled. "He told me about how he grew up with five brothers. Can you imagine? Five."

She prattled happily on for a while about all they had in common, and how she felt so comfortable with him. "I think he will make a good husband," she murmured, blushing.

I wrapped my thoroughly washed hair with a scarf and stared at my sister. She looked so happy, so content.

"I hope he will be," I whispered. "You deserve the very best. I liked what I saw of Xanda and am thankful you had such a good experience with him today."

She smiled at me and came to sit on my bed with me. "Thank you. That means so much to me coming from you."

I squeezed her hand. "Just please make sure that if he is not kind to you—if he is anything like our father—then you will tell me. I will always be here for you, no matter the distance. I love you and will do anything for you, Tega."

She gripped my hand tighter, resting her head on my shoulder.

"I am so glad you are leaving this way. I don't know if I could've borne another secret disappearance. And now I can keep you in my life."

"Thank you for everything you did last time," I whispered. "I regret hurting you more than anything. And I am so grateful that you are my sister."

I closed my eyes, took a deep breath, and exhaled slowly.

I would always have Tega. I would always have home.

But it was time for me to leave.

The next day, I visited Moyo's house for the first time since I arrived back from Ewuare.

He was sitting on his porch, soaking up the late-afternoon sun.

"Well it's about time." He chuckled.

I gave him a rueful grin. "I've been a little busy."

"So I've heard," he replied, smiling. "But why am I hearing about it from Tamunor and not you? You know he is not a reliable storyteller. Surely you did not fight off two dozen Ebo and save King Brumeh's life."

I sat in the chair next to him. "For the first time in his life, Tamunor was not exaggerating."

I told Moyo everything, and he listened, rapt.

"I am so proud of you, Naborhi," he whispered. "You have done so much for yourself, for others, for this kingdom. I could not have hoped for more for you."

His words warmed me from the inside out.

"I wanted to thank you for everything you've taught and given me, Moyo," I replied, my throat tightening. "I wouldn't have been able to do any of this if you hadn't been there for me. You were the best father I could have ever asked for."

Moyo's eyes were glistening, but he smiled gently, his hand resting on mine.

"When do you leave again?" he asked softly.

"Tomorrow. I'm going back to Qua'i to work with La Hinan. I'll stop in Mbiabong first, to stay with Atai and his family."

"That sounds wonderful. Give my best to him and Inemesit."

"How do you two know each other?" I guessed.

He chuckled. "You caught that, I see." He shot me a bashful look. "We knew each other, years and years ago. Long before I met my wife, and long before Inemesit's father died, passing down the oracle title."

I read between the lines and chuckled back. "Ah."

"May I visit you in Qua'i?" he asked, switching the subject. "It's been years since I've been, and I would like to see this Red Tapestry."

I smiled widely at him. "I would be delighted if you did."

The next morning rose crisp and clear.

"Be safe and write to us as soon as you arrive in Mbiabong and as soon as you arrive in Qua'i," Imoni urged.

She, Unika, Tega, Tamunor, and I stood in the courtyard, saying our goodbyes.

"I will, I promise," I told her, hugging her.

Tamunor scooped me into his arms next. "Please don't drown on that ship."

I laughed. "I promise I'll try not to," I replied. Imoni and Unika had booked passage for me on a ship to Ewuare from Oron, where I would pay a visit to Senaga and King Ide before finally returning to Qua'i.

Unika held me tightly. "Keep making us proud, Naborhi."

I smiled into his chest. "I promise."

Finally, I turned to Tega. She had tears in her eyes, but she was beaming, joyful.

"I love you," she said, hugging me fiercely.

It was all she needed to say. "I love you too," I whispered. It was its own kind of promise.

Just as I was heading for the gate, Chipo rushed inside, a huge bag thrown over her shoulder.

"What are you doing here?" I gasped, gripping her arm.

She was out of breath, her chest heaving. "You didn't seriously think you could leave without telling me *again*, did you? I'm coming with you."

I blinked at her, shocked. "What?"

She readjusted her pack. "I'm coming with you. Birungi is dumb as dirt and his father frightens me. Besides, I'd rather be with you any day than with some odious man."

"But how . . . ?" I couldn't process this news, my mind trying to catch up with the increasingly wonderful situation before me.

"Imoni told me about your plans," she said. "You know she can't help but brag," she added in a whisper. "So I told my parents that Imoni and Unika were allowing your journey, and they should allow mine, too, since I was going to break off my engagement and join you. I didn't really stay long enough to give them a chance to say no."

I glanced back at Imoni, whose eyes were mischievous and knowing.

I smiled and turned back to my best friend. "I'm taking a ship from Oron to Ewuare first," was all I said.

"Good, because so am I."

My heart swelled. "You're really coming."

She gave me a wide, infectious grin. "I'm really coming."

Together. We'd lived this strange, beautiful life together for so long, and now we'd take on the future together.

As we set off for the Oron Forest, waving goodbye to my family, I reflected on all that had brought me here, the people who had gotten me through it all.

I was unstoppable as the mightiest river, but my friends, my family, were what fed my strength.

And with their love, my strength would thunder throughout the world.

ACKNOWLEDGMENTS

Thank you to God, always, for His Grace.

Thank you to my daughter and son, who will get to read this book someday and hopefully love it.

And thank you to my sister, Odes, whose delicious foods and drinks fueled me as I wrote and edited this book.

Many, many thanks to Sarah Odedina and Accord Literary, who gave me and my story a chance.

To my editor, Kristin, whose emails and notes have both elevated and stabilized my heart rate. Thank you for your guidance.

A massive thank-you to the team at Norton Young Readers for making this book a real thing, and to Hana Anouk Nakamura and Michael Machira Mwangi for the jaw-dropping cover. I still get teary-eyed when I look at it.

And to my Erhudites, my readers: finally an Urhobo girl on a front cover! Thank you for your immeasurable support.

ABOUT THE AUTHOR

Erhu Kome was born and raised in the great city of Benin, Nigeria. She went on to study medical biochemistry and genetics, a venture that has since taken a backseat in her life.

Now she writes stories centered on her Urhobo tribal roots, where myth and magic come together. "Writing Urhobo characters has helped me deeply learn about the history and ways of my people," she says. "It is important to know where we are from."

She hopes her stories will find a place in the hearts of readers who, like her younger self, read late into the night, who rummage through old family shelves to read any book they can get their hands on, and who will take a book anywhere they go.

Erhu is also the author of *Not Seeing Is a Flower*, the first bizarro novella written by a Nigerian female author, which was shortlisted for the Nommo Awards. She is an anime enthusiast and a huge fan of *Bob's Burgers*, and has a soft spot for any TV show or movie that will make her laugh. She lives in Asaba, Nigeria, with her two children and sister.

ABOUT ACCORD BOOKS

Accord works with authors from across the African continent to provide support throughout the writing process and secure regional and international publishing and distribution for their works. We believe that stories are both life-affirming and life-enhancing, and want to see a world in which all children are delighted and enriched by incredible stories written by African authors.